Praise for Lisa Tawn Bergren and "Until the Shadows Flee"

"I am a Lisa Tawn Bergren fanatic! I can't begin to tell you how wonderful and entertaining each book has been. I get lost in her words for hours. I truly believe that God guided me to her books and to have a source of entertainment for my soul."
—*Heidi Endicott, Wisconsin*

"I was truly blessed through reading 'Until the Shadows Flee' and enjoyed every minute of it. It's amazing how real Lisa can make the characters in such a short time. Lisa is a gifted writer. I am thankful for such uplifting, positive, spiritual fiction!"
—*Cheryl Crawford, Washington*

"Lisa Tawn Bergren has deeply touched me with many things she has written; God has used her words to help me heal, open my heart to my husband and family more, and to love him more as I follow him. I am grateful to God for giving her this tremendous gift."
—*Roberta Reed, Minnesota*

"I finished 'Until the Shadows Flee' last night and loved it! I especially loved Ari's love letters and the Scriptures Samuel and Charissa wrote as their own kind of love letters. The way Lisa brought two sad, lonely souls together was romantic, but the way they helped each other strengthen their love for God while falling in love was uplifting."
—*Sharon Morgan, California*

Praise for Maureen Pratt and "Dear Love"

"Wonderful! 'Dear Love' is a graceful story of faith and true love."
—*Linda Beck, California*

"Maureen's vivid descriptions of deep color, sweet fragrance, and dashing movement bring her characters to life in ways that make the reader feel witness to the events unfolding. A joy to read again and again."
—*Carolyn Conkling, Virginia*

HEART
QUEST®

romance the way it's meant to be

HeartQuest brings you romantic fiction
with a foundation of biblical truth.
Adventure, mystery, intrigue, and suspense
mingle in these heartwarming stories of
men and women of faith striving to build
a love that will last a lifetime.

May HeartQuest books sweep you
into the arms of God, who longs for you
and pursues you always.

Lisa Tawn Bergren · *Mauree*

LETTERS OF

Pratt · Lyn Cote

THE HEART

Romance fiction from
Tyndale House Publishers, Inc., Wheaton, Illinois
www.heartquest.com

Visit Tyndale's exciting Web site at www.tyndale.com

Check out the latest about HeartQuest Books at www.heartquest.com

Until the Shadows Flee edited by Traci L. DePree; *Dear Love* and *For Varina's Heart* edited by Diane Eble

Designed by Dean H. Renninger

Scripture quotations within the novellas are taken from the *Holy Bible,* King James Version.

Scripture quotation in the epigraph is taken from the *Holy Bible,* New Living Translation, copyright © 1996. Used by permission of Tyndale House Publishers, Inc., Wheaton, Illinois 60189. All rights reserved.

Library of Congress Cataloging-in-Publication Data

Letters of the heart / Lisa Tawn Bergren, Maureen Pratt [and] Lyn Cote.
    p. cm.
    ISBN 0-8423-3580-3 (softcover)
1. Christian fiction, American.   2. Love-letters—Fiction.   3. Love stories, American.   I. Bergren, Lisa Tawn. Until the shadows flee.   II. Pratt, Maureen. Dear love.   III. Cote, Lyn. For Varina's heart.
PS648.C43 L48 2002
813'.085083823—dc21   2001004003

Printed in the United States of America

06   05   04   03   02
9   8   7   6   5   4   3   2

Contents

UNTIL THE
SHADOWS FLEE

Lisa Tawn Bergren

Prologue

SEATTLE, WASHINGTON · JUNE 1888

"Step away from this patient," Charissa Nadal demanded, striding around the examination table. Her long Bellevue nurse's skirt impeded her progress, and she pulled the heavy cloth aside. She'd had enough, seen enough. Nothing was going to stop her from kicking this, this quack out of her office.

"Wh-what?" the man said, looking over at her with a mixture of surprise, fear, and bemusement on his face. He set down a brown bottle he had pulled from his bag.

"You heard me. You are not going to touch this woman. Get out. You may not buy the business." She pulled the stethoscopic tube—her own Ari's old instrument—out of his hand and looked up at him, daring the man to defy her orders.

His expression changed from shock to rage. "You, why y-you . . . who are you to think—"

"I am Charissa Nadal. I own this building and this business, and I am in charge here. You are nothing but a trespasser." She stood up to her full height, which as a petite woman, didn't amount to much, but she would use every inch she had.

Dr. Gallatin—if one could call him a doctor—stared at her and then at his patient, a young Caribbean woman who was plainly suffering from the ague. She needed rest and plenty of water and broth, perhaps a dose of quinine, not the calomel that Dr. Gallatin was giving her.

"Now, Nurse Nadal, perhaps there's been some misunderstanding." A slow, deep red blush climbed his neck as he attempted to suppress his obvious fury.

"No, Dr. Gallatin, there has been no mistake. I simply will not stand by and see you misdiagnose or mistreat another patient. You can't give this poor woman calomel. Have you not seen what that can do to a patient over time? It leaves one's gums and teeth a bloody mess! And it does nothing to cure the disease for which you are prescribing it. Have you not read the latest findings on these things?"

Dr. Gallatin's mouth clamped shut, and with cold eyes he studied her for a moment. The red tide along his neck reached his cheeks. "I will not forget this," he finally said, shaking a finger in her face.

"Fine," Charissa said. "See that you don't." She followed him out the door and watched him stride into the dusty, busy street. He would have no difficulty finding another position in the burgeoning city of Seattle—that was the real travesty.

She sighed, giving in to the trembling that always followed an argument. When she and Ari had quarreled she could hardly remain on her feet afterward. . . .

The young woman's cough brought Charissa back to the present. Ari was gone, dead these long two years. And she had driven out yet another doctor—the fifth—who might have taken his place in his practice. She returned to the patient's side and eased the black woman's back onto the table. "There, there, dearest, you rest. I'll take care of you. Don't you worry. You'll be fine, just fine."

Salma, Charissa's loyal friend and maid from her years as a child in Boston, appeared in the doorway. "Where's the doctor?" she asked suspiciously.

"I sent him on his way to see about other positions in the city," she responded. "He was not right for us. His type of care is worse than no care at all!" Charissa wrung out a cloth and laid it on the sweating patient's brow. The poor girl was suffering from a malarial fever, probably picked up just as she left her native island for the Panamanian crossing and dreams of America. With the prejudices that permeated the town, how could she find a competent person to care for people like this woman? What would happen if Charissa closed her doors and said good-bye to the whole mess? Not that she hadn't considered it now and then.

"We needs a doctor, miss," Salma said, her voice rising in concern.

"We are faring just fine on our own, Salma."

"We needs a doctor. The town council, they don't like you operatin' without a doctor. You can't keep on seein' patients all on your own."

"I can and I will, until we find the right doctor to see to our patients." Charissa gripped the tall woman's arm and pulled her out of the examination room and into the front parlor, where they could discuss things in private. "I will not stand by and see Ari's patients mistreated. And it's only a small group of old biddies and some insecure doctors on the city council who make a fuss about me seeing anyone." She let out a dry laugh. "Whoever heard of anything so ridiculous! I am a woman. Just a nurse. Seeing the people they refuse to see. And yet, somehow, they're still threatened by me. Just boys in men's clothing, that's what they are."

"Them boys can make trouble for you, miss."

"Oh, they'll fluster about, but they'll let me be. Soon, the right doctor will come to us, Salma." Charissa reached out to take her friend's hand. The black woman's fingers were long and slender, an artist's fingers, as compared to her own olive-toned, short, stout digits. "I promise. If Seattle keeps growing at this rate, we'll have five new doctors on our doorstep tomorrow, all wanting the job." Since the fire leveled the city, it was rebuilding at twice the previous rate, like a forest floor reseeding itself.

● ● ●

BOISE, IDAHO

Mrs. Alton put a wiry arm around Samuel Johnson's shoulders. He struggled to keep himself from shaking off her attempt to comfort him. It was her husband—her husband!—he had let die. He stared out the window into the coal black darkness. "There was nothing more you could do, Dr. Johnson."

"There must've been something. I'm sorry. I'm so sorry."

"I watched you myself, Samuel," she said. He'd known

her since he was just a boy. Her husband, Joseph, had been like a second father to him. "Everybody in this town knows there's not a one who takes care of his patients like Samuel Johnson."

"Still, I keep thinking there might have been some-thing . . . "

"Let it rest, son," the woman said, tears now making her eyes bright in the lamp's light. "My Joe is at peace now. You be the same. You did all that God could expect of you. It's certainly enough for me."

Samuel let out a shallow breath and turned to take the small, elderly woman in his arms. It had been she who had come alongside him after Mamie died. She had been the one who had consoled his spirit with gentle talk and fed his body with warm food. But still, every time he lost a patient, he was taken back to the night he lost his beloved wife, the night he lost the son who never got to take his first breath. Two years ago now.

Forcing a smile to her face, Joan Alton moved away. "I'll see to my man now. It was his time, Samuel. You just remember that. He struggled for so long, was in such pain. . . . If there had been something you could have done, you would have found it. You did your best. That's all anybody expects of you."

Samuel shook his head. "I'm sorry. You're the one who needs comforting, and here you are comforting me."

"I know what Joe meant to you." She brought an old, wrinkled hand up to her mouth and let the first tears fall. "Meant to us all," she added, her voice cracking.

Together, they turned to the old man who had lived a

full life. Joseph Alton had spread good cheer and a kind word wherever he went. Samuel Johnson wanted to be like him. If he could just rediscover that joy from within, that joy he had lost with Mamie. But he had no idea how to go about reclaiming it. As they stood looking at his old friend, now lifeless, growing cold, Samuel realized that he needed a change. Joe's death sounded an alarm bell on the old fire wagon. A call to wake up and move. Being here in the town where he had lost his family just brought it back to him again and again. The pain was easing away, and there were weeks when he didn't think of them. But then there were days like today that seemed to bring it all back, as fresh as a storm on the wind.

Yes. He needed a change, a new challenge. New surroundings, new people—people who didn't watch him with wise, wary eyes, waiting for him to make a mistake again. In some place new, he could live his life as Joe Alton had lived his, how Samuel's wife, Mamie, had lived hers. He would practice long, slow, generous smiles and care for his patients. Do the best he could, as Joan put it. The best he could. And find some peace in it.

His eyes went to the lithograph above the Altons' bed, the bed they had shared for over forty years of marriage. It was a picture of a wharf in Seattle, sent last Christmas to the Altons from their son, a ship's mate. The grand, tall schooners were lined up in a row, their sails furled, their decks empty of men or cargo, waiting . . . waiting. For what?

Seattle. It would be nice to see the Pacific Ocean. And who knew? Maybe he would sail on one of those ships himself.

Chapter One

Salma reached over and dabbed at Charissa's brow with a cloth as Charissa worked on the gash in the Chinese man's chest.

"I need more light!" Charissa barked, frowning as she worked to stitch up the wound.

"They's no more lamps, miss. The wall lamps are up as bright as they'll go."

Dark had descended just as the railroad boss brought the Chinaman into the office and dropped him off like a load of horse dung from the stables. Fight at the tracks, he had said, shrugging his shoulders as if bringing someone to the doctor with a knife wound were an everyday occurrence. Then he'd walked out without saying another word.

Tensions were high between white settlers and the Chinese these days. There was talk daily of driving all Chinese out of town. "They steal all the jobs from us hardworkin' white folks," she'd heard a particularly surly man at the mercantile say. Charissa knew there was plenty of work in this new, untamed land. But such reasoning didn't seem to matter one whit to such idiots. Who was next? Charissa wondered. Would they target Greeks, like herself? Demand she leave her home and her husband's business behind because of some narrow-minded paranoia?

The Chinaman moaned and moved, and Charissa prayed he would not awaken. She needed to stay on with her stitching, hadn't time to give him another dose of ether. "Salma," she muttered, "I'm going to need your help." Her eyes widened when she saw a bit of the man's intestine; it had been sliced open. Ari had always told her it was deadly when that happened. It was too hard to stitch the intestine and keep it clean. Never mind that it made the wound itself toxic. Most likely it had already released poison into the abdominal cavity. Septicemia was probable.

"Give him a dose of that ether," she directed the maid. "No more than five breaths. Be sure you count."

"Yes'm."

She closed her eyes for a moment. If only there was a doctor with her. This was beyond Charissa's capability, her training, even with her years working at Ari's side. Perhaps she should have insisted the railroad crew boss take the man to the hospital, but even as it crossed her mind, she shook her head. They would have never accepted the man with his slanted eyes and yellow-toned skin. His long, black hair, neatly braided, was enough to make him a target of their prejudice.

"Miz Nadal, you bette' come and see this," Salma said. She had moved over to the window, where the sounds of men's voices rose. There was fear in her voice, anxiety in her wide eyes. For the first time, Charissa saw torchlight bouncing around the window behind her maid, accompanied by the sounds of men's voices. They were coming closer. A knock sounded on the front door. Salma went to answer it, but returned with a grim face.

"It's the city council. They wants to talk to you now, Miz Nadal."

"Oh, for heaven's sakes." Charissa finished stitching the intestine as best she could and then laid a blood-soaked cloth over the rest of the wound. "Open the door, Salma. Then see that the patient rests quietly."

"They don't look too agreeable, miss. I'll go fetch the gun," Salma whispered. "They's some rabble-rousers with the councilmen."

"You do that." Taking a deep breath as the pine door creaked open, Charissa walked out to the porch. There were eight or nine of them, their faces lined with concern. When she left the porch and approached the men, they parted for her like the Red Sea before Moses, mouths agape as they spied the bright red blood on her hands and her nurse's uniform.

"Who you got in there?" one man asked, looking toward a companion.

"You're not licensed to practice surgery, Mrs. Nadal!" Fred Hastings said. "We've been hearing a lot of complaints again."

"Gentlemen!" she barked. Surprisingly, they quieted for a moment to hear what she had to say. "I have a patient who will likely die if I don't see to him. Can we not have this discussion tomorrow morning?"

"Take him to his own," said one in a soothing voice.

"What do you care that I am seeing to his wounds?" she asked calmly.

"We can't just go on letting anybody practice medicine about town. We have rules, standards. If we can't appease the people of Seattle, I'm afraid we'll have upheaval, riots even."

"I see how it is. You kowtow to your racist constituents and let a whole segment of our town suffer and die because of their ignorance," Charissa interrupted.

"The other doctors in town tell us—"

"Tell you what? That I am practicing medicine? Well, I'm the best some of our townspeople have since these doctors refuse to treat them. I had formal nurse's training at Bellevue. I served as my husband's nurse for years, and I have seen a great deal. We've spoken of this before—I am interviewing doctor candidates."

"Whom you keep firing," said a red-faced man from the back. That was when Charissa noticed the men beyond the lamplight's glow. She took a half step backward, suddenly realizing that the men were pushing subtly forward. She cast a furtive look about. There were faces in the windows of her neighbors' shops and homes, but few dared to come out. Nobody wanted trouble. There were a couple men riding by on horseback, and one edging closer . . .

"You either show us your new doctor or close up shop," the first man said, taking a step closer to her and whispering so the others wouldn't hear. "Or there will be more trouble in town than we'll be able to handle."

She looked up and for the first time felt fear. John Napier, a no-account who was continually in trouble with the sheriff, looked at her from the back of the group. His slitted eyes moved over her from head to toe, sending shivers of fear down her spine. "This isn't a place for a lady, Mrs. Nadal," he shouted. "We'll take your patient to his own, and you can see to womanly things. You seem to have a hard time grasping the fact you're not a doctor. With your man gone, we're here to make the decision for you."

"That would be a bit premature," said a man of medium height. He edged through the passel of men about Charissa and came to her side. "Mrs. Nadal, I am Doctor Samuel Johnson. I believe you received my cable about an interview?"

Charissa looked up at the man who had warm, kind eyes behind his wire-rimmed spectacles. Gently he took off his bowler hat and gave her a curt bow. She didn't know the man from Adam, had received no telegram. "Doctor Johnson!" she said with relief. "I wondered when you might arrive." She turned halfway to show him in and cast a glance back at the mob of men. "You all go on home," she said, taking the tone of a chastising mother. "We have a life to save. See to your own business and leave me to mine."

"See that you keep the good doctor around this time," Councilman Hastings said. "Or we won't have a choice but to shut you down."

"I shall keep him on if he is suitable for the job," she said, reclaiming her pride. And with that, she turned on her heel and followed the waiting doctor—if he was who he said he was—over the threshold and into the building. She shut the door and leaned against it for a moment, eyes closed, and fought against the trembling that tried to claim her. When she gazed up, she saw Samuel Johnson staring down the length of a rifle that Salma held on him.

"I am no threat," he said, his hands raised in submission. Charissa shook her head at Salma and the gun slowly lowered. Dr. Johnson drew a deep breath and took long, purposeful strides into the examination room and removed the cloth over the patient's wound. "Nice stitches," he said. He looked over at Charissa with admiration in his eyes, then down at her dress in a gentle perusal, not the leering glance of the man outside, but with a shy, sweet expression. "Bellevue nurse, eh? You look like you could use a few minutes off your feet. May I take over for you here for a bit? I am not just your knight in shining armor; I truly am a doctor."

Charissa pursed her lips. It was true; she was dying to get off her knocking knees for a minute or two. "If you are a doctor of at least three years with a legitimate medical degree from a legitimate medical institution, you may scrub your hands in the kitchen and see to that wound. I was forced to stitch a bit of his intestine." She looked to the patient uncertainly. "If you could review my work and do what you can about the rest, I would be most appreciative."

"Done," he said, turning away at once and heading for the kitchen.

Charissa immediately sank onto the red brocade settee in the front parlor, which was directly opposite from the examination room and had served as Ari's office. Charissa tilted her head toward the kitchen and said in a low voice, "Can you keep an eye on our mystery doctor?" Salma nodded and followed the man into the kitchen.

Charissa was suddenly tired, so tired. And angry. What

did those men care if she looked after the medical needs of the Indians and Chinese and Negroes and all the rest? It all boiled down to one thing: They didn't want anyone else here at all, at least no one who was different from them. Never mind that Seattle wouldn't have their builders for roads or railroad tracks or workers for their mines or drivers for their lumber wagons without those who were willing to take on their dirty work.

It probably irked them that she, a woman, was making a living on her own without the help of a man. A woman more competent than some physicians. And a woman who had the audacity to fire those same men. A slow smile grew across her face.

Salma returned with a damp rag for Charissa's hands and a cup of tea for Charissa and another one for herself. Together, they sipped the tepid liquid and watched the doctor emerge from the kitchen with a white apron on. For the first time, Charissa spied the small black bag he carried. He set it on the long table behind him in the examining room and quickly, efficiently laid out his meager supply of instruments.

"Use what you need of ours," she invited with a soft call as she continued to observe him from her seat in the parlor.

He looked up at her as if in surprise that he wasn't alone, so intent was his focus, and nodded once, then returned to his work. Selecting a bottle from his bag, he turned and began inspecting the patient's wound. "Has he had ether?" he asked quietly, still staring at her stitching when the man moaned and moved.

"A bit. But it's likely wearing off."

Unable to curb her curiosity any further, she joined him in the examination room. He began to work, irrigating the wound to better see Charissa's work, looking at the remaining damage, and washing away anything that might cause septicemia. "You've done well here. . . . What shall I call you? Nurse? Mrs. Nadal? I take it from the idiot outside that your husband has passed on."

"He has. Two years ago . . ." Her voice faltered, and Samuel glanced up at her with wise, knowing eyes, a compassion in their depths. Was that a hint of shared sorrow? "You may call me Nurse Nadal or Mrs. Nadal for the moment; it matters not to me. I've been searching for the right doctor to take my husband, Ari's, place ever since he died," she said, raising her chin.

"Probably not a man who could do that. Take his place, that is," he said softly, kindly. He cleared his throat. "*Make* his own place—now that's another matter."

"True enough. Ari was the best of doctors. He was always reading and reading, eager to learn, to expand his knowledge so he could better treat his patients."

"I do my own share of reading," Samuel said, his concentration back on his stitching again.

"That is good to hear. A surprising number of men who call themselves doctors do not."

"True. There are a good number still trained by the apprentice method. Unfortunately," he said, pausing to make a quick knot, "that leads to a lot of old, unfit practices still being used."

"Like administering calomel," Charissa muttered.

"What?"

She shook her head. "Forget it. Where did you take your medical training?"

"At the University of Pennsylvania. And where did Dr. Nadal receive his education?"

"Harvard."

"Ahh. No wonder your standards are high. And you, yourself a Bellevue nurse." His eyes again traveled to her uniform.

"Indeed." She squirmed under his steady gaze. Did he always look at people that way? As though he could see right through them?

He worked on in silence, closing the wound and bending to listen to the patient's respiration. "Know his name?"

"No. He was dropped off by a crew boss who seemed relieved not to have him bloody up his wagon anymore."

"That kind, eh?" Samuel said.

"Better than those who would let a man die by the tracks without even trying to save him. The lesser of two evils, I suppose. At least he left him in my care. Which brings me to the job itself. Are you indeed interested in a position in Seattle, Doctor?"

Samuel let out a humorless laugh. "Well, I hoped to purchase a business outright. Begging your pardon, ma'am, but I don't care to work for anyone but myself. I'm my own man, and I have enough to handle pleasing myself with my work, let alone a widow who wants someone to fill her husband's obviously large boots."

Charissa bristled at his words. She didn't want someone to fill Ari's boots . . . did she? "I . . . I understand," she said, struggling to maintain her dignity. She couldn't afford to get angry with another doctor. "Perhaps you can keep this business in mind as you interview around town. The majority of our patients are people who generally shy away from seeing white doctors, mostly people of Indian and Negro and Chinese descent. Most of them have work in Seattle. They don't pay well, but they do pay; some have to pay in onions or beef.

"I would do my best not to . . . compare you—your work, I mean—to my husband. I might consider selling the business, but I would need to be certain that Ari's patients are well cared for. . . . I had hoped, however," Charissa continued, unsure of his reaction, "to remain on in my role as a nurse."

• ● •

Samuel studied the beautiful, petite woman before him. She was so brave, and yet there was a weary quality in her expression, a sadness that she was trying so hard to hide. He'd seen that look before. In his own mirror. How long had she been practicing medicine on her own? taking care of people nobody else cared to?

He looked back to the patient. He was still unconscious, and Samuel pretended to listen to his lungs. Anything to keep from staring at the woman across the table—so proud, so needy. What was this connection between them? He hadn't felt so instantly drawn to another woman since the day he'd met Mamie. Did Mrs. Nadal feel the same attraction? He shook his head. It was simply their shared experience in losing a loved one—at about the same time—that drew him to her. That certainly didn't mean anything romantic . . . did it?

A woman like Charissa would never look twice at a man like him. Ari Nadal had no doubt been her equal not only in medical aptitude but also in looks and fiery demeanor. Samuel was nothing of the kind. Still, he glanced up at her again and found himself fighting off the crazy desire to take her like a child into his arms and tell her that he would stay, that things would be all right. That he would make it all right.

His thoughts startled him. He'd never looked at another woman since Mamie, and here he was not half an hour after meeting this woman wanting to hold her in his arms. It was ludicrous! He was allowing his lonely heart to wander. He had to stay with what was best for himself and not let such silly ideas creep in. He had to strengthen his resolve.

"I'm sure this is a fine business," he answered her at last. "And that you're the finest of nurses. But since I just got to town, Mrs. Nadal, I think I will see what else is available and spend some time in prayer before I make any rash decisions." He dared to meet her gaze.

"I would expect nothing less, Dr. Johnson," she said. Was that a bit of triumph in her luminous eyes? "But I sense that you're the right doctor for this part of the city. And you'll soon see it too."

Samuel smiled. "Do you always get your way, Nurse?"

She tilted her head up to him, her long lashes curled around dark, beckoning eyes. "Nearly always, Doctor."

And that was what he was afraid of. Sweet heaven, she was beautiful. How could he resist this headstrong, gorgeous woman working at his right hand?

Chapter Two

Charissa Nadal began her day as she had begun every other day since news of Ari's death had reached her two years before: by writing a letter to her husband while seated at the desk he had given her. It was a tradition that Ari himself had begun, a means of reaching out to the one who had been dearest.

He had brought home the old captain's desk, carved with Oriental ornamentation, and let her wonder over its significance for weeks before finally showing her the secret compartment. It had been inside there that he had left her love letter after love letter, filling her with pride and honor and peace and pleasure as his words expressed his passion for his wife.

His last letter lay beside her, old and dirty after count-less nights of being clutched in her hand. *"Until my dying day, Ari,"* the closing had read. How ironic that it had been his dying day when he wrote that letter! Somehow she felt as if she should have known what was in store for Ari, that she should have read his letter and his last words as a sign and chased after the coach herself. She should have insisted he not go that day, demanded that he remain at home. She should have taken better care of him.

He should have taken better care of her. But he had not. He had left her side, forever. It wasn't as brutal to consider the fact anymore, didn't take her breath away; yet it still made her a bit melancholy and lonesome. If he had only put her first, for once . . .

"Please, Ari. Do not leave," Charissa had begged him, pulling once more on her husband's overcoat sleeve. She cast a worried glance to the window, where sleet hit the glass and slumped downward.

A horse whinnied outside, and Ari looked at her with a tender gaze. "I must, my love," he said, using his favorite Greek endearment for her.

She closed her eyes, wanting to let the sound of their native Greek seep deep inside her. She wanted to hold on to the nuances, the reassurance of his words, as long as he was absent from her side. "Surely your patient can wait until morning," she tried once more, already knowing the futility of her words.

"We have been through this," Ari had said, lifting her chin until she looked into his dark, dancing eyes. Even after ten years of marriage, he was still able to move her like a ketch on the windy Mediterranean. "I hate to leave you as much as you hate to have me go. But I must. The guilt would be too great if this man dies before morning and I did not try to reach him! Neither of us wants to live with such a thing, no?"

He waited until she finally answered. "No," she said, shaking away her sorrow and frustration as well as his hand. It made her angry, this devotion to his patients at the cost of her own security. Even if deep down, as a nurse, she understood. It still hurt.

"Charissa," he said lovingly. "Wish me well and I'll be off."

"Go with God, my husband," she said solemnly, "and return to me by sunrise."

"If I can, beloved," he had promised. Had he somehow known, wondered then that he would never return to her again?

She still found herself occasionally reaching for Ari at night, still found herself imagining what he might think of this or that, even though his pillow no longer contained his scent and his things had long been stored away in the attic. She pushed back the tears that longed to flow. There had been too many tears since she lost him, and for once, it seemed as though she had too few left.

Salma softly knocked at the partially open door. "I have your breakfast, miss."

"I am not very hungry," Charissa said, even as the maid entered with the tray.

"You say that every day. But you eat what I bring." She set the tray down and took a biscuit from it for herself, then sat on a nearby chair to eat it. "A man came from your solicitor's office. He'd like to meet with you this afternoon."

She knew what Sean Wilks would tell her; he'd said it often enough before, but she'd resisted. "The sale of the office building and Dr. Nadal's equipment, after paying off

his debts, will help you get along for a while longer. Ari
would want that. . . . Besides, the ledger is nearly empty now.
With some money of your own, perhaps you could return
home to Boston. Be with family."

He meant well. Ari had always trusted him; Charissa
should too. But she didn't want to return to Boston nor her
family, as dear as they were to her heart. She had discovered a
new life out west with Ari, and she wanted to continue onward,
not turn back. It would be like turning her back on Ari.

"Thank you, Salma."

"Not at all, miss."

Charissa dipped her pen and wrote a quick note to her
lawyer.

> Mr. Wilks,
> I'm considering selling the business. I believe I may
> have found a buyer. More in the next week.
> > Best,
> > Mrs. Ari Nadal

She stared at the words. A buyer for Ari's business, even
as she still signed her notes with his name. It seemed curiously impossible and not real. Her thoughts moved from Ari
to Samuel Johnson, the sad-eyed, kind doctor who had come
to her rescue the night before. She hoped he would see how
badly he was needed here and be led back to her door. Her
patients needed him. She . . . needed him. Charissa wanted to
remain in Seattle, continue on as a nurse. And the only way to
do that was to sell Ari's business to the right man. Right
away.

• • •

Samuel Johnson had worked like a madman ever since his
Mamie died. It was his penance. He could not do enough for
his patients, driving from one to the next in his buggy, forsak-
ing sleep. It was futile to go home, anyway. He could find
little rest in the bed he had shared with his wife; Samuel
would often sit up at night, gazing at the straw tick from
which his love had left for eternity. It had been too much to
bear. That was why he had had to leave.

He took a deep breath. Here in Seattle, where the cold
air blew in from Puget Sound and the Cascades sheltered him
from the east, he would build a new life. He would prove
trustworthy to his patients. He would not fail anyone again
with his own ineptitude.

And it was Charissa Nadal's plight that seemed to be
calling to his heart the most; with her husband's business, he
would be able to take care of the neediest in the city.

He found his way back to Charissa Nadal's building
again two afternoons later. It was a sufficient structure, two
stories tall. Nothing fancy, but big enough that he could house
a patient overnight should the need arise. Sometimes a patient
was not ill enough to be in the hospital but needed extra care.
His visit to the local hospital left him suspicious that it might
be a haven for disease and lackadaisical care. And his visits to
the other physicians in town had left him curiously cold.

Thoughts of Mrs. Nadal's caring, spirited demeanor, her
careful stitching of a poor Chinaman's wounds, kept surfacing
in his mind. So here he was, back at the Nadals' place of business, considering the ramifications of purchasing the business.

Would the people of Seattle look down on him for caring for the Negroes and Chinese in their town? Or would they respect him for being someone without regard for skin color or ethnicity? What would Charissa think? Somehow, that thought meant more to him than any of the townspeople's.

"How is our patient today?" he asked, referring to the stabbing victim.

"Doing better. In some pain, and swelling a bit, but all in all . . . alive." The wry smile she gave him warmed Samuel as if they shared a secret. Her lips settled back into a perfect rosebud, rounded and pointed in all the right—

"Shall I give you the grand tour?" Her words cut off his thoughts, for which he was grateful. "Make this an official meeting? I know you've seen it already, two nights ago . . . or do you favor mob scenes to provincial manners?"

"I'll take provincial manners today. Please, give me the tour."

"Let me show you around to the back, so you can see for yourself the fine workmanship of this building. My Ari saw to the construction himself. There's an entrance there, too, that leads to the kitchen."

"Very well." Obediently, he followed her, checking for cracks in the foundation as they walked, studiously curbing his desire to stare at her curvaceous body and her gently coiled hair. It was a lovely, if small and simple, house in the Victorian style, with well-maintained clapboard siding and a few cornices at the corners. The concrete was in good shape, the wood siding in equally good stead. They reached the back, which spread toward a creek.

"Spring fed," Mrs. Nadal said, noting his focus. "Fresh,

clean water for your practice and home, should I decide to sell. Please, come in. I have a teakettle on. We can speak more about it."

Samuel followed her into the tiny galley kitchen, in which a huge cast-iron stove dominated. He had noticed it two nights before, as well as much of the rest of the house, but he hadn't really inspected it as a potential buyer. "For boiling instruments and cloths," she briefly explained, then moved to check the teakettle. "It needs a moment. Let me show you the rest while it reaches a boil."

They walked through a swinging door to the examination room. It was spotless and smelled of fresh whitewash. Crisp linens were folded and stacked on the table, and tools were neatly spaced on a tray beside it. To the right were several shelves that displayed every instrument Samuel could imagine, far more than the meager, basic assembly he carried in his old, black bag.

"It is impressive," he mused. "Your husband amassed an amazing array of equipment."

"It is," she nodded. "My father-in-law gifted him with much of it upon Ari's graduation, and Ari believed in reinvesting any of his profits. He was about your age," she said, pausing to study him more closely. "He had recently moved into this building to better serve his patients."

"He must have had quite a large practice to afford this," Samuel said, probing, wondering just how many patients for which he was signing on.

"There are many," Charissa said carefully, "who cannot see the other doctors in town. And they have been without a physician for two years now, except for what meager help I've been able to offer." She lowered her gaze to the floor and then lifted her eyes to his, her concern for her husband's patients written in the lines of her face. "They need you, Dr. Johnson."

"To be absolutely frank . . ." His voice faltered as her eyes seared his heart. "The other doctors refuse to assist you because of the matter of race, am I right?"

She nodded. "It has been my main concern. Ari never saw skin color as a reason to turn people away, and it is my hope that you too would be able to look past such trivialities to the human beings beneath." Her words were impassioned, fervent, and Samuel felt a deep respect for her.

"I want to assure you, Mrs. Nadal, that nothing would keep me from doing the very best for my patients, least of all the color of their skin."

She gave him a weary smile. "I hope you still feel that way in a year. It takes some engineering to run a business with little cash, but Ari found a way." She sighed and looked out the window, seemingly lost in thought. "Upstairs are two bedrooms. You could sleep in one, and use the other for the occasional patient or for guests."

The whistle of the teakettle drew them back to the kitchen. "Upstairs are two more rooms. There is a large bed in one room, and in the other a narrow one. Both are in good condition. There is no other furniture, besides the small stove that stands between the rooms."

"I see there is gas lighting in each room down here. Upstairs as well?"

"Yes. They are equipped to go to electricity when the city gets this far out. I hope it's soon. As you've seen, it is difficult to attend to a patient at night, even with gas lights.

I bring the old kerosene lamps nearer, but it still is not enough. And then there's the mess of kerosene tanks."

"I am accustomed to the routine, so it is no hindrance to me."

"Please, Dr. Johnson, sit," she said, leading the way to the front parlor and setting a tray beside a wing-backed chair upholstered in a blue brocade. She poured a cup and handed it to him, then sat in another chair across the simple table. "Perhaps we should start at the beginning."

"By all means," Samuel said, unsure of exactly what she meant.

"I have no right to ask, but what brings you to Seattle?" She sat straight, tea cup in hand, her expression earnest. Samuel looked at his tea and then back at her. Deep within, he wanted to tell it all, to release the heartache and pain that had brought him here, but the risk of it, of having her look at him with disapproving eyes, was more than he could bear.

"I found I needed a change, a new start," he said simply.

Charissa stared at him strangely, as if seeing him for the first time. "I find myself thinking the same, of late. You have no family?"

A knot grew in his stomach. "No immediate family." He cleared his throat, searching for something appropriate to say. "You need a new start—does that mean you intend to move soon?"

"Ah, no. I was raised in Boston and could return, but Washington is my home now. Ari always wanted to head west, from the time he was a small boy. I suppose I adopted his dream . . . " She paused and then swallowed hard. When she gathered herself again, she looked him in the eye. "Dr.

Johnson, I find I am eager to be done with this and move forward with my life."

"Yes, of course." he said. What did she mean by "move forward with my life"? If she wasn't moving away, what was it? Had she found a new man to marry? The thought made him anxious.

"I have only one request."

He braced himself.

"That you hire the best nurse Ari ever had."

"Mrs. Nadal—" he said, simultaneously relieved that she wasn't leaving him and oddly discomfited at the thought.

"Please. I could find a job elsewhere. But I will be of more assistance to you here. I know the patients. And truth be told, I don't want to work anywhere but here."

"I thought you wanted a fresh start—" he said, wiping his forehead and knocking his hat to the floor.

"You are my fresh start," she said with a smile, and then colored prettily when she realized the double meaning of her words.

Samuel bent and retrieved his bowler. "Perhaps I am not the right buyer for your husband's business after all." He wanted a new beginning, true. But he didn't know if he could risk being near her, in a working relationship with someone whose sorrows mirrored his own. He didn't know if he could maintain a merely professional relationship. He stood, signaling his desire to leave.

Charissa stood too, pulling her shoulders back and lifting her chin. "No, Dr. Johnson, you are the right buyer. You are the *only* buyer. I can sense it. This town needs you. My patients need you. You can't forsake them!"

Samuel quietly regarded her for a long moment. Would he ever be able to say no to this woman? "Perhaps we can begin together, work together for a few weeks, but I cannot promise anything long term."

"There are no promises, Dr. Johnson, other than what fate allows. I want nothing, only what's best for our patients. What's best for you. It is the most I can ask."

Only his best. Joan Alton's own words. If Mrs. Nadal only knew what his heart seemed to shout.

•   ●   •

The next evening the tall, elegant, coal-black-skinned house-maid silently led Samuel upstairs in the modest Nadal home, six blocks from his medical office. Salma had a warm second-generation slave's accent and a graceful way of carrying herself—like an East African queen—and yet there was something in her eyes that gave Samuel pause. Not just protection for her mistress, for that was surely there. But there seemed to be something else as well, something in the way she gazed at his black bag and then ran her hand across her forehead . . . was she, herself, not well? Mamie had often teased him about looking for illness in everyone he met. He turned his attention to the patient at hand and studied the pictures on the staircase wall as he made his way up to Charissa.

Salma had come to get him late that evening. From her description of Charissa's condition, it sounded serious. She'd been unable to keep any food or liquid down for hours and was running a high fever. If it was cholera or influenza, it could be deadly. Samuel's hands grew sweaty at the thought and he quickened his pace.

A wedding portrait of the striking couple came into view and Samuel tried not to stare at it too long. It was difficult. Charissa was a classic Greek beauty and her husband had been her equal.

"How long has she been unwell?" Samuel asked, forcing his feet forward.

"Since she came home from work. She's burnin' up with the fever." Without another word, she slipped inside the Nadals' bedroom while Samuel patiently waited outside the door. "Come in, Doctor," she said a moment later, ducking her head back out.

"I am fine," Mrs. Nadal said with a furrowed brow. "You needn't have come."

"From what I understand, you're far from fine."

"Salma, you should have left the good doctor to his sleep."

"She told me you wouldn't look kindly upon a house call. I decided I should look in on you anyway." He glanced between the two strong, stubborn women. "Salma, would you be kind enough to stay and assist me?"

"Of course," the maid said, moving next to Mrs. Nadal.

"Fine. See to me and then see yourself out."

Samuel's eyes widened in surprise. "Now, Mrs. Nadal, illness does not give one license for rudeness."

"As I've said myself many a time," Salma seconded.

Charissa sighed in acquiescence, but without apology, and sat up straighter in bed. Salma helped her to reposition the pillows and Samuel opened his doctor bag. Without speaking, he soon had monitored her blood pressure and listened to her heart and lungs. After replacing his equipment in the bag, he turned her desk chair and sat beside the bed.

"Told you I simply picked up a case of the influenza."

"And you know as well as I that one mustn't trifle with the influenza." Samuel studied her. Her rebuffing tone did not fit with the fear in her eyes. Even ill, she was a beauty, classic, refined. As though she belonged in an Impressionist painting, surrounded by lively flowers, not stuck in a gloomy, stagnant bedroom.

"Sometimes I wonder if life is worth all the hard work it takes."

He looked down, and then to her, waiting for her to see him, truly see him. He'd been low before, felt the shadow of her musings. *Lord, give me the words. Give me the words to reach her.* He had never been good with words.

When her big, black lashes slowly lifted and her eyes found his, he said softly, "Life is something to be embraced, ah, treasured, valued"—hadn't he told himself these things a thousand times?—"something we shouldn't throw away. Dr. Nadal would want you to take good care of yourself."

She stared at him, almost not breathing, and he became lost in her dreamy eyes. Her lips moved but he heard nothing. Had she said something? "P-pardon me?"

"You have known great sorrow, too, haven't you?" she whispered. "Do you struggle like I do, to find the meaning of life? Wonder if it's all for naught?"

"Everyone on earth knows sorrow, at one time or another . . ." His words trailed off. "I've known my share. But God gives us reasons to go on. He's given me mine, and you

33

. . . you have your patients and Salma. They need you as much as they need me." The intimacy of his speech left him embarrassed. He looked away for a long moment and then back at her penetrating eyes. "If you will rest and take in adequate fluids, you will recover in time to return to work next week and then this silly mood will pass. You're not feeling yourself." He put his hand on her hot brow and rose to get a damp cloth from a wide-mouthed bowl nearby. He wiped her fevered cheeks and she closed her eyes for a moment.

He turned, suddenly weary, and placed his hat on his head and straightened his glasses. Charissa opened her eyes and gazed at him. "I read a quote last night from Phillips Brooks. He said that the worst thing in life is not to find no meaning in it." Samuel had her attention now and it made him itchy with nerves. He swallowed hard. "He said that the worst thing would be not to . . . um . . . miss life itself but to never find the delight one finds in friendship with the Father. It made me wonder if I had been missing it myself—missed something that might have seen me through many dark nights. I will pray for you this night, Mrs. Nadal, and through the week. And I will be back tomorrow to make sure you're feeling better."

Salma was at his side then. Tipping his head, he departed Charissa's room, taking his first deep breath in the hallway. The maid led the way, and at the bottom of the stairs, gave him a gentle smile. "You will be good for Mrs. Nadal, Doctor Johnson," she said. "And she will be a fine nurse for you."

Chapter Three

> "Two are better than one; because they have a good
> reward for their labour. For if they fall, the one will
> lift up his fellow: but woe to him that is alone when he
> falleth; for he hath not another to help him up. . . .
> And if one prevail against him, two shall withstand
> him; and a threefold cord is not quickly broken."
>
> Nurse Nadal, be ever sure that I shall see to your
> physical well-being. And remember that a friendship
> with the Father is the strongest strand to life. No one
> can conquer your spirit with the Lord by your side.
>
> Sincerely,
> Samuel Johnson

Charissa let the note fall to her side again, after rereading it for the fifth time. Life. Friendship with the Father. A relationship that could not be ended by death, indeed was transcended through it. Samuel's words echoed through her mind. Every day, the faithful physician came to visit his nurse, now a patient, each afternoon carrying with him new advice, new instruction. Not merely medical wisdom, but words of eternal value that she'd never considered before. There was a surprising strength, an iron will buried beneath Samuel's softer expressions. And she felt galvanized by his presence.

Salma entered the bedroom with her breakfast tray, and Charissa glanced in her direction. Was the long, lithe woman gaining weight? Perhaps she had been eating all the food Charissa sent away untouched in the last week. "I . . . I think I shall take my breakfast by the window," Charissa said, rising to move toward the sunlight. It surprised her that she felt so weak after six days in bed. Today was the first day she felt a bit of herself returning. Salma studied her with those wide, black eyes.

Charissa frowned. Salma did not look well herself this day.

"That Doctor Johnson is good for you, miss." Salma set the tray down on a tiny table by the window and drew open the drapes. She turned and lifted the cover from the plate, grimaced, as if disgusted by the food, then fled the room.

"Salma?" Charissa called in alarm. "Salma!"

Charissa followed her down the hall, trembling. What was wrong with the woman? Had she contracted the influenza as well? What if Salma became sick and died like Ari? Charissa could not bear it! If it hadn't been for Salma, Charissa would surely have perished during the long days since Ari's passing. Charissa might not be in this place, fighting for direction and life, as well as health. "Salma?" she asked gently, feeling as afraid as a lost child.

"Yeah, Miz Nadal, I'm here," she said from the other side of the water-closet door.

"Are you . . . ? You are ill. You must take to your bed."

"No, miss."

"I insist. It is obvious that you are not well. When Dr. Johnson comes to call today, he will see to you instead of me."

"No, miss."

"Why?" Charissa stared up at her tall friend as she at last emerged.

"Because I'm not sick. Expectin' a child, come April. That's all that ails me."

Charissa stepped back. A child. How she and Ari had longed . . . she shook her head. It was time to stop remembering the past and focus on the future, that was what Samuel had said. Salma's husband was away, working on the constantly expanding railroad. She would need Charissa.

"Of course, Samuel will see to you. What better reason than pregnancy for the new doctor in town to attend to you?" Charissa felt stronger than she had felt in months. A baby was on its way! Life drew near like the tide upon the beach, flowing closer, pulling her in. "His nurse will see to it," she added.

• ● •

Samuel bowed his head and listened to the silence within his home, the creak of saddle leather and the whinny of a horse outside. He sighed. Another patient, one of an endless stream, it seemed. The sheer volume of patients threatened to suck him under like a tidal wave.

A Mexican, with an unconscious man slung over his shoulder, banged the door open and started chattering in what Samuel guessed was Spanish.

"I only speak English," Samuel said slowly, holding up a hand. But he could clearly see what was wrong. The Mexican man's companion had been severely beaten. Another railroad brawl. Already, after being on the job for only a week, he had treated more than ten men for similar injuries.

There was talk on the streets of running the Chinese out of town, that they stole all the jobs. *"If we don't watch it, there won't be a living wage for a white feller"*; the words bounded from saloon to saloon, from the lumberyard to the hills surrounding Seattle. Of course it wasn't true. Few were willing to do what the Chinese did along the railroad tracks, in the shipyards, in the packing factories. But there always had to be a scapegoat. In Boise, it was the Shoshone Indians. In Ohio, where he had been raised, it had been the Negroes, a generation out of slavery. In medical school, it had been anyone who threatened a person's station. As Mrs. Nadal had threatened the doctors of Seattle.

By the time he finished, it was eight o'clock. The patient seemed to be resting comfortably, and Samuel gave a nod of encouragement to the man's friend. "I think he will see again from that eye," Samuel said slowly. "But we won't know for several days." He motioned to the bone above his own eye, where he knew the man had seen his friend's sunken brow for himself. "It is dangerous when this bone breaks," he said with a worried shake of the head. "It makes it more difficult for him to recuperate."

But then, he hadn't expected Charissa's Chinese patient

to make it—he'd been sure the man would succumb to septicemia. But he hadn't. He had made a good recovery and gone home a week after he had arrived.

The Mexican nodded quickly, as if understanding every word. Samuel tried to smile encouragingly, but he was frustrated. Caring for people who spoke no English called upon every resource within him—patience, ingenuity, strength, courage. And he felt depleted today, not strong enough for the task. In the last week alone, Samuel supposed he had heard over fourteen dialects and languages. How could one adequately care for his patients when one could not communicate? He needed to find several translators, and hope that upon Charissa's return, she would be of good help rather than a distraction. He needed to find a supplier for medical necessities, a good laundress for the office linens . . . the list went on and on. Most urgently he needed to connect with the other doctors in the city in order to confer on medical treatments when the injury or problem went beyond his field of knowledge.

He considered going over to Mrs. Nadal's home, but decided to let her rest. He comforted himself with the knowledge that she had been feeling better the day before. Besides, it was late and he was plumb tired, ready for some food, some prayer, and some big sleep.

• • •

"Where was Dr. Johnson last night?" Charissa asked the next morning, pacing.

"Missin' the good doctor?" Salma asked, placing her

breakfast tray on the table by the window. "I'd say if you's well enough to pace, you's well enough to traipse on down there yourself and ask him."

"I have simply come to expect him. And yesterday I was hoping he would come to examine you."

"Maybe he had to see to someone else," Salma said quietly, taking the cover from the tray—this time, not pausing to see or smell the food—and slipping out the door.

Another patient? Charissa was surprised by the thought, then startled that it left her feeling jealous. Had not her own Ari been constantly called upon by others? Had she herself not been continuously busy as soon as she opened her doors again, even if she was "just a nurse"? Only Samuel's notes assuaged some of her frustration; but then, what kind of friend was he to abandon her when she needed him, when Salma needed him?

She retired to bed that evening as she did each night— with one of Ari's love letters. She imagined him writing them at the old captain's desk. Imagined him sitting there, his black curls wisping errantly at the neck. Imagined him turning and smiling softly at her as she lay in bed, drowsy.

Tonight, his smile was wistful, making him seem more distant. She frowned and sat up straight in bed. She could not remember. Suddenly, Charissa could not remember exactly what he looked like when he turned to her from his desk, with desire and love in his eyes. How was it that he had held his eyebrows? What had it been that sparked in his eyes? Images of Samuel's kind eyes—eyes that truly beheld her, almost caressed her with their care—kept coming to her instead.

She pulled the love letters out en masse. Urgently, she

opened one, and then the next. *"You are like cold water to a thirsting man,"* Ari had written her early in their courtship, before they had even really known each other. *"How I would take to the icy mountains, the dry desert, any place to serve you,"* he had written later, in the midst of the crushing news that children were unlikely. She laughed without mirth. Hadn't he left her that fateful day even though she had begged him to stay? *"I would hunt down and throttle any man who hurt you,"* he promised. *"You shall never fear as long as I am by your side."* But where was he now? What was she to do now, with him gone? She felt weak, vulnerable. *"I long for the days of our elder years, when I have nothing to do but sit beside my beloved and prove to her that all I have done has been for her. The days of our youth shall fade, but our latter days shall show you that true love survives. Forever."*

Then the tears began to flow again, tears she thought had dried up, for what would never be. Charissa lay down amidst the letters, as if held in her lover's arms. As if she were held by an Ari forty years older, after a lifetime together. How she had longed for that! But it was not to be. She was alone. And expected to move forward, back into life without him. It was the hardest task she'd ever faced, but she would move back into life, embrace it, live it fully. She would investigate what it meant to have a friendship with the Father, and see if it was the missing key to the puzzle that had become her life.

• • •

Salma showed Samuel to Charissa's room at 11 P.M. He had awakened and was unable to fall back asleep, feeling as if he had neglected Charissa. She was a priority. In seeing her to a place of wholeness deep within, Samuel knew he would get a glimpse of wholeness himself—perhaps find the path all the way back to healing. Who knew what had transpired in the last forty-eight hours? Influenza could be nasty, deadly. She might have had a relapse, her fever rising again.

"She fell asleep hours ago," Salma said, leading the way up the stairs, holding a lantern aloft. She paused near the top and let him pass by, never allowing her watchful gaze to fall from him.

"I know. Forgive me. I tended to a man with a leg wound earlier this evening, then went to bed thinking she would be all right." He cast Salma a rueful glance. "Couldn't sleep without knowing for sure. Let me take her vitals, and then I will be out of here."

"Miz Nadal wondered where you might be. I told her the kind doctor was most likely seeing to other patients."

He turned around, halfway through Charissa's bedroom door. "She was expecting me? She asked about me?" he whispered urgently.

"Yes, doctor. She asked. She was none too happy when I said you hadn't come, though," she warned, a twinkle in her weary eye. She lowered her voice. "I think she's on the mend in more ways than one," she said, gazing at him as if she were in on a conspiracy. She offered him the lantern.

"Perhaps," Samuel allowed. "Perhaps." Lifting Salma's lantern high, he went inside, leaving the door open for Salma to follow. "Mrs. Nadal?"

Charissa was spread out on the coverlet amidst a smattering of letters, all in the same script. He took a step back.

She was lovely, so lovely, with her hair now in glistening, brushed waves of black oil, her skin a soft olive.

"Mrs. Nadal," he said a bit more loudly. "Charissa," he tried finally, bending low.

"Ari?" She sat up as though a shot had been fired.

"No," he said sorrowfully. "Forgive me, Mrs. Nadal, it's late. I just could not sleep until I had checked on you this night."

Red-rimmed eyes beheld him, disappointment clearly drawn. But there was a spark of life, a light he had not seen before, like a candle shining beyond a drawn shade. He wondered what it meant, what had ignited it.

She dutifully reclined and he listened to her lungs and checked her pulse. He asked her the now-routine questions about diet and liquid intake and output.

"You are improving," he said, nodding.

"I am well," she said. Was that a tinge of anger in her tone?

"You are not pleased?"

"Pleased enough."

"Mrs. Nadal, is there something wrong?"

"Why is it," she asked, sitting up straight, "that you have not come to see me in the last two days?"

"I had others to attend to," he said carefully, winding up his stethoscope tube.

She laughed under her breath, a singular sound. He looked up to find no merriment in her eyes. "Always another patient. You doctors are all the same." She fingered one of the letters.

"From him?" Samuel chanced, gesturing beside her.

She looked up and nodded, moisture in her luminous eyes. "From him," she said softly.

He moved to a chair by her bed, suddenly anxious for a little more distance from his patient. But there was an openness in her tonight, a gate cracked that he could not pass by. He glanced back to the doorway. Salma had disappeared.

She picked up a random letter, unfolded it, and began reading: "'*You are the beacon on the rocky coast, the mission on a lonely trail. You are the summer shower in the midst of drought. The sun-ripened wheat to a starving man.*'"

"He was a poet," Samuel said quietly.

"Indeed," she whispered.

"You must miss him very much."

"Every day. But tonight . . . I was frightened."

"Why?"

"I'm starting to forget. I wish I had a picture of him. A picture from every moment of the day. When he was happy, and when he was angry. I'm forgetting how he looked, how he held his brow, his chin . . . " She paused, embarrassed at sharing so much.

Samuel nodded. It was enough that she had dared to open up as she had. And almost too much for him to hear—how often had he felt the same fear about his memories of Mamie? He swallowed hard, finding his mouth suddenly cottony. Charissa looked so beautiful there, yet so alone surrounded by her love letters from her lost husband. It was humiliating, witnessing the depths of the Nadals' passion for each other, the testament to their love.

He had written Mamie two, maybe three, letters in their courtship. He had never been able to find words adequate to express all that was inside him. They came out flat and stilted. And yet Mamie never complained. Their relationship had been a simple one, but solid. He cleared his throat when his eyes met Charissa's questioning gaze.

"I am pleased that you are improving, Mrs. Nadal. Do you feel up to coming to work tomorrow for the morning or the afternoon?"

"I will be there first thing," she promised, and lay back down amidst her letters.

"Good night, Mrs. Nadal."

"Good night, Dr. Johnson. Oh, and, Doctor?"

"Yes?"

"When I come, I will bring Salma. She needs to be examined."

"She is unwell?"

"She is in need of a doctor . . . " She let the sentence drop and her eyes drifted closed.

He left her to her memories and gently shut the door behind him, but he felt her presence beside him all the way down the block and around the corner. He shook off the uncanny feeling. It was probably the urge to share his own grief over Mamie with her. No one could understand how he missed Mamie. Yes, Charissa mourned her husband. But their relationship had been passionate, perhaps tempestuous. His love with Mamie had been quiet, without bumps. Just as intense, but a different shade of red altogether. Different.

Samuel glanced up at the waxing moon amidst broken clouds, moving fast to the east. "Keep your hand upon us, Lord. Thank you for bringing us this far. I pray for Charissa's total healing. And mine," he added softly.

Chapter Four

"The missus was hollering at me to pay your bill, Doctor, but I ain't got it," Mr. Conner soberly explained the next morning at sunup. He gestured out toward the front porch. "I'm hopin' this piece I brought ya will settle things between us."

On his porch sat a beautiful, handmade, wooden rocker. "It's beautiful, Mr. Conner. More than payment enough."

The old man grinned at him. "The missus and I appreciate all you done, helping her with her consumption and all."

"You just make sure she takes plenty of liquids and rests up. Those coughs tend to resurface if you don't take care of yourself."

"You got it, Doc. G'afternoon."

Samuel closed his eyes and rocked back and forth, back and forth, hoping the headache right behind his eyes would ease, trying to block the busy sounds of an awakening city. It was good to be here, where patients came to him, rather than traveling out to see them. Seattle was booming, but had it changed all that much since then? He wondered if he would ever have the chance to make a housecall again.

Charissa quietly cleared her throat, and Samuel painfully opened his eyes and raised his head, straightening his glasses as he did so. "Why, Nurse Nadal," he greeted her with pleasure. "You are . . . up and about! And looking fine in your work clothes, if I may add. If things remain this busy, I'll be very happy for the extra assistance."

"Dr. Johnson." She raised her white-and-blue-striped skirts and climbed the stairs to the porch as he rose. "Were you up all night?"

"All night. Man named Ping was stabbed last night outside the Silver Tip Saloon. Almost lost him; he's resting upstairs now." His tongue felt thick, his thoughts fuzzy from lack of sleep.

"It looks like we're about to lose you," she said, gently studying him. "Why don't you go upstairs and rest a spell? I'll look after our patient."

"Our patient. Sounds like music to my ears, I tell you."

"Go then. I'll awaken you in a few hours, or if anything alarming transpires with Ping. Remind me when I do that I must speak to you of Salma. She wouldn't come with me this morning."

"If I can remember a thing." He rose and wearily made his way to the door.

"Are you sorry you've taken this on, Dr. Johnson?"

"Sorry?" he asked, raising his eyebrows. "I've never felt more alive. Especially now that the cavalry's here." He smiled at her, feeling relaxed and daring in his sleepiness.

The young woman looked down and then out to the

street. "I am glad that Ari's business is proving to be successful for you. He would have . . . " her words faded. "Tell me, have his patients been surprised to find you here?"

Samuel smiled gently. "Most had heard that I'd bought the business from you. Many spoke highly about your husband's skill as a doctor. Several told me he had saved a loved one's life."

Charissa remained silent, but Samuel knew by the spark of pride in her eyes that she was pleased.

"Your husband was obviously quite a doctor," he went on.

"He was," she said, nodding slowly. Then she looked directly at Samuel. "And you're just the man to take over his business."

"I'll do my best to cover his territory."

"Good enough. You have signed the papers I left for you?"

"I have. And I have the banknote for you too. How are you feeling today?"

"I am faring fine. I think I have gained back most of my strength in the last day, and as you can see, I'm even out and about." She paused, gathering herself. "Thank you, Doctor, for seeing to me." Her eyes locked with his, her gaze intense. "Thank you for everything."

"I have done little." He looked away, embarrassed.

"To me, it meant a great deal. Anyway," she said, dismissing the intimate moment, "you go and rest now."

"Yes, ma'am." Wearily he trudged up the stairs and closed his bedroom door to the chattering in Ping's room, filled with so many of his clan. His senses were alive, as if they were soldiers on alert. What was it about Charissa Nadal that made him feel like Lazarus back from the grave, when he was dead on his feet? Still fully clothed, he lay down, sure he wouldn't be able to sleep now. And then he was dreaming. Dreaming of Charissa.

• ● •

"Dr. Johnson, Dr. Johnson!" Charissa wondered if she would ever be able to raise the man, and indeed, she had been reluctant to do so; he had looked so peaceful, so happy in his dreamland. But Ping was spiking a fever again, and she had tried everything she knew of to lower it. She doubted Samuel would know of anything else to do, but she longed for a second opinion, a companion in the worrying, if nothing else.

"Wh-what?"

"Dr. Johnson, you have been asleep for six hours. You need to see to Ping. His fever is raging again."

"Oh. Yes, yes. And you need to speak to me of Salma." He swung his long legs over the side of the bed, sat up, rubbed his face, and stared at the wall in front of him. There was a tender quality to a man just out of sleep, childlike, uninhibited in his actions. Then, embarrassed at her intimate train of thought, she concentrated on the wide, clear pine of the far wall instead.

"I have wondered if she is well," Samuel said of Salma.

"Salma is expecting a child."

Samuel swallowed hard and paused oddly. "Oh."

"I would like for you to examine her and care for her. See her child safely into the world."

"I cannot do that. I do not see any obstetrical patients."

"What? Why not?"

He rose and looked down at her, his eyes wide and sad. "I had a rather unfortunate . . . experience with my last OB patient. I will see Salma now, to make sure all is well, but then I must transfer her care to a qualified doctor who specializes in obstetrics."

• • •

The young woman studied him until he could not meet her gaze any longer. She seemed to see right through him, as if she could see him that night beside his dead wife and child. "Are you certain, Dr. Johnson, that you cannot see to Salma's care? I was so certain—"

"I am most certain," he interrupted with a scoffing tone. "Listen. I give you my word that I will find an adequate physician myself." Her gaze was unflinching and he felt himself losing ground. "Until I find someone suitable, I will not abandon Salma's care," he compromised. "Is that acceptable?"

Slowly, with confusion in her eyes, Charissa nodded once. "Salma means everything to me, Doctor. Anything you can do will be most appreciated. We must get back to Ping now," she said. "Come. I will feel better about his condition once you've examined him yourself."

She led the way and then turned in the hallway to watch Samuel pass into Ping's room. He did not glance at her. She no doubt wondered about his refusal of her request to care for Salma. After all, what could make him afraid of delivering a child? He had trudged right past the angry mob of men that first night they met. He had been fearless then, but the thought of making a mistake with someone Charissa obviously cared deeply about made his palms sweaty.

He turned back toward her before disappearing into the room still crowded with Ping's visitors. "Trust me on this, Nurse Nadal. Salma and her child are safer with you than they ever would be with me."

As he saw to Ping, laid a fresh cloth on his sweating brow, sent his relatives scuttling away, Samuel's thoughts were on a night two years earlier, in his old house . . .

• ● •

"You listen to me," Samuel said, leaning close enough to touch his wife's forehead with his own. "You're going to get through this, Mamie," he promised.

Sweat poured down her pale face and she didn't respond. She had been laboring for hours. Was it just yesterday that she had met him at the door with the news that their child was to be born? She had never looked more radiant to him than she had at that moment, her light brown hair coming loose from her bun, her milk chocolate eyes alight. He had swept her into his arms and said, "You are beautiful, Mamie. And soon we will be three."

He leaned away from her and, hiding his worried expression, reached for the damp cloth. He rinsed it out in the basin beside the bed. The baby was making little progress, and Samuel knew they were at a crossroads. He either had to do a caesarean section on his wife or watch her die with their child inside.

He stood and paced, vacillating on what to do. He had

seen the procedure done in medical school, but it had been eight years ago. Only once in his practice—through over fifty deliveries—had he had to perform one on his own. The woman had finally fallen unconscious after losing so much blood, and with a nod from the husband, he had performed the caesarean and saved the child. Miraculously, the mother recovered too. But sadly, that was not often the case. Even now, in the relatively modern medical times of 1888, most caesareans were performed on mothers who were dead or expected to succumb anyway.

Samuel wiped his damp face. That woman had been a distant neighbor, not his Mamie. Not his sweet, loving wife. He wrung his hands and glanced over at her, her eyes closed as she rested between contractions. She was a strong woman, a good spouse, a best friend to him. They had been through much together. But finally he admitted that odds were she wouldn't make it. Everything in him told him it was wrong to take a knife to her. Wrong to admit defeat and give up on his Mamie's survival. But then he shook his head again. He couldn't do it; he just couldn't.

• ● •

Samuel swallowed hard, trying to focus on Ping, not the nightmare of losing his wife and son. It had been a year since the dream had returned to him, jolting him from slumber, a year since he had relived those last, awful moments.

It was his discussion with Charissa Nadal that had brought it to the surface of his subconscious and let it leak back into the painful threshold of consciousness. Seeing her amidst her husband's love letters, still grieving his absence. He felt empty, aghast at the abyss in his chest, as if he had just lost them again. It had been real, so real, and he ached to go back to the dream, daring to encounter that excruciating pain just so he could hold Mamie one more time, tell her he loved her, try to save her and the baby sooner. Why, oh why had he been such a fool? How could he have let them slip through his fingers?

He fought for breath and gave in to more tears. He had let them go, let this grief go, in so many ways. Would it always follow him around, just around the corner, ready to pounce on him any time, any place? *Please, God, release me from this agony. Spare me these memories! Let me leave their deaths behind and embrace my new life. I need to go on, not linger in the past. Isn't it you who has led me here?*

He heard no answer. Samuel dropped his face into his hands and silently wept again.

• • •

"Mrs. Nadal?"

With a start, Charissa realized that she had been standing stock-still, staring at her wedding photograph on the stairway wall.

"It still hurts, doesn't it?"

"What?"

Dr. Johnson gingerly stepped away. "You miss Dr. Nadal a great deal," he said, clarifying.

"Of course I do," Charissa huffed. "You presume to know me too well, Doctor."

"I beg your pardon, Nurse." He bowed slightly and

raised his face again to turn calm brown eyes upon her. There was a quiet quality about Samuel that Charissa found at once reassuring and yet disconcerting, as if he knew her and accepted her just the way she was, when he really didn't know her at all.

"Salma is ready to see me?"

"Yes. She awakened feeling poorly. More than her usual morning sickness. I am frightened that she has contracted the influenza. I'll show you to her room," Charissa said, uncomfortable under his penetrating gaze. "She stays with me when her husband is away."

Samuel gave her that shy smile again, and Charissa turned and rushed down the hall. What was it about this man that so unnerved her all of a sudden? She had encountered many men since Ari's death, but none that made her feel so . . . so cared for. . . .

She reached out and knocked on her friend's door. "Salma? May we come in? The doctor is here to see you." Charissa glanced back at Samuel, who was nervously fingering his medical bag.

Was he a bit ashen? What exactly had happened to his last obstetrical patient? With some trepidation, she opened the door, trusting the kind doctor to do his best with this patient, regardless of what had happened in the past.

•   •   •

"She's worried about you," Samuel said to Salma.

"Just a touch of fever."

"You're right," he said, feeling her head. "Nothing like

Mrs. Nadal's." He picked up her wrist and felt for a pulse, timing it with his pocket watch.

"She frets, the missus."

"You are important to her." Satisfied that the young woman was not nearly as ill as her mistress had been, he tucked her arm back under the sheet and looked into her luminous brown eyes. "Still feeling sick in the mornings?"

"Mos' every day."

"It will pass in time. You seem to be in good health. I will see to finding you alternate care at my first opportunity."

"You's afraid."

Samuel willed his eyes to meet hers. "Yes. Yes, I am."

She let his words seep into the air about them for a long moment. "Who'd you lose, Doctor Sam?"

"My wife and child. Two years ago."

Salma closed her eyes as if feeling a measure of his pain. "My momma always said there ain't no pain like losin' your own."

"Your mother was right." He rose and busied himself by packing up his few instruments. "You'll be better off in someone else's care, Salma. I'll see to it that you'll be seen by a competent, experienced doctor."

"You's that doctor, Doctor Sam. I know it in my heart. You just gots to see it too."

He didn't dare meet her knowing gaze again; he couldn't. "You just see to yourself now, Salma. You've got a touch of the influenza, and it's best if you don't let it get as bad as Mrs. Nadal's. Fevers are bad for babies."

Salma frowned and rubbed a hand over her slightly bulging belly. "I don't want anything bad to happen to my baby. You'll make sure?" She reached out a slender hand and gripped his arm with a strength that surprised him.

"I'll do what I can, Salma. Fevers have to run their course. You can do your part by staying in bed and resting. Don't be getting up and pushing yourself."

"Yessir," she said. Her eyes told him she had more to say, but he put on his hat and tipped it toward her. "I'll be back tomorrow to see to you, Salma. Good day."

• ● •

Charissa did not sit. She paced the hallway outside Salma's room. In ten minutes, Samuel emerged and shut the door behind him. "She is all right?" Charissa asked worriedly.

"I would agree with your diagnosis—I'm afraid she has contracted the influenza. Hopefully, she'll get better soon and this won't endanger her child. She's nearing the end of her first trimester. The babe is due this spring. I will need to find another doctor for her soon. Preferably tomorrow, with this turn of events."

"There is no other doctor. Not for anyone of color."

The doctor stared out at the dusty street and straightened his spectacles. "Give her some of Mrs. Gustavson's chicken broth tonight," he dictated. "I expect you to stay here and care for her tomorrow; don't come to work. She is your first priority."

"As ordered, Doctor," Charissa said in relief. Ari would never have thought twice about leaving Salma alone in favor of having his assistant beside him. She was startled to realize that she'd just compared the two men so.

"Very well." He patted his bag as if mentally going through his instruments, to be sure all remained with him. "Good day, Mrs. Nadal," he said softly, setting off down the street.

He was curious, the good doctor. Dedicated. Kind. Even when she was abrupt and less than kind to him. What drove him? motivated him?

She watched him walk down the street, away from her home, back toward his office. His shoulders were slightly hunched, his gait rambling. He seemed to have lost all the good cheer he had displayed for her.

"He lost his wife same as you lost Dr. Nadal," Salma said from directly behind her, scaring her half to death. The maid could move with the stealth of a plains Indian on the attack, but Charissa immediately covered her dismay. Salma would make a big deal of finding her staring after the doctor.

"What? What did you say? And what are you doing out of bed?"

"His wife. Dr. Johnson's," Salma said, ignoring Charissa's complaint, nodding after the form growing tiny in the distance. "You are looking after him; I see it with my own eyes. She died, about the same time you lost Doctor Ari."

Charissa felt deflated, utterly taken aback. She had suspected that Samuel Johnson had suffered a loss or two in life, but nothing of the magnitude that she herself had suffered. She returned her gaze to the street, no longer caring if Salma saw her or not. Here, he had been looking after her, coming even late at night to see to her health, and yet she had been blind to the pain that he buried deep within himself.

He was no longer visible along the street.

And the knowledge of it left Charissa curiously bereft.

Chapter Five

They had worked together for over a month now, and Samuel could not stand it any longer. He assumed Charissa knew about his wife's death because he had told Salma. This little bit of information she had made Charissa dangerous to his heart. The last thing he wanted was for her warm, sympathetic eyes to melt him and leave him a puddle on the floor.

He had made a concerted effort to be strictly business with her, discussing only patients' care and treatment, ever careful to steer conversation away from the personal. It was a daunting challenge, because the petite woman had a way of prying at the crevasses of his defenses. The only thing he did in a personal manner with Charissa was to continue to leave her small notes of encouragement, telling himself he was merely seeing to her moral and mental well-being, not reaching out in anything that might be construed as . . . romantic.

"Come with us to the county picnic," Charissa repeated as they cleaned up after a long day in the office. "What could it hurt? Everyone needs a little time to recreate."

"It isn't appropriate for a doctor to be seen socializing with his nurse."

"I used to socialize with the last doctor in this part of town. Nobody looked at us askance."

He let the smile grow across his face and shook his head. "That was entirely different."

"Only if you let it be." She looked into his eyes with a penetrating gaze.

"Do you always get what you want, Mrs. Nadal?"

"Nearly always," she said with a smile that matched his own. "Ari always said I was more persistent than a Mediterranean breeze. Besides," she returned to the topic of the picnic, "it's only a box social—odds are I could end up with a totally different gentleman for the remainder of the day."

"Well, when you word it so invitingly . . . how could I refuse?" He quirked a brow at her. "But at least give me the pleasure of being the one to ask. I am a gentleman after all."

"By all means," she said, another smile tugging at the corners of her lips.

"Will you do me the honor of joining me at the county picnic this Saturday, Mrs. Nadal?"

"Why, Doctor Johnson! This is so unexpected!"

He laughed then, louder than he had laughed in years. She was outrageous, impetuous, charming. And utterly irresistible. He would be delighted to spend the afternoon with her. Even if someone else bid on her box and stole her away, although the thought of that was oddly disturbing.

They stared at each other until they both shifted uncomfortably and then returned to their work of cleaning the examination room, working side by side.

"How is it with you, Dr. Johnson?" Charissa asked after a bit. "Are you feeling settled in Seattle?"

He looked over at her. Everything about Charissa Nadal made him feel increasingly unsettled. He laughed under his breath.

"Did I say something amusing?" She wiped a wet, black lock from her forehead. It was a hot summer day, and yet she wore her heavy wool uniform. Her olive skin glistened and there was a rosy hue in her cheeks.

"No, no. Yes, to answer your question—I think Seattle will be home for me. Eventually."

"Do you want a new home? Or are you running from your old home?" she asked softly. She stared at him for several long seconds and then turned to look at the examination table, crossing her arms.

"And what gives you the impression that I'm running from something?"

"I'm sorry. It's none of my business really. You don't have to be so strong though . . . you know?" Her eyes searched his, prying again, trying to loosen the chains around his heart.

Sighing, he reached inside his coat pocket and pulled out a scrap of paper. They were done cleaning, and for once, there was no one at the door waiting to see a doctor. Placing his hat upon his head, Samuel paused beside Charissa and then carefully handed her another note. "Granted, it takes the heart longer to heal than the body," he said quietly. "We do our best to make it through the hard times. We do our best to make the most of the good times. I hope I'm not running. I hope I'm here for good." Then he turned to leave.

"Where are you going?"

"To dinner." He cocked a brow at her. "Not because I'm running. Because I'm hungry. And you, Nurse Nadal, should go home and make sure Salma is still feeling better."

When she smiled, he left, and whistled all the way down the street to the new hotel for a supper of fried chicken, mashed potatoes, and fresh corn on the cob.

●　●　●

She waited until he closed the door behind him before she looked at the note the kindhearted doctor had left. Oh, how he intrigued her! He was a puzzle she wanted to figure out.

She paced back and forth, thinking about Samuel Johnson, and finally walked out to the front-parlor office. Her eyes moved over the thin wallpaper she had hung herself—curling in a few corners now—across the few paintings Ari had been able to afford, to Samuel's framed medical certificate where Ari's had once hung, and down to the furniture she and Ari had picked out together. Ari had wanted something welcoming, calming, like the front parlor of a house, not an austere and impersonal office.

The new doctor had added a hutch filled with different pharmaceutical supplies. Charissa nodded in approval. A wise business decision, to make medicines available himself and cut out the mercantile as middleman. Plus, Samuel could watch the inventory and not rely on another to keep on hand what patients often desperately needed. It had always aggravated Ari when the local merchants failed to order a bottle of quinine or sold his stock to another doctor.

Samuel Johnson was a smart man and arrogant. Not in the way that Ari had been—blindly, bullishly moving forward without a thought to the people around him—but in a prideful way that made him stubbornly hold on to his secrets as if no one else could quite understand him, quite empathize with what he had been through. Had she not been through the same? She had loved Ari with all she had in her. How could he have loved Mamie any more?

Suddenly miffed again, she went to gather her bag and stuffed the paper in her pocket. She would read it later. Later when she didn't feel so . . . unsettled. What was it about Samuel Johnson that made her so thoughtful yet so unbalanced? Unable to wait a moment longer, she reached into her pocket and ripped open the envelope. It was a long passage this time, uncharacteristic of her quiet doctor friend.

Blessed be the God and Father of our Lord Jesus Christ, which according to his abundant mercy hath begotten us again unto a lively hope by the resurrection of Jesus Christ from the dead, to an inheritance incorruptible, and undefiled, and that fadeth not away, reserved in heaven for you, who are kept by the power of God through faith unto salvation ready to be revealed in the last time. Wherein ye greatly rejoice, though now for a season, if need be, ye are in heaviness through manifold temptations: that the trial of your faith, being much more precious than of gold that perisheth, though it be tried with fire, might be found

*unto praise and honour and glory at the appearing of
Jesus Christ: whom having not seen, ye love; in whom,
though now ye see him not, yet believing, ye rejoice
with joy unspeakable and full of glory: receiving the
end of your faith, even the salvation of your souls.*

Charissa tied her hat bow beneath her chin and glanced
out at the beautiful evening, out into the twilight that would
last until ten or ten-thirty. She loved summer along the
Sound, but even the quieting city and soft lights inside the
houses along her route home did not keep her mind from
Samuel's words, God's words: *"According to his abundant
mercy hath begotten us again unto a lively hope . . . to an inheritance incorruptible, and undefiled, and that fadeth not
away. . . . Wherein ye greatly rejoice, though now for a season,
if need be, ye are in heaviness through manifold temptations:
that the trial of your faith, being much more precious than of
gold that perisheth, though it be tried with fire, might be found
unto praise and honour and glory. . . ."*

She paused at the crest of a gently sloping hill to see a
peekaboo view of the water, where forest met wave. She imagined the coastline looked much the same as it had for decades,
for centuries even, at least where the rebuilding hadn't
sculpted away the Seattle hillsides. Perhaps a newly carved
beach here, a redefined pebbled slope there . . . was God like
the ocean? Ever expansive, sometimes ebbing and flowing
from a person's back, sometimes pounding one into a new
formation? Her eyes scanned Samuel's poorly crafted script
again for the jewels buried within. *"Begotten us again . . .
lively hope . . . fadeth not away . . . are in heaviness . . . more*

*precious than of gold . . . tried with fire . . . found unto praise
and honour . . ."*

She studied the sun, making a steady path toward the
western waters. God seemed to come around after her, like
the sun came back around every day. Was this what she was
missing? the answer to the uneasiness in her soul? She smiled
as she felt a wave of the sun's last burst of warmth cast over
her face and send a tingle down her arms. Was this the beginning of what Samuel had quoted from Brooks—about a
friendship with the Father?

She was still thinking about the note the next morning,
still in a reverie about the hope Samuel's words had instilled
in her heart, and about how she and Doctor Johnson were
getting along like cucumbers and onions in a Greek summer
salad, when the office door burst open. "It's my wife," said a
young man, his arm around a slender girl as they entered the
office. "She says her head feels as if it might fall off it hurts so
bad."

"Doctor!" came another voice from outside. "We needs
a doctor!" Looking desperate, a black man appeared in the
door frame behind the young couple. Sweat poured down his
face as if he had run a mile. "My friend—a cowpoke done
shot him! You gotta come with me, Doc!"

Samuel looked urgently from the three before him to his
present patient, Mrs. Foraker, who was in because of a stomach-
ache, and then over to Charissa.

Charissa stepped forward and took the young woman's
arm. "Probably a migraine attack," she said softly, conscious
that loud noises aggravated headaches. "Have you been

eating?" She led the girl upstairs to where she could find rest and quiet. A dark shade, a cool cloth, a dose of digitalis . . .

Behind her, Charissa heard Samuel efficiently finish with Mrs. Foraker before he grabbed some instruments and bandages to care for the gunshot victim. He pulled up short at the bottom of the stairs. "Mrs. Nadal?" he said softly.

"Yes," she said, turning to look down into his eyes.

"Thank you. Thank you for being here."

"You're welcome, Dr. Johnson. I wouldn't want to be anywhere else."

• • •

It had been an exhausting day. Patient after patient had poured into the office. Samuel and Charissa had worked together all day, until finally, he sent Charissa home. If only he had done it in better fashion.

She had been trying to help, obviously dead on her feet herself. Reaching for some alcohol, she had tipped over the tall glass, sending it shattering to the wood floor. Then she went to roll the gunshot victim, to keep him from lying too long in one position, and inadvertently rolled him onto his wound. He had cried out in agony, and she had blanched in horror.

"Go! Go home! You're so tired you're no good to any of us. Go get some sleep," Samuel had shouted. Even now, he cringed at the memory of his gaffe.

Tears had risen in her eyes, ringed with purple from weariness, and then she had turned and fled.

Now he had to go and apologize for his foolery. "'A word

fitly spoken is like apples of gold in pictures of silver,'" Samuel muttered. "'A word fitly spoken is like apples of gold in pictures of silver,'" he repeated, using this verse from Proverbs as a means of berating himself. He had fouled things up. Again.

He had never been any good with words, never a poet, never good at explaining things in depth. Not like Ari. And yet Mamie had always understood him, had been able to translate his intentions and look past his bumbling and see his true self within. But she had always been like that, ever ready to see the best in people. There were few like her.

Charissa was certainly nothing like Mamie. She had probably gone home to read all those love letters from Ari Nadal, a man who had never said a cross word to her, never said anything he didn't mean, and always spoke eloquently.

Samuel was good at getting to the bottom of an ailment and prescribing a simple, clear-cut treatment. His methods were sufficient, but far from the elaborate ministrations that he had heard Dr. Ari Nadal had lavished upon his patients. He felt out of his depth in comparison, both with his patients and with Charissa. Maybe his choice to come here had been ill conceived. Maybe Charissa was right: perhaps he was running.

He turned the corner and wearily climbed the front stairs of the Nadal home. He knocked, forcing himself to not just tap and then walk quickly away with the excuse that he had tried to see her.

Salma opened the door and looked him over suspiciously.

"May I see Mrs. Nadal?" Samuel asked.

"Salma, may I see Mrs. Nadal?"

"That depends."

"On what?" he dared.

"On if you 'tend to be a gentleman and not upset her no more."

Samuel sighed. "I promise."

The door shut abruptly in his face. Samuel blew out his cheeks while he paced. "I guess I'll wait out here," he said to no one in particular.

Finally, Charissa appeared on the porch. Her eyes looked puffy. The fear that he had been the cause of her crying made him want to beg her for mercy. "Oh, Mrs. Nadal, forgive me. I was so thoughtless. It was late, and we were both so tired. But I was an idiot. Completely out of line. Can you forgive me?"

"I suppose," she said, staring at him meaningfully.

"Please. Will you sit with me for a moment?"

She didn't answer, merely led the way to the porch swing. He sat as far from her as he could, not wanting to crowd her yet simultaneously wishing he could be nearer. He turned his bowler hat in his hands. "That wasn't like me. I mean, not saying the right thing at the right time—that was me. But getting so angry. I'm sorry. I do hope I haven't ruined everything between us."

"No, Samuel, you haven't ruined everything."

His breath caught when she used his first name for the first time, but he passed it off as trivial. "Then you won't resign? I need you. At the office, I mean," he quickly added.

She studied him, searching his eyes, and he dared to return her gaze. "Of course," she said finally. "At the office."

Samuel swallowed past the lump in his throat, completely ill at ease. "Well then, I will see you tomorrow for the picnic, and pray that you will find it in your heart to forgive me." He rose and was stepping down from the porch when she spoke again.

"You are forgiven already, Samuel. Your notes . . . thank you. They mean a great deal to me." She paused for a second, while Samuel struggled to find an appropriate response. "Why do you write them?" she went on.

"Do they help you?" he returned, deciding that answering with another question was the safest course.

"Yes . . . no one's ever written Scripture to me before, and the verses you choose seem to be exactly what I need . . . as if you can read my heart."

Samuel glanced away, embarrassed yet flattered at her admission. Then he said, "Scripture has a way of addressing human needs, whatever they may be." He cringed inwardly. *That was impressive, Samuel. She opens up and I give her a platitude.* "I've wanted to write you myself, Mrs. Nadal. My own words. But I can't seem to say things much better than the good book."

"It says enough, Samuel. More than enough. I've been . . . moved."

"Oh . . . well . . . that's good." Things were going better than he'd expected between them. He chanced a grin in her direction. "I suppose I should go then," he said awkwardly.

"Well, then, good evening, Doctor Johnson."

"Good day, Nurse Nadal."

• • •

Charissa wrapped her box for the charity auction with a ribbon of deep green. She disliked box socials, but it was all for a good cause. Even married women packed baskets, knowing their husbands would bid for their luncheons as well as their company. Yet as a widow, it was a bit awkward; just who would she be stuck with today? Would Samuel Johnson dare bid on her box? Would he recognize the green ribbon she used in her hair?

As they had arranged, Charissa and Salma met Samuel on the park grounds, near an old maple tree on a hill overlooking Puget Sound. It was a lovely summer day. The smell of humus and salt water filled her nostrils, and she squinted at the bright light that reflected off the sea. Deep green forests hugged the edges of the meadow, threatening its borders, but for now, the open space belonged to the townspeople. And more than five hundred had turned out for the event.

"Your Doctor Johnson set my Hayden's arm late last night," Mrs. Crawford said, tucking her arm in Charissa's as they walked. Charissa ignored her suggestive use of *your*. She was certain that since she was working side by side with Samuel and was officially out of mourning, tongues were wagging.

"He did? Late last night?" Charissa asked.

"Yes," the bedraggled mother of eight said. "Hayden was out jumping from the hayloft with his brothers. I was so glad when the good doctor answered his door. I thought we'd never awaken him." Charissa could see Samuel's broad back just ahead and his slow smile in profile as he bent to speak with a boy. Mrs. Crawford raised her voice so Samuel could overhear the last part of her comment as they neared. "But when he finally dragged himself out of bed, he was the best doctor in town for my Hayden. Why, you should have seen how he tended to my son!"

"It wasn't much," Samuel said.

"More than I would have been able to do for him," the poor farmer's wife said gratefully. "Might've lost the use of his arm had we not had you, Dr. Johnson."

Samuel shrugged off her praise. "I hope he rested well when you finally got him home."

"Oh, he's right as rain." She nodded at a group of boys chasing girls, Hayden in their midst, sling and all.

"Good to see he's back to his old self." Samuel smiled at Mrs. Crawford, and she took off after her son, scolding him as she went.

Samuel turned to Charissa, a vague uneasiness in his eyes. "Are things still okay between us?" he said, referring to his blustering at her the day before.

She smiled and tucked her arm into his. "Come, Doctor. Salma is setting out a blanket over there. I think she's missing her husband, especially today. Let us go and keep her company."

"Any word on when he intends to come back?"

"He's only been on the job for a couple of months. It pays well, so he'll stick with it until the end of the line. They're reportedly going all the way to the Yukon."

"I suppose with a pregnant wife at home, he feels all the more responsible to earn a good wage."

"Especially for a colored man, finding a job that pays well is a rare thing indeed. Even if employers do pay him less than the whites. It gets lonely in my house when she goes." She glanced up at him. "I feel as if they're my family now that Ari's gone."

"I understand," he said meaningfully.

She supposed he did. He was often alone too. Charissa grinned. It felt good to be away from the office and outside on such a glorious day.

"Hello, Salma," Samuel greeted when they drew near. "This looks like a mighty fine spread." Before them was a jug of fresh lemonade, oranges shipped in from California, ginger cookies that smelled freshly made, and cheese and bread.

"You should see what Miz Nadal packed in her box," Salma deferred. "Hoo, yes, you should be biddin' on that woman's box today, if you know what's good for you."

"I'll do my best to choose the right one," Samuel said with a smile. When they had entered the park grounds, women from church collected the boxes and squired them away, conscious to at least attempt to keep their makers a secret.

Charissa and Samuel sat down with Salma and looked around, taking in the aroma of roasted nuts and the sounds of salesmen pitching candy sticks and molasses taffy. Down the hill toward the water, booths were set up with various carnival games. And to the right, children tried their best at a three-legged race.

• ● •

"I always did like a sweet before my noon dinner, much to my mother's dismay," Charissa said, as she bit into a cookie and poured lemonade for all three of them. The new sparkle in her brown eyes caught Samuel's attention. After handing out the glasses, she leaned back on her arms, looking relaxed as she lifted her face, eyes closed, to the noonday sun. She was so

LISA TAWN BERGREN

beautiful. He fought the urge to stare at her. All across the grounds were women perched beneath sun umbrellas; yet Charissa looked like an island queen, with her copper, glistening skin and dark hair—

"So tell me, Doctor, how do you find it here in Seattle?" Salma interrupted his thoughts.

"I'm adjusting." Samuel quickly recovered. "I like the growth of the city; it keeps things interesting. Sometimes, though, I get overwhelmed. Exhausted. Like yesterday. Mrs. Nadal, I can't help but apologize again for—"

"I think we're getting along just fine."

Samuel glanced at her. Charissa's use of those two words—*getting along*—ran through his mind again and again. What exactly did she mean by that? That they weren't fighting or that there was hope for more?

"Dr. Johnson, Dr. Nadal and I had a wonderful life, a wonderful love together. But you are not the first man to be cross with me. My marriage was . . . tempestuous. In fact, Ari was cross with me on an almost daily basis. And not nearly so intent upon apologizing," she added softly, stirring her lemonade with a silver spoon.

Her admission humbled him. An image of Charissa Nadal amidst a bed of love letters flashed through his mind. He'd assumed she had romanticized and idealized her life with her first husband. That he would forever have Ari's ghost to overcome, but this . . . this cast a whole new light on the situation. Perhaps Charissa Nadal wasn't lost to the past as he had assumed; perhaps there was hope for a future.

He frowned slightly. What was he thinking? Had she so affected him that now he was considering a future with her?

"Oh! They're calling people over for the box social," Salma interrupted his musings. She stood up, and so did Charissa.

Charissa looked up at Samuel as he rose next to her. "You are a good doctor. Different from my Ari, but nonetheless, quite good. Ever since I came to work with you, I feel more alive than I have in two years. Working with you has given me purpose again. I have much to thank you for." She glanced down at the ground and then back into his eyes, looking more winsome than ever. "I'm glad to be working for you, Dr. Johnson. I know my position sort of came with the property. But I'd really like it if my employment was by your choice and not my cajoling."

"Do I have a choice?"

She paused until he met her dark eyes. "Yes, Samuel. You do."

He broke their gaze first. "Yes, of course, I want you there. If my rudeness doesn't drive you away, stay on as long as you care to do so."

She shook her head and Samuel winced. Would he ever have the right words around Charissa Nadal?

• • •

They were crossing over to join the auctioneer. The crowd gathered around him when John Napier, the man in the mob who'd threatened Charissa, stepped away from several other swarthy men and leaned toward her. "That your pretty box all tied up with the green bow?"

"I would never be so foolish as to tie my box with one of

my hair ribbons," Charissa returned. She hoped the man would be confused, wonder at her logic. The last place she wanted to be was under some tree for an hour with this leering idiot, just because he had bid the highest for her box.

"A lady such as Mrs. Nadal would never agree to go with a lout such as you, anyway," Samuel interjected.

"Depends on who has the most money," John said, tilting his chin back in subtle challenge. "The cards were good to me last night," he added.

"Ladies and gentlemen!" the auctioneer shouted.

Samuel used the opportunity to extract Salma and Charissa from the heckler's presence. They walked a good distance away and settled in to watch the goings-on. "Welcome to the fifth annual Seattle social! As we have done in previous years, today's proceeds will be donated to the county orphanage. We appreciate all the ladies who have given their time and resources to donate to the cause."

Several men let out catcalls while the rest of the crowd politely applauded. For the first time, Charissa noticed a group of sailors from the wharf. John Napier might be less of a problem than any of them, she thought. She fought off the urge to tell Samuel which box was hers. She would leave it in God's hands. If she ended up with a no-account like John, she would simply insist on sitting some place very public. Besides, she knew that money was tight for the good doctor after purchasing Ari's business. There had been days when he had had no cash for fresh gauze or other necessities, and he had to put them on account at the mercantile. No, she wouldn't put this on his wide shoulders as well. What was to be would simply be.

Still, she grew more and more nervous as the bidding

continued. John Napier never bid on another box, simply stared over at her with his big, empty eyes. He smiled at her, showing those yellow teeth, and then winked. Charissa felt shivers of dread creep up her spine. He was definitely a man she wouldn't want to meet alone on the streets at night.

"Are you trembling?" Samuel asked her, looking down at her in concern. His big, warm hand covered hers.

"Nerves," she said with some embarrassment.

"Do not fear," he said, tucking her hand closer to his body. "A dollar!" he shouted, bidding on a pretty box, daintily tied with a yellow bow.

"What are you doing?" Charissa hissed.

He leaned closer. "That's it. Talk with me in hushed tones. If we keep our heads together, conspiring like this, that idiot will think—"

"Two dollars!" shouted John Napier.

Samuel grinned at Charissa, and she took her first breath since the auction had begun. "Coming to my rescue yet again, are you?"

"I do my best," he said. "But it won't be convincing unless I pull as much of the gambler's money from his pocket as I can. Three!" he shouted.

"Four!"

The crowd gasped. This was getting interesting.

"Five!" Samuel called.

"Dr. Johnson," Charissa said between her teeth, still grinning like a proud peacock to further their charade, "what if you actually win? Do you have five dollars?"

"I'll have to trade medical services for the balance," he said easily. "Orphans need a physician's care too."

"I hear five dollars," shouted the auctioneer. He looked over John Napier's way. "Do I hear six?"

Napier hesitated for a telling moment. But he was a gambler. Perhaps he was calling Samuel's bluff. "Six," he called.

"Seven!" Samuel said calmly, a second later.

"Seven on the table; do I hear eight?"

"Eight!"

"Nine!"

Charissa could feel her eyes growing larger. It would take a lot of calls to the orphanage to pay off nine dollars.

"Ten!" John responded.

"Ten dollars, do I hear eleven? Ten dollars, do I hear ten-fifty? Ten dollars, do I hear ten-twenty-five?" He looked Samuel's way, and the doctor gave him a shrug of resignation as if he had just passed his limit. Charissa breathed a sigh of relief, but then began worrying over who would be stuck with the thug if not her.

"Ten dollars buys the box lunch with the lovely . . ." The auctioneer paused to read the card his assistant passed to him from the box. The crowd was silent, all eager to hear who had spurred on such lively bidding. Charissa chanced a glance in John's way. She grimaced as he looked her over as though she were a slab of beef he'd just purchased from the butcher. " . . . the Widow Kollwitz!"

The crowd erupted with laughter and surprise. Mrs. Kollwitz, the elderly proprietor of Kollwitz's Ladies' Home, hobbled out and joined John Napier at the podium. She shook her cane in her hand as if already giving the man the what-for.

Charissa covered her mouth with her hand and giggled.

"That is just too perfect. The town's biggest prude with the town's biggest reprobate. Well done, Dr. Johnson."

"Why, thank you, Mrs. Nadal," he said, obviously proud of himself. He watched Napier stalk off, leaving behind his money, his potential date, and his box lunch. "Now, it is a box with a green bow that is worthy of my bidding, is it not?" he whispered. His eyes searched hers and then glanced at the forest green ribbon in her hair.

"Well, Dr. Johnson," she said, surprising herself with the note of flirtatiousness that entered her tone, "I could never tell you that." She hoped he understood. There was no one else on the park grounds she would like to share her lunch with more than Doctor Samuel Johnson.

• • •

Charissa awakened late the next morning, when Salma brought her a tray with steaming mush and hot coffee.

"It was a big day for you yesterday, miss," the maid said lightly.

"Indeed," Charissa responded, rising to accept the bed tray. "Tell me, how are you feeling today?"

"Better and better." Out of the corner of her eye, she saw Salma reach for a white scrap of paper on the floor. "What's this?"

"Oh, something the doctor left for me last night. I forgot about it. It must've fallen out of my pocket."

"May I read it? Or is it too lovey-dovey?"

"Oh no! Things are not that way between us. Please. See for yourself."

Salma gave her a doubtful glance and then read aloud:
"*'Hast thou not known? hast thou not heard, that the
everlasting God, the Lord, the Creator of the ends of the earth,
fainteth not, neither is weary? there is no searching of his understanding. He giveth power to the faint; and to them that have
no might he increaseth strength.'*"

Salma glanced up at her mistress when she finished
reading. "It is beautiful, this word from the Lord. Makes a
person feel loved, cared about, when they read these verses.
You sure the doctor doesn't have feelin's for you?"

"It is beautiful," Charissa whispered. He had left her a
stack of them. Not a love letter like Ari would have written,
but something familiar and warming, like a mother's lullaby.

How long had it been since she had opened her Bible?
Since before Ari's death, to be sure. Ari had never loved the
poetic nature of the Scriptures, didn't enjoy deciphering its
meaning as she had. He preferred the classics, complained
that the Bible was for the needy. At some point, she had
ceased trying to show him the joy she had found in it as a
child. Yet somehow, Dr. Johnson had found that joy. Was
that what had kept him from falling into the crater of his own
grief volcano, ever ready to erupt? "A friendship with the
Father," he had said. A friendship with the Father. She
almost understood that phrase now. Charissa smiled to
herself. "God is so faithful," she uttered.

"So is your Samuel."

"Hmph."

"Not a'tall, ma'am." Salma stepped toward Charissa
and placed Samuel's script on her tray before leaving. "Something of a balm," he had said, an encouragement. They were

soothing, those words. Hopeful. Charissa picked up the scrap of paper again and read: *"They shall run, and not be weary; and they shall walk, and not faint."*

For the first time in many months, Charissa smiled toward the ceiling, smiling at God himself. Perhaps she could discover something new in life, something she had never known before. That safety and comfort that were never far from Samuel. She considered his broad shoulders and sure hands, those eyes that knew a person before they were even introduced, his way of quietly coming to her aid when she most needed him.

Perhaps.

Chapter Six

Samuel Johnson finished his morning reading of the Word, removed his wire spectacles, went to the washbasin and splashed his face, then stared into the small mirror above it. He looked as tired as he felt. Part of him wanted to retreat to bed, but he pushed the desire away. The only way to face the hard things in life was to charge forward, through them, like a buggy through a thick patch of mud. If he slowed, if he tarried, it would suck him down and wouldn't let go.

His thoughts moved to Charissa. She, too, had obviously struggled with the shadows that lingered after losing a loved one. He could see it in the wrinkles of sorrow at the corners of her eyes, the hint of wariness in those large, brown-black orbs. And even now, she was just learning what might truly bring her into the light for good: a friendship with the Father. Today again in his readings he had come across the perfect Scripture to pass along to her, like many others that had passed through his hands and into hers.

She hadn't commented again on the fact that he had taken to leaving a verse or two with her each day as she left work for home. He took that as silent affirmation. If she found it distasteful, surely she would have said something about it by now. And this morning's verse—*"Come unto me, all ye that labour and are heavy laden. . . . Take my yoke upon you, and learn of me; for I am meek and lowly in heart: and ye shall find rest unto your souls"*—was just the same as the others; he knew in his gut that it was meant for her as well as for him. In their shared grief of the past, the constant struggles of the present, he knew that the passages that brought him comfort and hope would do the same for her.

In a way, since Mamie's death his faith had deepened beyond anything he had ever imagined. It came as welcome consolation, this soulful gain in exchange for a heart full of pain. He had had to lean daily on his Lord for his very existence and sanity. It astonished him, really. He had always considered himself a good Christian, but grieving had forced him into a devout belief.

Jesus had known his kind of suffering; God had known what it feels like to hold a dead son in his hands. Samuel needed that understanding, was drawn to the kinship of shared sorrow, comforted by finding a meeting place of light and hope during the solstice of his life. And in some small way, he hoped he had reflected to Charissa Nadal a bit of what he had been shown. That hope in Christ.

Sighing, Samuel turned from the sink to his bed, where his brown summer suit was laid out for the day. As he pulled on his socks and trousers, he frowned. It was lonely here. He longed to share more than work with someone again. He longed to connect with someone in that deepest part. So far, his friends were mostly patients who were of a kindly spirit, floating in and out of his life as they needed assistance. He had met precious few at church services, and because of his long hours, seldom had the opportunity to cultivate friendships within the flock. If only . . . if only he and Charissa could be more than coworkers, even more than . . .

He was a fool to think that she might desire anything more than friendship with him. He was not anything like Ari Nadal. Who was he to think that he could shed any light, share any of his faith with her? He was hardly an ordained minister! He couldn't even do his own job—seeing Salma's child safely delivered. And as for adopting the peace the Scriptures promised, well, that was something he needed to work on too.

Charissa Nadal was a solid aide in the office and on house calls. But she'd never given him cause to view her as anything more. True, she had flirted with him at the box social, but that didn't mean anything. She was merely a friend—nothing more.

He consciously turned his thoughts from her to his list of today's patients. He prayed for each one, and prayed over Salma and her babe for a long time. He needed to refer her to another physician. One who could care for her in the way she deserved. One who could give her the best chance of safely bringing her child into the world. He had been putting it off. Charissa had limited experience as a midwife, and she was obviously nervous about bearing the full responsibility for her friend's well-being. "I love her too much to risk making a mistake when her time comes," she had said. If only Samuel had listened to that advice with his dear Mamie! Charissa insisted Salma have a full-fledged doctor on hand in case anything went wrong. Samuel couldn't blame her.

He buttoned up his shirt, getting more frustrated with himself. Why was he hesitating to refer Salma? Because of Charissa? What did it matter if she looked down her nose at him for his refusal? Scoffing at himself, he picked up the Scripture verse, crumpled it in his hand, and stuffed it in his pocket. He would work alongside Charissa Nadal today. But he would keep his nose out of her emotional and spiritual well-being and stick to what he knew had to come next. Even if she grew to despise him for it.

· · · ·

Charissa dipped her pen in the inkwell and paused over her letter to Ari. She was running out of things to say. Why was there nothing to tell her beloved? The sun was shining, sending a bright silver sheen across Puget Sound. Again, she rose and went to the window. The verse that Dr. Johnson had left for her the previous week came to mind: *The Lord will give strength unto his people; the Lord will bless his people with peace.*

Enjoying her regained spirit, she paced back and forth, constantly checking the clock to see if it was time to go to work. She had awakened this morning with a smile on her face and couldn't wait to share her sudden joy with Samuel. She would wait until he asked of her well-being, as was his custom each morn, and then she would tell him that the world seemed somehow brighter since she had given her heart to Jesus. There were still moments of sadness, but overall her perspective had changed, shifted. And she was thrilled with it.

Charissa frowned at herself. It felt disloyal and wrong to be looking forward to sharing an intimate smile with anyone but Ari. And yet she sensed that Ari would be pleased that her sadness had ebbed. Inspired, she hurried back to her desk and took up her pen, its tip glistening with the blue-black ink.

> *Ari, my love,*
>
> *Today I awakened with a smile, as I used to when you were with me. I am grateful I will hold your memory, our memories of us, in my future days, even though you are most decidedly in my past. You will always have a place in my heart, and I will always treasure the years we shared together.*
>
> *Oh, Ari, I miss you. But I am coming back. It tears at me a bit, knowing that returning to myself and facing the future means pulling further away from the life we lived together, but it feels right. I am coming back to life, Ari. Living. Forgive me, my love! I longed to die alongside you for so long. But suddenly, I find myself longing to live to be an old woman. I—*

A loud knock sounded on Charissa's door. "Miss?" Salma asked. "It's time to eat." She entered, as usual, without waiting for an invitation. "'This is the day which the Lord hath made,'" she said cheerfully.

"So it is. 'We will rejoice and be glad in it,'" Charissa responded with a grin.

• ● •

There was the tiniest hint of autumn in the air on this bright, sunny morning. When Samuel's office door opened and Charissa entered with a quiet smile, it took his breath away. The woman was always beautiful, but when she smiled . . . he coughed, looking down for a moment to break the spell. He had resolved to be entirely professional, to look after his patients, be cordial to his nurse.

"Good morning, Mrs. Nadal," he greeted her briskly. "You are looking well." He found it impossible not to match her grin and busied himself in taking her coat. When he turned back to her, she was still smiling. He cocked his head. "What is it? You have news for me?"

"Only that I awakened with joy in my heart for the first time in months. The last time I awoke this happy, it was when I dreamed Ari had simply been away on a holiday and had returned. This time when I awoke I was still all right."

Samuel felt his smile grow across his face. "That is glad news. It means you are truly on the road to healing." He smiled encouragingly at his nurse, noticing the new glow of her smooth olive skin and the way her grin tugged at her lovely, round lips. Samuel looked away, unable to look upon her in a purely professional manner. Her blue-and-white uniform only brought out those round, dark eyes with the incredible lashes. Quickly, he turned his back to her, busying himself with the papers on his desk.

"May I help you find whatever it is you're looking for?" She took a step forward to stand beside him, and he caught a scent of rosemary and lemon in her hair.

"What?"

"May I help you find something? You're over here messing up my organization of the patients' records."

"What? Oh, sorry. No, no. It's not here. What I'm looking for, that is." He stared at her, unable to take his eyes from her. She was his nurse . . . certainly not interested in him.

She glanced up at him with curiosity, an openness in her brown eyes. Was that an invitation? A tilt to her chin, asking for a kiss? Certainly not! It was preposterous. But . . .

Just then, Salma came through the door. "Oh," Charissa hastily explained, "I asked her to come in this morning for you to check on mother and child. She is more than four months along now."

Samuel frowned. "I am still hoping to transfer your care, Salma, to another doctor. I've checked with those in town . . ." his voice faded. "It is rumored that another is moving in from St. Louis. Perhaps he can see—"

"I do not want another doctor," Salma annunciated slowly. "I want you to care for me and my child."

"That . . . that is impossible."

"Why? You done took care of me until now."

"I thought you understood," he said seriously. "I'm not . . . skilled in that particular area of medicine."

He glanced from Salma to Charissa, his eyes hesitating over Charissa's smile that was fading as he spoke; the last thing he wanted to do was disappoint her. He was attracted to

Charissa Nadal, he finally admitted to himself. No one else knew the depth of pain he had suffered.

The realization came fast and hard for Samuel. It felt as though a sword had severed his chest as surely as the knife that had sliced Ping's chest. He found himself perspiring and forgetting to breathe. Then guilt flared. It was dishonest, his attraction. Impure. Unfaithful to Mamie's memory—his beloved, sweet Mamie. She had only been gone what, a little over two years? "I will do further research," he mumbled, turning his back toward Charissa again. "I will find a reputable doctor for you," he said to Salma.

He forced himself to turn toward Charissa.

"You are the most reputable doctor in town. And the only one who is not a bigot," Charissa stated emphatically.

"Surely the new doctor will agree to see the maid of the deceased Dr. Nadal. Out of respect for the profession, if nothing else." His voice held little hope. Who was he fooling? "You, yourself, Charissa, have delivered quite a few babies. Perhaps we can find a midwife to assist you. I will inquire about it."

"You do not understand," he said after a short pause.

"No, I do not."

She didn't understand, couldn't understand . . .

•　●　•

Mamie moaned and her brow wrinkled in pain. Another contraction. Samuel cursed himself for his indecision, for burdening his wife with a child that would not come. He turned and went to his medical bag, reaching for ether and a scalpel, then went to the woodstove and stoked it after placing another pot of water above to boil. "Oh, Lord," he begged, "please be with me. Guide my hand. Give me the courage. And most of all, protect Mamie and our baby."

Mamie moaned again and opened her eyes. He went to her. She gave him a weak smile. "I've been sleeping," she said.

"Fitfully. As best you could." He swallowed hard. "Mamie, I think this baby refuses to arrive as he ought. Something's wrong, Mamie. I think I'll have to perform a cesarean."

Her eyes widened a bit but she nodded once. "I trust you, Samuel."

He grabbed his stethoscope and listened for the baby's heart. The familiar fast beat did not greet him. Thinking the baby had simply moved, he checked the other three quadrants. Nothing. His own heart skipped and he fought for the courage to meet his wife's gaze.

"Samuel—"

"Here," he said, hurriedly dumping ether onto a rag and placing it over her nose and mouth. "Breathe deeply." He didn't wait for an answer, just ran to the boiling water and fished out his scalpel, which bounced over the bottom among the bubbles. In haste he tried to take it without a rag and let it drop when the hot metal scalded his fingers. "No!" he cried in frustration. Every second counted, and here he was bungling away precious moments! Unable to wait any longer, he pulled out the scalpel, this time taking it with the clean rag, and rushed to Mamie's side.

It was then he saw the cloth still over her mouth and nose. "No!" he yelled again, ripping it aside. He bent low, listening to her chest. She was breathing, but very shallowly. He checked her pulse, chastising himself for the fool he was. He squeezed back tears of frustration and fear, glancing from his beloved's face to her abdomen. Was he endangering her life in performing a risky procedure to save a babe who from all appearances was already dead? Or should he give her time, hope that she hadn't inhaled an overdose of ether, let the effects diminish so he could take the child when she was stronger? He placed a hand on her bulbous womb. She was still contracting. And she would never forgive him for not trying everything he knew to save their baby, even at her own peril.

He cleaned her abdomen and sliced through the layer of skin and muscle in the direction of the linea alba, to the lining of the uterus, then through it as well. He spotted a tiny arm first and pulled the infant from her womb.

A perfect baby boy.

A beautiful baby boy, fully formed.

And blue, not breathing, not crying huskily like the other babies Samuel had delivered. He wiped the mucus from the child's nose and mouth, then gently thumped him on the back between the shoulder blades. "Breathe, baby Joseph," he said, calling his son by the name Mamie had chosen. "Oh, please, breathe," he whispered as he wept.

His tears fell upon his son's waxen face. There was no response, no heartbeat. He had waited too long.

Painfully, he looked upon his wife, staring at her still chest and the blood that soaked the sheet around her. He didn't have to check with his stethoscope to know.

She was gone too.

•   •   •

Samuel sighed and picked up his bag. "Mrs. Nadal, the last baby I delivered was my son."

"Oh, I know, Samuel—"

"And because of my lack of foresight and care, both he and my wife ended up dead. It is in Salma's best interest that I pass her case along to another." Samuel swallowed hard, not wanting to weep here in front of patient and nurse.

He mumbled something about a house call, hurried through the door, and scurried down the stairs. He was lost in thought again, unable to think of anything else now.

•   •   •

With the agonizing steps of an old, arthritic man, Samuel carried the newborn to his wife. He laid the dead infant upon her chest and bent to whisper in her ear, his tears dripping to her shoulder.

He struggled to gain enough breath to speak. "It's a boy, Mamie," he sobbed. "Our Joseph. He's beautiful."

Then he rose and covered his family with a sheet, sank to the wood floor on his knees, and let out a keening cry. He pulled his hands from his face and stared up at the ceiling. "Oh, God, my God. I've failed them. I'm sorry. I'm so sorry."

He was a failure and a weakling.

He could do nothing right.

Who did he think he was fooling?

. • .

Charissa sat down hard on the chair, unable to watch the doctor leave the office.

There at last was the truth of the matter. The reason for his sad eyes. No wonder he had reached out to her, above and beyond most doctor-nurse relationships. She had known of his wife's death, of course, but had never been able to venture into imagining what he had gone through. It was enough to have weathered her own sorrow, to move through it as through a storm upon the sea, each wave threatening to break her.

Here, on this day, safely past the eye of it, she was finally able to look back at it with a little courage, for the sake of fully empathizing with Samuel.

. • .

It was still raining that night when Charissa heard the creak of saddle leather and the wagon pull to a halt in front of their home. When she didn't hear the familiar footsteps of Ari's large feet upon their front steps, she frowned and hurried to the door. Just as she reached for the knob, a pounding fist assaulted the door, and she frowned again.

Charissa opened the door to find a drenched man, hat in hands, hair plastered to his head. "Ma'am, I'm afraid I have bad news," he said immediately.

Charissa couldn't breathe, knew by the look in his eyes what he had to say before he said it. She tried to focus on his words.

"—went over and the doctor was thrown out. He was

crushed by the rolling wagon. I'm so sorry. I brought his body back for you. I knew you'd want to bury him here. I'm so sorry . . . I'm so sorry."

His body. The driver had brought back Ari's body, and her dearest lay in the back of an open wagon, the blanket askew, rain pelting his beautiful, cold face, as she went to him to cradle his head in her lap and scream out at the sky, begging for one more chance to hold him, one more chance to tell him of her love, one more chance to feel his lips on hers. "Oh no, Ari. Oh no!"

* ● *

Charissa shook her head. No wonder Dr. Johnson was unwilling to bring Salma's unborn child into the world. The thought of failing again, of leaving Salma's husband as alone in the world as Samuel probably felt sickened him with fear and dread.

"Let's go home," Charissa said to Salma. "It will be good to get some air." She unfolded the crumpled sheet of paper. It was as she expected—a Scripture from Dr. Johnson. She smiled as she read the words of care and understanding: *"Ye shall find rest unto your souls. For my yoke is easy, and my burden is light."*

Perhaps there was something she could do for the good doctor, something she could do as a true friend. Or more.

Chapter Seven

OCTOBER

True to his word, Dr. Johnson referred Salma to the new doctor, who agreed to see her at month's end. Charissa was returning from accompanying Salma to the appointment, her mouth set in a grim line, thinking about the man who had taken over her husband's business and the incompetent racist he had sent Salma to see. And she was angry.

Lifting her chin higher, she walked faster, with a more determined step than ever. How dare Dr. Johnson abandon her friend! How dare he send her to such a priggish, awful man and expect her to be grateful! She would tell him exactly what she thought of him. Tell him she knew better than anyone what he had been through, but that he had a social obligation, an oath to care for his patients. Through anything.

Why, it felt like he had done the same thing to her; built her up with notes of encouragement from the Word, gestures of friendship, even the occasional glance that said he might be interested in more, when all of a sudden, it all ceased. They still worked alongside each other with skill and compassion, but what had begun between them had certainly dwindled. Yes, she would have a word or two with him. And she would begin with this nonsense about Salma.

With a self-satisfied nod, she rounded the last corner and strode down Eighth Avenue. Her pace slowed, almost involuntarily, as Ari's old office building came into view. So many memories . . . Ari's eyes sparkling as he unfolded the architect's drawings before her . . . Ari picking her up in his arms and swinging her around, the first time they stepped inside the framed walls . . . Ari proudly giving her a tour of the finished building . . . Ari, radiant with joy, facing a room full of patients. He had been a passionate man, her husband. He had lived his life like a fast-burning flame moving through a decade-dried log. Hot. Bright. There had always been something about him that made Charissa want to shield her eyes, as though he was too much to gaze upon. Too intense.

Suddenly, she realized she had stopped in her tracks, and people were filing around her, giving her quick glances as if to ask if she was all right, but too busy to pause. Charissa forced herself to move forward, remembering that she used to put two hanging baskets of flowers outside. She hadn't put any out in two years. Maybe next summer . . .

Charissa slowed again, evaluating her memories, of life and love and sorrow. At least she could breathe and walk and be angry again. And tell Dr. Johnson just what she thought of his "reference."

She resumed her quick pace toward the medical building. She threw open the door and ducked her head into the examination room, then bit her lip. He was with a patient. Turning abruptly away, she sighed and paced the length of the front parlor, waiting for doctor and patient to emerge. After a while, she sank to the settee, feeling a bit deflated at not being able to vent her anger immediately.

Five minutes later, she watched as Samuel guided an elderly woman to the door, his reassuring hand on one shoulder. "You do as I ask, Mrs. Miller, and see to it that you get plenty of rest and some decent food. Those dizzy spells should be gone within the week. If they aren't, I want you to send someone to fetch me."

The older woman turned to the doctor and smiled, revealing two gaping holes where several teeth used to be. She reached for his hand, gratitude in her eyes. "You are such a dear, Doctor. Thank you for everything."

"Not at all, ma'am," he said, patting her hand. "I'll have my nurse, Mrs. Nadal, check in on you tomorrow out at the house."

If I'm still working for you, you big lout . . .

"That will be fine. Just fine," she said; then the old woman spied Charissa across the room. "Oh! Another patient for you. I'll be out of your hair before you can say Jack-be-nimble."

Smiling, Dr. Johnson's eyes followed the woman's gaze, softening in genuine pleasure when he saw her. "Mrs. Nadal!" He hurried over to her and reached for her hand. His kind manner melted away a bit of Charissa's anger, her reason for charging over, and she faltered. "Are you all right?"

"Dr. . . . Dr. Johnson," she greeted him in return. "I am fine." She took his proffered hand and rose. "You probably wonder why I am here. On my day off."

"Indeed. Would you care to speak of it here or in the back?"

"No. Here in the parlor is fine." Charissa smoothed her skirts, then looked back to Samuel who was about six inches taller than her. Ari had towered over her, making her feel diminutive. Dr. Johnson's stature came as reassuring, protective, but was not so overwhelming. She bit her lip, suddenly trying to choose her words. All the way over here, she had ranted and raved, told the phantom Dr. Johnson exactly what was on her mind! But now, staring into his warm, brown eyes, with wrinkles at the corners that spoke of sorrows and a deep inner peace, the words fled.

She turned away and paced to the window, trying to gather her thoughts. She had missed the warmth and camaraderie he instilled inside her with his shared passages of Scripture that had suddenly stopped coming. But those were not reasons she could share with him, reasons for her anger, her arrival here today. "I need . . . I would like for you to see Salma as your patient again." Charissa did not turn to hear his response, did not want to see his expression of confusion and consternation.

"I do not understand. Is Dr. Gibson not treating her well? We had a lengthy conversation during which I made absolutely clear that I wanted—"

"His care is . . . barely sufficient. Barely." She turned to him then and walked across the space that separated them. "Dr. Johnson, I want you to usher in the new life that represents my friend's future. She means so much to me. Dr. Gibson is a quack in comparison to you—"

He shook his head, his moss brown gaze going to the window. "We've been through this, Mrs. Nadal."

"Please, we have known each other long enough. Call me Charissa."

He glanced at her quickly, then shook his head. "All right . . . Charissa." His eyes lit up for a moment, then faded. "I simply cannot." A weary hand went through his hair, but all Charissa could think about was the way he had said her name, like an astronomer naming a star. "The business continues to grow. It is slow right now, but you know as well as I that most days, I work from dawn until late at night. Seattle is booming, and so is the need for good doctors. I have no idea if I'll even be in town when her time draws near. What about those weeks that I am absent for two or three days, one patient asking me to see another, taking me farther and farther away?"

"It will be late March before this child arrives. Surely you will be doing less traveling as the weather turns."

"I do not know that."

Frustration furrowed her brow. "You're making excuses, Dr. Johnson."

"Please," he said ruefully, "call me Samuel."

"All right . . . Samuel," she said softly, finding herself concentrating on his name. *Samuel* was such a nice, solid, warm name. Was it her imagination, or did the room suddenly feel hotter?

He took a step away from her, and then back, his hand going to his chin. "And I hardly need an excuse—"

"You told me that you would not deliver Salma's baby because of what happened with your own child. Isn't that the real reason?"

He nodded softly, never letting his eyes leave hers. But his gaze hardened a bit. "Yes. That is the other reason."

Charissa sighed. She hated the flash of pain in his eyes, hated to bring the dear doctor back to the unpleasant. But she was determined to win him over. To show him that he wasn't disabled in this area—he was an excellent doctor. She had seen it for herself, time and time again. She didn't want the distasteful Dr. Gibson for Salma. She wanted dear, sweet Samuel. And while she could serve as an able midwife, it wasn't the same as having a doctor on hand . . . "Please. May we sit?"

Hesitating a moment, he sat down across from her in the wing-backed chair. Charissa dived in. "Surely you know that the God you wrote me about has forgiven you your mistakes of that day?"

"They are not my words. They are words from the Bible that others wrote."

"Still, they spoke to you. Enough that you shared them with me. Did those verses of love and light not pierce your heart as they did mine?" Her hand went to her breast in agitation. "Your wife and son, Samuel, are with God right now. And they want nothing more than for you to embrace life and live it for all it's worth. Yes, it's a struggle. But you have to go on—and honor your Mamie's memory and love—by not giving up."

"That is why I work so hard."

"You hide behind your work ethic, Samuel." Her voice softened and she reached for his hand. "Have you really discovered forgiveness? Or are you punishing yourself for what happened? If God can forgive you, you need to forgive yourself too."

Samuel sat back in his chair as if she had struck him. Still, she pressed on, driven. "I know that caring for Salma and her child would be a risk. But life is about risks. What more wonderful thing can life offer than greeting a new baby? Seeing a child take its first breath? You could be there. You can do this, Samuel."

Her voice softened to a quiet plea, and she pulled back her hand, looking at him shyly. "I . . . I need you there. Dr. Gibson might be able to attend to her physical needs. But from the beginning, I've seen that you do so much more for all your patients. Please, Samuel. Will you think about it at least?"

He was silent, staring at her. His Adam's apple bobbed a little as he swallowed. "I . . . you ask . . . Charissa . . . " He looked away to the window again. Then he suddenly stood. "I cannot. You ask more from me than I can give."

Charissa nodded slowly, suddenly ashamed. She spoke of receiving life as if it were easy. She stood and then dared to look into his compassionate eyes again. "People are drawn to you, Samuel. As a doctor, of course," she rushed to include. "Salma wants you to deliver her child. She refuses to beg it of you as I do today. I know you do not wish to do this. But I . . . feel as if God has led me here. It is tragic what you faced that day. I know what it is to face tragedy such as that. And I know delivering a baby is tricky and often ends with tragic results. That you can't promise . . . please. Simply think about it. I will not take no for an answer today. But at least consider it. We will speak more of it next week."

"No, we will not," he said, turning away from her. "It is not in Salma's best interests," he said over his shoulder. He turned at the door of the examination room "Please, Charissa. Take Salma back to her new doctor for her scheduled visits. Do not think of bringing her here. Promise me you will not."

Charissa lifted her chin a bit. "I cannot do that. Salma needs you to deliver her child. You need to deliver her child."

He flushed at her impertinence. "Of all the presumptuous . . . that is—"

"Rude? Improper?" She laughed. "Samuel, just as you felt some higher urge to see to my spiritual welfare, I feel I must see to yours."

"I stepped into a world that was none of my business!"

"It was your business. It was because you took to leaving me those Scripture verses that I have found a new life in Christ, that I've come out of the darkness of my mourning, and—"

"Charissa," he interrupted her, "I am no preacher. I did not belong in that realm."

"Oh, you are wrong, dear Samuel," she said, stepping forward. She winced and doubled over, gritting her teeth against the sudden pain. "Oh!"

"What is it?" he asked, rushing to her side.

"I don't know," she ground out. "Sharp pain."

Samuel swept her into his arms and carried her immediately into the examination room.

"Samuel!" she protested.

"Hush, Charissa. For the first time this morning, just hush."

Chapter Eight

"Put me down, Samuel," Charissa directed.

He did so, but on the examination table. The pain was subsiding, and Charissa managed a weak smile. "That was lovely! Just when I had a head full of steam, too!"

He glanced at her face quickly, as if to ascertain if the whole thing was a charade. "How are you now? What is happening?"

"I am . . . I'm fine. It's gone now."

"Where was the pain? Was it localized?" For the first time, Charissa noticed his ashen face, the beads of sweat along his receding hairline. Gently, he prodded her abdomen.

"I do not know. It was a sudden, sharp pain. Mostly right here," she said, motioning to directly below her ribs on the right.

"And it's gone now?"

"Yes. It only lasted about ten seconds."

Samuel blew out a long breath and studied her. "We'll

wait a half hour to see if there are any other attacks, but I wonder if it might be your gallbladder. It's not your appendix. Or it simply could be . . . indigestion."

"Oh," she said, partially relieved, partially embarrassed for her own rash concerns. "It's simply a matter of my diet getting the best of me, is it?"

"Perhaps," he said, a small smile tugging at the corners of his lips. "Did you have something unusual for breakfast?"

"Salma fixed eggs Mexican-style," she admitted. "With spicy tomatoes and potatoes. The hazards of living with a pregnant maid," she added.

"It can be difficult," Samuel said, giving her a relieved smile too. "I will let you rest a bit," he added, tenderly touching her arm. "You stay here and I'll check back on you in another twenty-five minutes. If you have another pain, shout. I want to make sure we are right about our diagnosis, Nurse."

"Yes, Doctor," Charissa said. She tried to catch his eye while he carefully pulled the Hudson's Bay blanket to her chin, but he avoided looking at her again.

She adjusted her head on the barely stuffed pillow and stared at the clear pine ceiling. Ari had helped hammer those boards there himself. He had put everything he had into his work, wanting to make his parents proud.

But what drove Dr. Johnson? There was a similar need to perform, but was it for similar reasons? She just couldn't see Samuel needing to obtain anyone's approval. But he worked constantly, without end. She remembered what she'd accused him of before—working to make up for the mistake he made with his wife, the guilt he couldn't seem to rid himself of. How could she help him past that pain as he had helped her past hers? Tears streamed down her face, rolling back toward the pillow. They weren't tears for herself; they were for Samuel.

• • •

Samuel shut the door behind himself and leaned against it as if she would come after him like an apparition. Charissa wasn't just a nurse he had hired; she had become so much more. It pained him to say no to her. But he couldn't deliver Salma's child . . . he couldn't. He couldn't bear the responsibility.

He ran a hand through his short hair. Why did it have to be him? Why was Charissa so determined to enter this dark part of his life, his past? His thoughts ran wild, from the western forest of his distant memories to the eastern coast of today's events. He needed air, space to think. Quickly he ducked through the parlor doorway, strode through the kitchen, and let the door slam behind him as he walked to the creek behind the office. It was a good place to mull over his situation and all that had transpired.

• • •

After a while, Charissa rose and peeked her head into the kitchen. There was a pot of boiling water, with the familiar metallic clink of instruments. But no Samuel. She scanned the other rooms. Not finding him inside, Charissa walked out to the backyard. Fifty feet beyond the house, the narrow creek sliced its way through the property like a grass snake on the prairie. She could see Samuel sitting in the knee-high grain, staring at the water. He was deep in thought, his spectacles in the hand at his knee, the other one behind him, supporting his weight. The soft, late-afternoon light, coloring the October grass a deep gold against the fading green of the brook grasses, splashed about him, making him look as though he were frozen in time. He seemed somehow warmer, more approachable, and Charissa found herself staring at the man she wanted as a friend, and maybe more.

He looked up finally and shook his head with a friendly chuckle. "I thought I told you to stay put."

"Since when do I listen to the advice of a man?"

He laughed again as if exasperated, but he was smiling. "Sit down, Charissa. Are you all right?"

"I'm fine. Must've just been indigestion, as you guessed. See? Finest doctor around. You should be caring for me—and Salma during her confinement."

"I thought you said you wouldn't bring it up again today."

Charissa smiled gently and reached for his hand. The doctor looked over at her in surprise. "Samuel, you helped me. I found myself . . . looking forward to the Scriptures you used to leave me. They lightened my load. May I not help you with yours?"

"Is that what this really is about?" he said, rising and dusting off his trousers. "You don't have to save me, Charissa."

She stared at him for two long seconds. "I'm not trying to save you. I just want to help ease your pain as you helped me."

"The only thing that could do that for me would be if you could erase my memories, which you can't do, can you?" He reached down to help her up, his voice softening. "Here . . . " She stood next to him, staring at his warm, liquid eyes.

"Charissa, I can't," he said gently.

He was being so stubborn, it was infuriating. "You can," she insisted, putting her hands on her hips in a stance of defiance.

"I can't! I won't!" His voice bellowed out at her, making her take a step away. "I'm sorry. Please forgive . . . " He walked toward the stream in irritation and then turned back to her, splaying his hands in question. "What is it you want? Maybe Ari would have done this, but I cannot. I can't be your husband, Charissa. I am hardly anything like him."

Now she was angry. "I don't want you to be Ari! No, you are not like him! But you are a fine doctor, the best I've seen. I want you to care for Salma. Nothing else. If you're suggesting—"

"No, no. Of course I wasn't," he hedged. "You've pressed so hard, you make my head spin. You . . . you . . . " He searched her face, as if searching for the right words. Then he stopped and just stared at her.

In that moment, Charissa felt as if she had been truly seen from the tip of her toes to the roots of her hair and loved for every inch in between. Never had Ari looked at her that way, not in all the years they had been married, not during all the passionate nights they had spent in bed together. Ari had always moved so fast, his mind racing in so many different directions. Yet Samuel saw her, knew her. There was something deep within him that connected so surely with something deep within her that it took her breath away. She felt as if she were being carried away.

He was the first to break their long stare, and he seemed slightly out of breath himself. "Well . . . I suppose I better go get those instruments out of the pot." He looked at her uncertainly and then left.

Samuel was at the back door of the house when Charissa again found her voice. "I will come to fetch you when Salma's labor begins."

He did not look at her. "Do not. I will not come." He passed out of the light and into the dark kitchen without another word.

Charissa pulled out a note card with her name embossed on the front and a Scripture verse in her handwriting on the back. She left it on the back porch, between the screen and doorjamb, silently repeating the words her Lord had given her, now the words she left for Samuel. Dear, wounded Samuel.

> *I cried with my whole heart; hear me, O Lord: I will keep thy statutes. I cried unto thee; save me, and I shall keep thy testimonies. I prevented the dawning of the morning, and cried: I hoped in thy word. Mine eyes prevent the night watches, that I might meditate in thy word. Hear my voice according unto thy lovingkindness: O Lord, quicken me according to thy judgment.*

Chapter Nine

As the snows of winter melted into the first vestiges of what promised to be a hearty spring, Charissa continued leaving Samuel Scripture verses on the backs of her note cards: *"O God, thou art my God, early will I seek thee; my soul thirsteth for thee, my flesh longeth for thee in a dry and thirsty land, where no water is."*

The rain had begun in late October, tearing the colorful leaves from the trees, and making Samuel wonder if Charissa's persistent hope that he would tend to Salma would finally fall too. Throughout the winter months the note cards kept appearing—through the melancholy holiday season, past the lonely third anniversary of Mamie's death, and into the new year—usually every other morning and often accompanied by other items like a freshly baked pie, a bundle of kindling, a plate of baklava, and once, a bushel of russet potatoes.

Was she just a friend reaching out to him as he had to her? a nurse caring for a coworker? Or did she want more? Could she really care for anyone again as she had once cared for the mighty Ari Nadal?

Charissa's attentions ministered to his heart in ways he had no idea that he needed. And yet their relationship was chaste, platonic. They had not even seen each other outside their professional office environment since that day beside the creek. He could still see her then, the late-afternoon sunlight creating a golden halo over her shiny black hair, a soft coil escaping at the nape of her neck. She had stared at him as if she had seen through to his heart, to the deepest secret place that harbored his feelings for her, his desire to hold her, to pull her to him with all the passion inside him and kiss her as she had never been kissed before. Ari Nadal might have once had the words that Samuel Johnson would never master, but he certainly could not have desired Charissa more than Samuel desired her now.

Her Scripture verses—he reminded himself, getting back on track—often familiar to him, were well timed and seldom failed to speak to him in a fresh way. And a forkful of her apple pie or a piece of divinity or a hot baked potato satisfied his stomach, and he fell asleep in peace, often to awaken refreshed. Samuel set today's cobbler on the kitchen counter, grabbed a fork, and took a bite.

"I hope that is not dinner," Charissa said, pulling her coat on over her white-and-blue striped uniform. She reached for her scarf, wrapping it around her neck and face, and then for her muff. It was snowing outside.

"Maybe." He took another bite. The rich taste of cinnamon and nutmeg and sweet apples caused him to close his eyes in the joy of it. This was a woman who knew how to get to the heart of a man! What was the matter with him? Mamie had been gone three years, and he'd never had such thoughts about another woman. He considered his relationship with Charissa to be professional, a friendship at most, and yet their notes to each other implied something entirely different. Even if they were verses from the Bible rather than the Bard's poetry. There was a deeper connection between them that he couldn't deny.

After an awkward silence, she asked, "Do you have anything else to eat?"

"Uh, no. Maybe . . ."

She waited expectantly, an eyebrow raised.

"Perhaps . . . would you care to join me for supper at the hotel down the road?"

Charissa studied him and then quickly stared at her muff, fiddling with it as if she were having difficulty finding the holes on the ends. When she finally looked up at him, he steeled himself for her refusal. "Yes," she said, making it sound almost like a sigh.

"Wh-what?"

"I said yes," she repeated, smiling now. "It's Salma's day off, so why not?"

"Oh. All right, then. Let me just fetch my coat and we'll be off." He hurried into the coatroom, stood staring at his boots for a full minute before remembering he had come in search of a jacket, took his blue coat with the ripped sleeve from the hook, started to put it on, shook his head in irritation at himself, replaced it on the hook, then took his good black overcoat and headed back to the kitchen.

It had been a long time since he had had company for supper, and his stomach roiled in sudden nervousness.

Charissa smiled shyly as he returned. She moved toward the front door with him. Outside on the porch, they paused together, as if holding their breath, wondering if this was right, this move.

Oh, for heaven's sake, Samuel thought. *It is only supper.* "Shall we?" he asked, offering her his arm. She slipped her small hand into the crook of his elbow, and they walked toward the hotel.

• • •

It felt good to be out and about on the arm of a gentleman again, Charissa mused. It seemed forever ago that she and Ari had last gone to a restaurant together. Many months before he died.

Salma had a friend who cooked at the new roadhouse, and many townsfolk raved about the quality of food there. She glanced up at Samuel, who was grinning as if he couldn't help himself. "You did a fine job with Mr. Price today," she said. "When I saw the extent of his burns, I wondered if you might send him to the hospital."

"Never. Until they modernize their laundry and kitchen facilities, I will never subject a patient to their care. It is atrocious, what they call 'clean.' He is better off at home. We will make a house call tomorrow to change the dressings, monitor his vitals, and see if we can alleviate some of his pain."

Charissa stifled a smile. He was quite smug about his own cleanliness and care of his instruments and linens. Few

LISA TAWN BERGREN

would measure up. Ari had never cared much about this, had seen it as a "nonessential." His main concern had been that everything looked good on a surface level so he could move forward to the next patient. Samuel was all about taking care of the person, from illness to complete recovery. He was a servant at heart, not in it for the glory.

Charissa liked this facet of Samuel's care, of considering the patients, not only in their physical need but emotional as well as spiritual needs, and following up until he knew they were well on their way to good health. It was little wonder that Samuel needed assistance. That kind of diligence took a great deal of time, attention. "You are a different kind of doctor than Ari," she said. She felt Samuel's arm stiffen.

"Better? Or worse?"

"Different," she said again. "Ari was quick, able to diagnose in seconds, and he was seldom incorrect. But you are more thorough, and I appreciate that. I like how you attend to your patients, as if they are old family friends. Ari . . . well, he saw them more as just another case, to think through as one might a word puzzle or mystery that ought to be solved."

Samuel lifted his chin as if in understanding, and his arm relaxed beneath her hand. "I have greatly appreciated your assistance as my nurse, Charissa." He pulled them to a stop, almost unconsciously, and she noticed how his eyes danced in the porch lights of the mercantile, how the snowflakes, big and fat, settled on his hat and then melted away. A few caught on his eyebrows and long lashes. He had a good face, a kind face. "I could never have made it through these months here without you," he said, staring intently into her eyes.

"Oh," she said, "I'm sure you would have managed."

"Not as I have. I was drowning . . . in more ways than one, I'm afraid. Your . . . friendship means a great deal to me too. I've appreciated the cards and the pies and the baklava. . . . You have been most generous."

"If you hadn't come to town, I might have been forced to return to Boston."

"That," he said, reaching up to softly stroke her left cheek, "would have been most unfortunate." His eyes burned with an intensity she hadn't seen in them since that day in the backyard, but then he hesitated awkwardly, as if it dawned on him that he had touched her. He coughed nervously. "Shall we continue on?"

"Yes, Samuel." She hoped her eyes conveyed all she carried within her heart. Did he know that if he wanted to kiss her that it would be all right—more than all right? How long would it take him to figure out that she had feelings for him?

• ● •

He picked up Charissa's latest card and shuffled upstairs. In the bureau by his bed, he took out the box of cards she had sent him since September, maybe forty all told. Each had a Scripture verse, nothing more. But each card had her name embossed on the front. Mrs. Ari Nadal.

"What do you want me to do?" he whispered to the pine ceiling. God had led him here, to take over Ari Nadal's practice. And Samuel had followed God's call when he passed along encouraging Scripture to Charissa. Now what was he supposed to do with this nurse who had not only ministered to his heart but truly had captured it?

He thought again of their moment on the street when he had dared to touch her. She had not shied away; she actually seemed to draw closer, to invite a kiss, to desire more of their relationship. Over dinner together, with sometimes halting but constant conversation, their eyes had been locked in an intimacy he'd forgotten could exist between a man and woman. They were both still guarding their hearts, and yet the door between them seemed decidedly open.

For the first time, the guilt fled as he considered Charissa and his desire to kiss her on the snowy street. In that moment, Samuel distinctly felt the memory of Mamie and their son take a step away. He took a deep, sudden breath, as if relieved and able to breathe freely, and then it became strangled by the fear that the memory of his wife would disappear forever.

He sat down on the bed and untied the green felt ribbon around the box he'd purchased at the social. He planned on opening and adding the newest note to the stack, but ended up going through them all again. *"Thou art a God ready to pardon, gracious and merciful, slow to anger, and of great kindness,"* said one. *"Be of good comfort; thy faith hath made thee whole,"* said another. *"For as the heaven is high above the earth, so great is his mercy toward them that fear him. As far as the east is from the west, so far hath he removed our transgressions from us."*

On and on they went, reminding him over and over how his failures were made victories through the cross, that God longed to heal him, to welcome him home, to step alongside him once again. He picked up the last: *"Stand ye in the ways, and see, and ask for the old paths, where is the good way, and walk therein, and ye shall find rest for your souls."*

Slowly, he acknowledged that he indeed stood at a crossroad and looked upon the "old paths" as if from a distance. "I don't want you that far from me, Lord," he said, sinking to his knees. It was then that he felt his heart cracking, letting in a bit of the same light he had shared with Charissa. The light he had instinctively known she needed but hadn't thought he deserved himself. He realized that it was a gift that could never be deserved, or it would diminish its greatness. It was freely given to all, even a man who'd let his wife and son die.

Samuel smiled through his tears, opening his arms to the ceiling of his room, welcoming the Lord into his heart. When he looked down again after several long moments, he spied the missive Charissa had left with the cobbler; it was still encased in a luxurious, ivory envelope, sealed with a red wax N. He passed a callused forefinger beneath the seal and slipped the note card from its hiding place.

> Dear Samuel,
> You remain in my prayers "until the day break, and the shadows flee away" and beyond.
> Devotedly, Charissa

He squinted, trying to remember where today's Scripture was from, wondered if it was Song of Solomon. He dismissed the ludicrous thought, rose, sank to the bed, then rose again. Shaking his head at his own idiocy, he lit the lamp, picked up his Bible, and paged through to the Songs. It was from Song of Solomon, chapter two.

He nestled his chin in his hand, staring out into the black night and wondering . . . wondering. Had she meant something more by this verse? by quoting from the romantic poem? Her words repeated in his mind. *Devotedly, Charissa.*

Was he imagining it, or was Charissa Nadal inviting him to pursue her? Was she pursuing him? Samuel Johnson? A plain old doctor from Idaho?

• • •

MARCH

A month after their first supper together, Charissa sat at the captain's desk, trying to write to Ari, but her mind was on Samuel Johnson. What was he doing? Tending to a late-night patient? Upstairs reading by the light of the parlor lamp?

> *Dearest Ari,*
> *Forgive me, my love, for speaking of another man, but I must. The doctor who has come to take over your practice fills my thoughts. You would have liked Samuel, Ari, though you are quite different. Where he is quiet, you were boisterous. Where he is passionate, you were silent. Where you were forthright, he is secretive. I want to know him, know what drives him. He is simple and yet utterly complex. Why does he not openly court me? Am I so ugly, after the ravages of mourning have passed, that he is not interested?*

She laid down the pen, deep in thought. She remembered the time by the creek behind the house when Samuel had stared at her. She recalled the image of him looking intently at her amidst the falling snow on their way to supper, when he dared to touch her and sent a shiver running down her back.

No, Samuel Johnson did not find her repugnant.
She picked up her pen again.

*Why does he not ask me to supper again? At the very
least, why does he not agree to be Salma's physician?
We need him, Ari.*

Charissa raised her head and shook it. What was she
doing? She was writing to her dead husband, the love of her
life, about another man! With a guttural cry of disgust, she
crumpled up the paper, getting ink on the palm of her hand.
She threw it to the ground and began pacing the floor.

What was going on inside her? Why was she falling for
a man whom she would never before have looked at twice?
What was it about Samuel? That he was kind to her? Was she
so desperate for a soft word, an encompassing glance that saw
more than just the doctor's widow, that she was desperate to
fall in love again?

She stopped suddenly and gasped. She was not ready to
fall in love again. And yet there she was, she admitted. She
was in love. In love with Samuel Johnson. Just as surely as she
had been in love with Ari Nadal. She sat back down at her
desk and started her letter to Ari again.

*Dearest Ari,
Oh, how I've loved you, darling. You have been
everything to me for so long that I could see little else. I
wish you were here with me today as I greet Salma's
child. I wish you could hold me through this fear, this
concern for my beloved friend, making me believe as
always that nothing could be bigger than you—*

"Miz Nadal!" came a weak cry from outside her door. "Miss!"

Frowning, Charissa rose and hurried to the top of the stairs. Salma was at the bottom, doubled over in pain.

• • •

Freezing rain pelted his windowpanes, and thunder rumbled in the distance. Samuel had just stocked the woodstove and settled in beneath the covers of his bed when he heard a loud rapping at the door downstairs. Sighing, he rose and pulled on a robe over his long underwear, then hurried down the stairs.

He opened the door to find Charissa, with wet hair plastered on either side of her face, and shivering in her soaked clothes. Samuel held his lamp higher and studied her up and down. "Come into the kitchen, where you can ward off a chill."

"It's Salma," she said between chattering teeth as they walked to the back, through the swinging parlor door. She began speaking as soon as they were seated, her words coming out like a rushing waterfall. "I know you didn't want me to come for you this night. I went to Dr. Gibson, but he's been out calling on Germantown patients struck with typhoid. His maid told me he's gone another four or five days, and then I went to Mrs. O'Shea's—the midwife—and she would have agreed to take care of my Salma, but she already had her hands full with a young mother with twins on their way and, and—"

She took a deep breath. "Samuel, you must come. You

must," she said, reaching for his face and cradling his cheeks in her small, trembling hands. "I cannot do this alone. If something were to happen to Salma . . . please come," she pleaded.

How could he deny such a request? From her? He rose and paced, as Charissa reached her shaking hands out toward the banked and glowing embers of the woodstove.

Samuel sighed and glanced up at the ceiling. Finally he shook his head. "I can't," he whispered.

"What?" Charissa sputtered. "Of course you can. I understand your fears, I do, Samuel. But this is our Salma I'm speaking of. And me. *I* need you there." Her tone changed from pleading to demand. "You have to go, Doctor. You must." Her eyes convicted him as much as her tone. "I've been all over the city trying to keep from asking this of you, but there's no one else. The Lord has it in mind to happen this way."

Instantly, Samuel knew he had as much hope of saying no to her as a scholar would have surviving in a gladiator's arena. He shook his head, fleetingly searching his mind for the right answer. It was cold, but already sweat was pouring down his face.

"You're a doctor, Samuel," Charissa pleaded. "Better you than me, if things get complicated!"

"You don't understand. What if she dies?"

"Dies?" Charissa rose, fear and panic outlined on her deeply shadowed face. "Why would you say such a thing? Is there something wrong with her? Something that makes you so afraid?"

"No, no. The woman is fine, ready to bear this child. It

is my skill that I doubt." He stared at the fire in the stove, aware of her gaze upon his profile.

"Your fears are unfounded. From the deliveries I've attended, it's the mother who does most of the work."

"Indeed," Samuel admitted.

"Come, Doctor. We must hurry! Salma is all by herself. Probably as scared as a wet kitten on a stormy night. She's counting on me to get back to her with help. And you are it."

It was the image of Salma alone in her room, bearing the pain of labor, that finally mobilized Samuel. He left Charissa and went to the adjoining room and gathered his bag and supplies, his breath coming in ragged heaves. What was he doing? Terror assaulted him. He had so carefully avoided this sort of scenario! He brought a hand to his head and the room seemed to spin. He dropped to his knees. Desperately, he sought a visual object to fasten his eyes on, and they fell upon a simple, wooden cross hanging on the wall.

It was then that it hit him. What if Salma lived? What if the child lived? He'd never considered that possibility! What joy there would be!

Tears slipped down his cheeks and a deep, single sob erupted from his gut and came out as a mournful gasp. As he opened his arms, still staring at the cross in the flickering candlelight, a deep, abiding peace entered Samuel and made him feel as though he were being held in a mother's tender embrace. Was this what the Lord had in mind when Samuel had asked for direction? A calm settled on him, and he felt God's blessing as surely as a trusted professor's hand on the shoulder in the midst of a troublesome exam.

Charissa appeared at the door of the examination room,

saw him on his knees, but barely wavered. "Are you ready, Doctor?" she asked gently.

"I am," he answered. Samuel's voice held a note of confidence, and he let out a small laugh of wonder. He rose and took his overcoat from the hook and reached for the other coat for Charissa. "Come," he said to her, already by the door. "Let us see to Salma and this babe who is bent on being born on such an inhospitable night."

Chapter Ten

Inside the front entry of Charissa's house, Samuel took a step back as Salma screamed from upstairs. Her cry came after him like a mountain lion on a wounded stag. His heart pounded with renewed fear.

He was soaked after their run through the cold March rain and muddy streets of the six blocks that separated Charissa's home and Samuel's office. The doctor lifted his wet, white hands in front of his face and prayed for strength to overcome his fear.

Salma cried out again, and Charissa pointed to the stairway to direct him to the laboring woman. She studied him a moment, obviously wanting him to hurry, but she remained silent. She was a silhouette in the creamy light of the doorway, and Samuel couldn't take his eyes from her. She simply reached out her hand like a beckoning angel.

Lord, I can't, Samuel silently cried. *I cannot do this.*

Charissa did nothing more than move her hand in a

tiny, upward circle. Samuel knew if she had said a word, he would have turned, but her quiet gesture was drawing him, soothing him, even as he heard Salma moan and gasp.

The spirit of calm peace entered him again as it had at his office. The light behind Charissa seemed just a bit brighter, just a bit warmer. The stove was probably banked in Salma's room; he could get warm. He could help.

He could help.

The thought encouraged him, forced him to ignore his pounding heart and hasten up the stairs. Charissa gave him a small smile and moved aside. His eyes focused on the bed where he found Salma, her long, kinky hair undone and falling in damp, black waves upon the pillows and partially over her face. She was in a white nightshift, and the bedclothes were in disarray.

Samuel moved to the side of the bed, waiting until her contraction ceased and she opened her eyes. When she looked at him, he was taken aback by the expression of surprise and utter relief on her face. Why had he made her wait? Why? He cursed himself for his lack of courage. Even if she did die, did he want her to do so alone? The poor woman was frightened out of her mind and had labored for hours on a cold, stormy night that was screaming of winter on its last breath.

"The kind Doctor Sam, at last," she whispered.

He knelt by her bedstead, his knees suddenly shaky at her words.

"I knew you'd come."

"As did I," Charissa added. Grateful tears slipped down her cheeks.

Samuel pulled off his wet coat, giving Charissa a small smile. "Plied by pies and called by cobblers," he quipped.

Something warm and soft slipped from her eyes, and Samuel frowned.

"Is that the reason you are here?" Charissa asked softly.

"One of them," he said, wanting to soften the excuse, yet not wishing to express anything more. "Get me a cloth and a bowl of cool water," he said gently to Charissa. "Then set more water on the stove to boil."

"Done," the nurse said, leaving the room at once.

Samuel rolled up his sleeves, examining Salma. "How fast are the contractions?"

"I don't know. Every two or three minutes, it seems."

"How long have you been laboring?"

"I felt the first pain this morning when I arose."

"It will be all right, Salma. You'll be all right."

Hungry, searching eyes met his. Dark and wide, like spreading pools of hot chocolate on the candy maker's white marble worktable. "I will?"

"Yes," he said firmly. "I'm here, Salma. God's here. We're not leaving until your baby has come safely into the world."

He turned to go and wash up, but her long fingers gripped his, pulling him back. "Thank you, Doctor," she said. "I know that tendin' to me hurts you."

He nodded once and then gently set her hand back on the rumpled sheets. "Turn to your left side; it might help you tolerate some of the pain to alternate your position." He lifted the sheets so she could move easily and then moved to the other side until he was in her line of vision. "I will be right back, Salma. I am going to wash my hands."

She nodded quickly, biting her lower lip as if she hated to see him go even for a moment. He paused at the door to hang up his coat and caught sight of the letter on the small desk. Unable to curb his curiosity, he glanced down the dark hallway where Charissa had disappeared, to Salma, who lay with her back to him, then cocked his head and read the beginning lines.

> Dearest Ari,
> Oh, how I've loved you. . . . You have been everything to me for so long. . . . I wish you were here with me today. . . . I wish you could hold me through this fear . . . making me believe as always that nothing could be bigger than you—

A moan from the bed brought his head up quickly. He forced himself to speak. "Another contraction?"

"Mm-hmm," Salma muttered through clenched teeth.

Hurriedly, he left the room, curling around the door and resting his face on the cool plaster of the wall beside the frame. He was a fool. Charissa would always love Ari, just as he would always hold a part of his heart for Mamie. He was feeling his wife's blessing to move on these days, to continue on with life without the weight of her death upon his shoulders, but Charissa apparently did not feel the same. His call here was for one reason only—to bring Salma's child into the world. He had no other business here. No other business.

But as he returned from washing his hands at the end of the hall, his eyes were once again drawn to the light emanating from Salma's room. It was such a soft, yellow, warm light, coming from the gaslights inside . . . so welcoming, so inviting . . .

Samuel was brought back to the present by his patient's mournful wail and hurried back to her. Charissa passed him, carrying a deep pot of wet cloths. They exchanged a quick glance and together rejoined Salma in the makeshift labor room.

• • •

The sleet ceased just as Salma was ready to bear down and push her child into the world. "Go to her other side," Samuel directed Charissa. "Hold her right under the shoulder, like this," he said, demonstrating. "That way, when another contraction comes, you can help lift her up as she pushes."

"This gonna help?" Salma managed to quip, even as her eyes were closed and Charissa wiped her sweating, flushed brow.

"Gravity always helps," Samuel said.

Salma looked at him and smiled. He could see the beginning of a grimace, the sign of an impending contraction. "I am glad you're here, Doctor Sam," she said through gritted teeth.

"As am I," Charissa seconded.

He returned his attention to the laboring mother, moving to the foot of the bed and studying Salma's desperate face as she leaned back into the pillows, as if she wanted to retreat from the front. "Salma, this time, push. You said you're feeling the urge. Don't back away from the pain, borrow from its flow." He nodded at Charissa as she lifted the laboring mother. "Now push and keep pushing." He could see the long-limbed woman tense and hold her breath as several slow seconds passed. She relinquished her efforts as the contraction passed, and Charissa gently lowered her to the bed again.

But the next contraction was immediately upon them. Groaning, Salma looked as though she wanted to weep at the effort it would take.

"This baby wants to be born, Salma. Come on, you can do it," he coaxed.

"A little bit more and you'll be a mother," Charissa added.

Salma squinched up her face, but was able to keep pushing longer, relaxing as the contraction eased. "Salma," Samuel said, grinning from ear to ear, "I can see his head. Two more pushes and he'll be in your arms," he informed her.

"Right . . . now . . ." Salma said, unable to do anything but concentrate on the task at hand. She sat up a little faster this time, and bore down through the contraction. Samuel remained at her knees, waiting to receive Salma's babe, while Charissa supported her back.

"One more push, Salma. You're doing well. The child is beautiful! Perfect features! One more—" The contraction itself interrupted his coaxing, and all of a sudden, an unblemished, squirming child lay in Samuel's hands.

The moment seemed suspended in time. All at once he was back in Boise, holding his own son. But Salma's and Charissa's cries of delight catapulted him to Seattle, where he cradled not a blue, still child, but a wailing, healthy, black boy. Samuel started and rushed to hand the baby to Charissa so he could cut and tie the umbilical cord. He sent Salma and Charissa a reassuring smile.

Then he gently reached for Salma's son and laid him at her breast, as he had done with his son, Joseph, and Mamie. But this time, instead of feeling as though he were being sucked into the path of a tidal wave, he felt higher than a redwood treetop. He had done it. Charissa had done it. *Thank you, Lord,* he prayed.

Love flooded through his heart and outward, and before he could stop himself, he threw an arm around Charissa, kissed her temple, and grinned down at Salma. "You have a beautiful, perfect son, Salma," he said in delight. "You did it."

Tears crested Charissa's lower lids and slid down her cheeks. "It is a big day for all of us," she said.

Samuel smiled at her, unwilling to drop his arm. "Indeed." He suddenly became aware of Salma staring at them, and he wondered why he didn't care at what she saw. God had given him a fresh start, and he had no choice but to follow all that was in his heart. Whether or not Charissa returned any of his feelings.

He knew it would be better, smarter, more logical, to pursue another—one more suitable for him, more plain, not so demanding or stubborn—but as his eyes flickered to Charissa, he knew logic was as lost to him as an iceberg letting loose in the sea. Somehow, he had to find a way to win her heart.

Tentatively, she covered his hand on her shoulder, sending a surge of joy and hope through Samuel.

"I think I'll call him Alex," Salma said, gazing down at her perfect son. "It means 'helper of mankind.' I think his comin' has helped us all."

"Little Alex," Samuel said softly, looking from Salma to the child, who squirmed about. "That is most appropriate."

Charissa leaned down and kissed the boy on the forehead as the child gathered up steam for another cry. "Welcome to the world, little Alexandros," she whispered. "We are most happy to greet you."

Chapter Eleven

APRIL

Samuel and Charissa's friendship deepened with the last of the winter's snow. As April's rains melted the white away, Samuel knew for certain that love had once again found him.

They talked of their spouses, celebrating what each had shared, but also looking ahead. Samuel sensed that Mamie would approve of this headstrong woman who had captured his heart again, even though Mamie would have stared at her like a strange, stubborn creature of another species. What he did not know was if Charissa had truly left Ari behind. The letter he saw on the night of Alex's birth still haunted Samuel, the words coming back to him again and again, despite his best efforts to banish them.

"What are you thinking about?" Charissa said, taking his arm and breaking him from his reverie.

Eager to make the most of a rare, temperate spring afternoon, they walked along the boardwalk, strolling behind Alex's buggy—giving his newly reunited parents an afternoon together without the infant. They ignored the curious looks of passersby at a white couple with a black child. Samuel paused, feeling the tinge of warmth from the April sun on his brow, and he turned to her. "I must confess something, Charissa."

"What is it?" Fear cascaded across her face.

"On the night Alex was born, I happened to see the letter you wrote to Ari. I'm ashamed to say that I read it."

"You . . . read it?"

"Yes," he painfully admitted. "And it has been haunting me ever since. I apologize for not respecting your privacy. There is no excuse."

"No. There is no excuse." She pulled her hand from his arm but did not move away. A tiny smile tugged at the corner of her mouth.

"You look angry, but also bemused," he said, puzzled.

"Both," she agreed lightly.

"Then you forgive me?"

"I do. But I also think you've paid your penance, Samuel. Because I never finished that letter. I kept it anyway, as a memento of Alex's birth, but it is obvious that you did not read all that was in my heart that day."

"Wasn't what I read enough?"

"No." Coyly, she smiled, turned, and began walking away from him.

After a moment's hesitation, Samuel followed with the buggy, rushing to catch up. "Why?"

She laughed, her delight making her maddeningly fetching. "No, no, no. I will not be the first to say it. I am, after all, a lady. You read about my love for Ari. What you did not read was my confession to him that I had certain feelings for another."

Relief rushed through him like a flood over cracking, dry ground. "You did?" he managed to ask. "You do?"

"I do. But do not ask me to tell you exactly what I said. You must promise to respect my privacy from now on."

"Indeed."

"And it will be you, Samuel Johnson," she said, tapping his chest lightly, and smiling into his eyes with one cocked brow, "who will confess love to me first."

He laughed with her and shook his head. "Of course I love you, Charissa. I think I've always loved you. I just never dared believe that you would really love me."

"Hardly the love confession of Shakespeare."

Samuel cringed at her words, but then shrugged his shoulders. "I am not Ari, Charissa. I will never be able to adequately describe what I feel for you here as he did," he said, gesturing toward his heart, hoping the longing he felt was seen in his eyes, "through the words of my mouth or what I write. I am sorry."

"Shh," she said, moving two fingers to tenderly cover his lips. "It is not how you say it, Samuel; it is how you show it. And you show me your heart all the time."

He smiled. "May I kiss you, Charissa?" His heart skipped as she smiled at him.

She did not answer for a moment. "Right here? In front of everyone?"

"Yes. I intend to marry you tomorrow if you'll have me."

Her eyes widened with joy and then softened with tears. "Of course I'll have you, my sweet Samuel." She lifted her soft, perfect lips in gentle offering, and he sank into the opportunity to do what he had longed to do, pulling her to him in a fierce embrace. When they parted, their gaze did not break.

"'Awake, O north wind; and come, thou south,'" Charissa quoted, speaking tender words from the Song of Solomon. "'Blow upon my garden, that the spices thereof may flow out. Let my beloved come into his garden, and eat his pleasant fruits.'"

"'I am come into my garden, my sister, my spouse: I have gathered my myrrh with my spice; I have eaten my honeycomb with my honey; I have drunk my wine with my milk.'"

Charissa grinned. "And you say your love cannot be expressed adequately? Is that not the ultimate love letter?"

"I suppose it is," Samuel agreed. And before he ruined the moment with lame words of his own, he kissed her again.

It was not the stares of the passersby that broke them apart; it was Alex's cry. Charissa rushed around to pick him up out of the buggy and offered him to Samuel. "You would be a good father, Samuel. I am not sure I am able to have children. Would you object to adopting?"

"It matters not to me, Charissa." He pulled her close, and she looked sorrowfully at the babe for a moment. "I would like to have a child with you, but the important part is that we are together. We can be a family on our own, just the two of us, or perhaps adopt a child. There is time enough to decide."

She glanced up at him, and the uncertainty in her eyes made him want to cry himself. *"Truly,"* he said, emphasizing the word.

As Samuel cradled the cooing child, sorrow faded from Charissa's expression and changed to curiosity. "Do you think that Mamie would have approved of me?"

"I do. She was a quiet woman, but she approved of living life to its fullest. She would have gone on to quote Song of Solomon after us: 'Eat, O friends; drink, yea, drink abundantly, O beloved.'"

"What a blessing she must have been to you!"

"She was." He looked at her then. "And I have been blessed again. With a beautiful wife-to-be. Thank you, Charissa, for loving me."

"Oh, Samuel, dear Samuel. There is no thanks needed. 'I sleep but my heart waketh. . . . I am sick [with] love.'"

"Well said," Samuel murmured, placing the child in the buggy again and turning toward Charissa's home, walking with a distinct spring in his step. He threw her a sidelong glance. "You loved me until the day broke and the shadows fled, Charissa. Can you love me forever more?"

She looked down at their feet and then back to him. "I think we've seen that forever doesn't always happen, Samuel. Let us love as much as we can, as fully as we can, all the days of our lives."

"For every day of our lives," Samuel happily promised.

And, as if in full agreement, Alex cooed.

A NOTE FROM THE AUTHOR

Dear Reader,

Thank you for picking up *Letters of the Heart*. In "Until the Shadows Flee," I wanted to explore the differences in love relationships, and how one love can equal another, even if it's not shaped the same. Ari and Samuel are quite different heroes, but each is dramatically qualified to win Charissa's heart! But then I always melt when it comes to the underdog; I frequently root for the losing team in any sport (much to my husband's chagrin). In my mind, Samuel Johnson was made for the quintessential hero role.

I also was curious about losing a great love and finding love again. There is great hope in the fact that there is always good potential in our future, regardless of what heartache we pass through. Many of us have suffered much, and it often holds us back, rather than freeing us to explore other potential routes toward happiness and fulfillment. God has good things in store for those who love him; we just have to give him the opportunity to show us the way.

More important, I wanted to explore how Scripture provides the best love letter of all—to each of us. Christ is our bridegroom, and we the ever-winsome bride. Whether you have experienced love and lost, are in love now, or desire to one day be in love, I hope you can rest in the fact that Jesus stands at your door waiting, ready to hold you in his arms and love you for all eternity.

Every good thing—
Lisa Tawn Bergren

ABOUT THE AUTHOR

 LISA TAWN BERGREN, a best-selling, award-winning author, lives in Colorado with her husband, Tim, and two small daughters. She has worked as an editor for Multnomah and WaterBrook and is currently devoting herself to faith, family, and writing her own fiction. In addition to her novella for *Letters of the Heart*, she has written ten novels—including *Refuge, The Bridge,* and *The Captain's Bride;* a children's book, *God Gave Us You;* and two gift books as well as three other novellas. Her works total more than 700,000 books in print.

Lisa invites you to visit her Web site at www.LisaTawn Bergren.com. She also welcomes letters written to her in care of Tyndale House Author Relations, P.O. Box 80, Wheaton, IL 60189-0080.

DEAR LOVE

Maureen Pratt

Chapter One

"You'll look lovely in the deep green velvet, Fern. I can't wait until Mrs. Davreaux finishes the dress so you can try it on."

Violet Milton looked up from her writing table and smiled across the cozy parlor at her best friend, Fern Lafferty. "There will no doubt be quite a competition for your hand once everyone sees how beautiful you look. You're sure to be the next one to walk down the aisle."

"You're very kind, Violet." Fern smoothed out the piece of embroidery in her lap. "It is beautiful material, and the style is flattering, to be sure." She seemed to hesitate. "But I still can't help but ask, isn't planning a wedding before you have a fiancé a bit . . . well . . . rash?"

Violet tossed her head. The light brown curls that framed her face danced merrily. "Nonsense, Fern. It makes all the sense in the world." She stretched her hands, then counted off her reasons on slender fingers. "From the time I was a young girl, I dreamed of marrying by my twenty-second birthday which, as you know, is January 11 of next year. My parents, too, have hoped for nothing but the most happy of marriages for me, and they have always promised me a wedding that matches my desires. While they have, at times, questioned my reasoning in making so many plans without telling them who the groom will be, they are, nonetheless, still eager to see that my very fondest dream of childhood becomes a sweet reality. Furthermore, you know how ill Grandmother Milton has been this past year. I would be devastated if she were unable to be present at my wedding, as close as she and I are.

"Perhaps it would be easier on all concerned if I waited for a warmer time of year, but—" Violet's cheeks grew warm as she continued to explain— "Christmas is the most beautiful, romantic time of year. The holiday colors are ideal for decorations, and I adore the scent of evergreen indoors." She paused for a breath.

Fern shook her head gently. "But Violet, without knowing the likes and dislikes of your betrothed—"

Violet rested her hands on the papers at her elbow. "True, there is no end of detail to making a wedding the occasion it ought to be. But it is also exhilarating. And by planning the whole affair, from start to reception, I am saving myself, my parents, my betrothed, and his own family no end of headaches."

She stared out the window at the slate gray clouds that promised snow before long. "Which reminds me, I must see about which flowers the florists will have available the third week in December. It has been exceptionally cold, and snow will undoubtedly have fallen by then. Perhaps there will be white roses, grown in the hothouse . . ." She dipped her gold filigree pen into a crystal inkwell and wrote something on the paper before her.

The sound of light laughter from across the room made Violet stop writing. She frowned. "What is so funny about white roses? They would look splendid with the red-and-green garlands. Very Christmas-like."

"It isn't the roses, silly." Fern carefully placed her embroidery aside and smoothed her blue silk skirts. "It's the idea of your so seriously orchestrating an entire wedding without having the faintest idea whom you will marry."

Violet pushed back from her desk. She was finding it more difficult to hide her true reason from her best friend and had to search for the right words. "If you doubt my reasoning, didn't you hear Reverend Crandal's sermon on Sunday? He said that there is a time for everything and that the Lord has someone for each of us."

"That is true. But I don't think he meant—"

A wave of disbelief struck Violet. "Or do you think I haven't any possibility of prospects? I thought you were my loyal friend, Fern."

Fern stood. "You know I have been your staunchest friend ever since we were babes. And this season you've been more popular than the rest of us girls combined. I'm sure any number of young men would give the world to become your husband. Why, I wouldn't be surprised if you didn't have a special someone already picked out. It would certainly explain your parents' willingness to agree to everything thus far." Fern dropped her voice to a whisper. "Am I right, Violet? Are you in love with someone?"

Violet felt the color rise afresh in her cheeks. She shuffled some papers on the desk. "I haven't decided . . . that is, I don't quite know . . . but perhaps, well, there might be someone."

"There is?" Fern stepped back, her eyes wide. "Who?" She crossed the room, treading quickly on the plush carpet. "Tell me, Violet. Who is it?"

Violet hesitated. For seven long months, she had managed to hide the source of her affections beneath the flurry of her preparations. The feelings she experienced were so new that it had taken her some time before she was comfortable with them and could believe with certainty that they were requited.

But four weeks remained before Christmas, before her scheduled wedding. Her parents, though patient, thought she was past time in announcing to them which young admirer she'd chosen. Reverend Williams told her Sunday that he was looking forward to announcing the banns of marriage to the congregation.

And of course she needed to be sure herself of the man she would marry. Even though she felt she knew him better than any other suitor, she did not wish to discover his identity at the eleventh hour!

Her resolve to keep her secret crumpled. Violet had to tell someone or her heart would burst. And while she valued her parents' counsel, Fern had a better sense of the young people in their circle. She would be the most help in Violet's next step toward planning her wedding: learning the identity of her one true love.

Reaching into the deep pocket of her mauve day dress, Violet drew out a thin sheaf of envelopes wrapped in a thick lavender-scented ribbon.

"I've received a letter a week for the past seven months. Ever since the ball at the governor's house. They're from him. The man I think . . . that is . . . I believe . . . that is . . . I wish more than anything to marry."

Fern gasped. "Seven months? You've kept this secret from me that long? Violet, this must indeed be serious." She fixed her eyes on the stack of letters. "Who is he?"

Violet drew one of the envelopes from the slender packet and slid a thin sheet of paper out of it. Her eyes beheld the letter, and she felt heat rise in her cheeks. It wasn't that the contents were particularly impressive. There was no grand style to the words or thoughts, no elaborate flourishes to the penmanship. But the spirit of the lines of prose was so strong as to make Violet's heart flutter.

She offered the letter to Fern. "This was the first letter I received."

Fern took the letter and read while Violet closed her eyes and recited the contents word-for-word to herself.

Dear Miss Milton,
I fear you will think me impertinent for writing to you unannounced and unbidden. Rest assured I have no wish to offend you, nor do I intend to bring you anything other than my most sincere admiration for the kindness you showed to the servants last evening at the governor's ball. Many in attendance took no heed to the inclement weather. But the way you insisted that the carriage drivers and doorkeepers remain sheltered from the elements was, indeed, moving. Your graciousness will be remembered long after this season

> *of rain is past and summer blossoms. You are a rare*
> *jewel of a lady.*
>
> *Your humble admirer*

Fern looked up. "It is a good letter. Strong and perceptive. But—" her brows knit together and she tilted her head to one side—"two things strike me most at the moment."

Hanging on her friend's words, Violet could scarcely breathe. "What are they?"

"First, that this is not a very romantic letter."

With only a little disappointment, Violet took the paper from her friend and read it over. "That is true, at least for this one alone." Gently she returned the sheet to its envelope and drew out another. "But his eloquence increases with each missive. His perception of me—the way he knows me—is uncanny. And his admiration, well, see for yourself how it increases." She handed the next letter to Fern, who read through it with a more critical expression.

"Perhaps," Fern said when she'd finished reading. "But my second question is even more of a tangle. Why doesn't he just say who he is?"

"That's the difficult thing of it." Violet held tight to the packet of letters. "I have no idea. No messenger delivers these; they appear out of nowhere at the front doorstep, always accompanied by a single, fresh flower. The writing belongs to no one I know, at least no one from our school days. But the details lead me to believe he is part of our circle. How else would he know about the ball and the picnic at Starved Rock? Or the donations my parents and I made to the Hanlin family in August? That, especially, was kept very quiet; only our closest friends were aware of it."

Fern looked at the letter in her hand. "I'm afraid I'm at as much of a loss as you. I don't recognize the script, and there are no telltale turns of phrases."

Her emotions rising, Violet clutched the letters. "Oh, Fern. If you read through these as I have, you would sense, you would know . . . I do believe he will soon propose marriage! Just in time!" She pitched her voice lower. "Will you help me find out who it is?"

"My dear friend, this is a puzzle you've found yourself in. I honestly have no idea how to begin." Fern sighed. "It seems more of a case for an investigator than either you or me. Perhaps you could take these letters to the Pinkerton people and—"

"No." Violet shook her head. "We mustn't tell anyone else about these just yet. I want to find this man myself, before other people start meddling."

Her eyes began to mist as the months of secretive wondering and hoping came to the fore. "It's like we imagined, Fern. Remember? All the while we were girls, we used to pray about the men we would marry. Remember how we would sit in the garden and look up at the clouds and sigh that our future husbands might be looking up at that very same sky?"

Fern nodded, her expression turning thoughtful as Violet continued. "With these letters, it's as though the dream has become real. It's so romantic! And yet, at the same time, so sensible."

"Sensible?"

"Why, yes. You know how social conventions can

sometimes stifle the reality of a person. Rather than approaching me at a party or an outing where there are hundreds of pairs of curious ears, he is opening his heart to me and me alone." She clasped the letters to her bosom. "He is my friend, my soul mate."

Fern laughed. "It still seems strange to call this unknown scribe your love. I'd always considered that respect and friendship, even affection, must be shared directly between two people. Have you shown these letters to your parents?"

"Of course not. They would think I was taking the entire situation out of proportion."

"Because you're planning the wedding of the season and your beloved is courting you in secret?" Fern asked.

Reluctantly, Violet nodded.

"Well, they may have a point, you know. Any person can write anything and make it sound like the stars and the moon all rolled into one."

Violet lifted the lavender-scented packet to her nose and inhaled the springlike aroma. "But this man is honorable. I feel it; I know it. Oh, Fern, you will help me find out who he is, won't you?" A new wave of desperation rose in Violet as she remembered again that there were only four weeks until her scheduled wedding. Her chin began to tremble, and tears slid from her eyes to her cheeks. "I must know soon. I must."

"Shh." Fern took a handkerchief from her skirt pocket and dabbed Violet's cheeks. "Silly, dear Violet to fall in love with a man she hasn't met."

Gulping sobs, Violet nodded.

Fern wrapped her arms around Violet's shaking shoulders. "There, there. It's all right. Shh. I'll help you. If we put our two heads to this, we're sure to reveal this love of yours and have you sailing down the aisle in church as you've dreamt."

"Thank you." Violet sniffled, dried the rest of her tears with her own lace handkerchief, and settled at her desk once more.

She slid another envelope from the ribbon-tied packet and unfolded the letter it contained. The paper was soft and warm in her fingers, the writing careful and plain.

"He sounds so strong, so brave and honest." Violet's sorrow lifted, and she smiled. "I believe he is the most handsome, articulate, intelligent man in society. Well mannered but compassionate. Caring for the plights of others in his employ or even of strangers. And he knows me well, even as to when I help Dr. Farraday at the orphanage."

"Then it can't be one of the Harelson twins." Fern perused the same letter and shook her head.

"Why not?"

"As handsome as they are, neither of them cares a fig about the orphanage. I doubt either of them even knows you go there, let alone cares that you do."

"True." Violet took out another letter. "This one arrived just after the church bazaar. He compliments me on my peach and apple pies."

"Ah, a man with a good appetite." Fern winked at Violet. "Can't be Henry Seaford then. He's skinny as a rail."

"And not altogether articulate. Why, his voice would nearly spook a horse. And I don't think it's Mason Jones, either," Violet said, smiling. "He is so portly I'm sure he can't remember the particulars about what he consumes each day."

"Right you are again." Fern set down the letter she was currently holding and picked up another. "And I cannot imagine him writing this." She traced a line of prose with her finger as she read: "*'Your smile lights the very night with a radiance that comes from within, from a spirit filled with God's grace and your own pure loveliness.'*"

Violet knew she was blushing. "I told you his eloquence increases, didn't I?"

"And his astute estimations of who you are." Fern tilted her head and furrowed her brow thoughtfully. "Violet, could it be someone even closer? Perhaps someone in the household?"

"One of the servants?" Violet hesitated, then shook her head. "The only unmarried man in my parents' employ is Adam MacGreggor, the stable manager. But I am sure he is not able to read or write."

"How do you know?"

"We have become good friends, and I know he is very intelligent. If he had a proper education, he would undoubtedly be working at some other less menial position."

Fern looked at Violet for a moment. "I see. Well, could it be a colleague of your father's, perhaps? There are bound to be eligible young men at the bank."

"There is Frederick Hallsworth. But somehow he does not strike me as the poetic kind."

"And poetic he must be," Fern said, perusing another letter. "Oh, to have someone write such letters to me someday! You are right, Violet. It's so much better than mere words spoken in haste or because silence is too tedious." Fern took the next letter that Violet offered and read the salutation.

"Hear what he does with a simple hello. *'Dear Love, I saw you running yesterday and must say that, although not a dainty pursuit, it only added to your beauty. The way the wind brought rosy color to your face and tousled your hair was a treat for my eyes, and I thanked the Lord that he brought me near enough, that blustery day, to behold you.'*"

Fern handed the letter back to Violet. "He is smitten, isn't he?"

"If only I knew who he was." Violet sighed.

She read and reread every letter in her packet, handing each over to Fern, who also studied them carefully. But by the time the afternoon light lengthened to shadows in the parlor and the maid had closed the heavy curtains and laid a crackling fire in the hearth, neither she nor Fern was any closer to guessing who had written the letters.

Carefully folding her embroidery into a quilted carryall, Fern said, "I had best be on my way home or my parents will worry."

"I will tell Maude to have Adam bring your carriage around," Violet said. She set the letters aside and sighed. "It can't be hopeless. But it does seem so."

They moved into the hallway, where Fern donned her warm woolen traveling coat. As the clop of the horses' hooves grew near, Fern gave Violet a hug.

"You, of all the people I know, have always had such faith, Violet. Keep your resolve to discover this man's identity and eventually you shall. As you know better than I, nothing is hopeless if the Lord's hand is guiding events."

The Miltons' stable manager, Adam, helped Fern climb into her carriage. Violet shivered as she waved good-bye to her friend. Snow had begun to fall. The air smelled moist and fresh. Christmas would come quickly now.

Was she making a fool of herself to plan a wedding without knowing the other half of the wedding party?

Violet thanked Adam for his assistance, and he touched his hand to his cap before walking back to the stables. As she turned to go back inside, she spied something bright amid the falling flakes. Violet's heart beat faster and the chill left her.

A single, slender pink rose rested on top of another envelope. Another letter!

Violet snatched up the rose and the letter, tucking both into the warm pockets of her skirts as she hurried into the house.

"Violet, dear, you'll catch your death of cold." A tall, slender woman with gently coifed gray hair and kind blue eyes met her in the hallway.

The letter radiated warmth from where it rested in Violet's pocket. Violet kissed her mother's cheek. "I'm sorry, Mother. You know how Fern and I go on."

Violet's mother smiled. "Hurry upstairs and change for dinner. Gracie's soup will warm you in no time."

Violet sped to her room. But rather than change her clothing, the first thing she did was open the envelope.

Perhaps this one would reveal the identity of the writer.

Perhaps it would contain the proposal of marriage she expected.

Perhaps, with this letter, Violet would finally know her true love.

Chapter Two

Early the next morning, Adam MacGreggor stood in the center of Chester Milton's study. Were it not for the import of his visit, he would have become impatient. There was much work to be done at the stables, and he also needed to visit the bankers before close of business. But Adam held his impatience in check, keeping his thoughts focused on his purpose for requesting this unusual meeting, apart from the normal business discussions he had with his employer.

Milton read through a long document on his desk, then added his signature to the last page with a flourish. He blotted the ink and blew on it to be sure it was dry. He then set aside the papers, took a pipe from the rack on his desk, cleaned it, filled it with sweet-smelling tobacco, lit it, and breathed delicate smoke rings into the warm air.

Adam's nose crinkled as memories came to mind of a time, years past, when he would sit at his father's knee and inhale the very same aroma. How long ago that was! And how much distance and time now lay between him and his Scottish roots.

What would his family—and particularly his father—think of his plans now? Would there be praise for his frugal saving, his carefully thought-out course of action? Or would there be derision for having defied the course his parents had set for him when they sent him to live with his uncle? Would they belittle him that he still had not overcome the defect that had caused him to be sent far from the midst of his loving family and home?

As more fragrant smoke wafted in the air around him, Adam suppressed the urge to cough. Better to think of the future, which certainly held a brighter promise than the dim past.

Finally, Milton spoke. "So, MacGreggor, I must admit I was a bit surprised to receive your request to have this meeting. All is well with the stables, I trust?"

Adam spoke slowly, carefully reining in his unruly tongue, which made his speech a mixture of Scottish burr, American flatness, and unpredictable stuttering. "R-R-Right as rain, sir."

"Good. Good." Milton puffed another smoke ring. "I hope this isn't regarding a raise in your salary. You know we don't discuss such things until after January 1."

"I'm aware of that, s-s-sir," Adam said, anxiety rising within him, and along with it, a more pronounced recurrence of the speech defect that had marked him from youth.

"Then what do you want to speak about? As you can see, I'm a very busy man. If this isn't important, then I suggest you get along with the day."

Squaring his shoulders, Adam looked directly at his employer. "It is important, sir. But it isn't regarding anything of a p-p-professional n-nature."

Milton raised an eyebrow and continued to puff on his pipe.

"It's regarding your d-d-daughter, sir."

Milton took the pipe from his mouth and spluttered, "My daughter? You mean Violet? What about her?"

Adam had written down his speech and practiced it several times. But still the words seemed to tangle in his thoughts and on his tongue. Steeling himself, he prayed, *Lord, be with me now. I've entered the very lion's den, and I so need you to give me courage and carry me through.*

"What about my daughter?" Milton asked again, his eyes narrowing into slits.

Adam squared his shoulders again. "Sir, as you know, I'm a God-fearing m-m-man. A churchgoer and a hard w-w-worker."

"Yes . . ." Milton said warily. "And . . . ?"

"I . . . that is, the Lord has been guiding m-m-my l-life for years, sir. And I feel he is leading me in a particular direction, which I m-m-must d-discuss w-w-with you."

Milton sat forward in his chair and fingered the pipe stem. "Out with it, MacGreggor."

Adam's throat suddenly became dry and his hands moist from nerves. He hadn't felt this way before, not even when he had boarded the ship that would take him away from home and toward his uncle's home in New York.

"W-w-well . . ."

What made him think that Milton would be open to

what he was about to ask? His own father had rejected him as soon as he realized he could not cure his son's speech defect. Sending him to his brother, a stern minister in America, had only reinforced Adam's feelings of inadequacy; as much as his uncle had insisted he speak up in services, his stuttering had grown worse and his uncle's punishments more severe. Adam's belief in a benevolent God was sorely tested then, and his faith had teetered on the brink of disillusionment.

Just when he was at his lowest moment, Adam had spotted a leaflet tucked among the prayer books he collected after Sunday services. The page was well worn, but the message seemed fresh and full of hope: There were many jobs farther to the west, in Chicago, and a need for skilled, deter-mined workers. After much prayer, Adam had surmised there might be a chance for him to have a better life there.

Adam clung to the belief that the Lord was leading him to run far away from all family, and so he did, carving a life for himself in Illinois. Here, his speech improved, his dreams became clear, and his faith was reborn.

He had fallen in love, too. In love with Violet Milton. The very thought of her gave his life a meaning and his heart a warmth that he had long since thought was impossible.

She had been friendly from the start, always kind and cheerful, a very rare flower among the stiffer social set in which she moved. They had instantly struck up a friendship that had grown with each passing day. And if Violet's heart and soul were lovely, her physical beauty was beyond that of any other woman Adam had ever seen. She was the perfect woman to share his life and dreams.

It had been so easy to begin writing letters to her,

personal communications where he was free to express himself without the burden of social division or his stutter. And once he began, he could not stop writing. He did not know exactly what Violet thought of the letters, but he hoped she was moved by them. Certainly her expression the evening before, when she found his latest missive, gave him hope.

If Adam had overcome his speech troubles and stayed in Scotland, and if he had met Violet there, there would have been no question of his suitability as a husband for her. Their families were at least on a social par, and he was sure their fathers would have been able to strike a satisfactory agreement.

But here, Adam was at a disadvantage. However, he had seen much of the American dream and had experienced it himself in his ability to amass considerable savings and look forward to a business pursuit of his own.

Adam breathed deeply of the tobacco-scented air and oddly drew strength from its warmth. The Lord had guided him thus far. Surely, he would not forsake him now.

Suddenly, the words flowed more strongly. "Sir, I would very much like to c-c-court your daughter, Violet, and I ask your blessing that I be allowed t-to approach her, with all propriety, to enable her to consider if she finds it the Lord's will, as I do . . . to . . . well . . . become my w-w-wife. I can offer her—"

Milton cut Adam's words short. He did not sound offended or angry, but rather astonished. "I know you and my daughter are on friendly terms, MacGreggor, but what can you offer her beyond the friendship you already have? Do you honestly expect her to live the life of the wife of a stable manager?"

Adam drew in a breath. Milton knew nothing of his plans, nor of the sizable sum of money sitting in an account at the man's very own bank. How he wanted to challenge Milton's attitude of condescension! But to do so would destroy any chance Adam had of persuading the man to think otherwise. And, in fact, Milton might find some way to thwart Adam's plans to buy the farm that would mean so much to so many people.

No, he must keep a level head and pray that the Lord would work through him now, as always. Carefully reining himself in, Adam steadily met Milton's gaze as he spoke. "I understand that m-m-my current situation is not exactly the most desirable for a man such as yourself to entertain for his own daughter. But what I appear to lack is, I hope, overshadowed by what I do possess in character, faith, future prospects, and g-genuine . . ."

He paused, wrestling with his feelings and his tongue.

He loved Violet.

But the cherished word would not pass his lips. Instead, he uttered the softer sentiment. "G-genuine affection for your daughter, M-M-Miss Violet."

Milton spluttered and coughed, looking very much as though he were about to begin laughing.

Adam was not to be put off. "All I'm asking is that you give me a chance, Mr. Milton. I'm well aware that your daughter has many other suitors. However, I assure you that n-n-none is as honorable as myself. And out of that honor, I assure you that I will n-not approach Violet until I have your p-p-permission."

The silence that followed Adam's speech was nearly

palpable. Adam's thoughts and feelings skittered like a nervous colt between hope and despair and back again as he watched Milton weigh what he had just said.

Finally, the older man spoke. His voice was tight. "You are correct in saying my daughter has many suitors. Many wealthy, well-positioned suitors. You are perhaps the finest stable manager I've ever seen. I've had no complaints in the five years you've been in my employ, and I would be loathe to have to replace you. But to think of you as a son-in-law . . . well, I am afraid that is out of the question."

Adam's face grew hot. He had not come this far to retreat. "Sir, there are some things you do not know about me, who my family is, and my future plans. If-if you would listen—"

"I gave you the opportunity to tell me about your parentage once before, and you would not do it." Milton waved a hand toward him. "Now is past time to try to convince me you are other than you have been and will continue to be—a stable manager." Milton steadied his voice. "My daughter needs someone who is well educated, articulate, well positioned socially, and can provide a comfortable, secure, and honorable life for her. I will not go into a detailed comparison of yourself based upon those things, however; suffice it to say you are unsuited to be my daughter's husband."

Adam opened his mouth and then quelled the urge to blurt out who his family really was, the standing they held in Scotland, and what growing up in that position of privilege had given him in terms of education and ability. But the promise made between him and the Lord so many years ago prevented him from doing so. He had vowed he would overcome his failings on his own, with support only from the Lord's forgiveness, promise, and salvation.

Adam was determined to succeed or fail on his own merit. Merit that he knew was as good as, if not superior to, that of any other man who might be seeking to court Violet Milton. Why, Milton himself would probably never consider doing what Adam planned for the land he was going to purchase!

Despite his earlier resolve to abide by Chester Milton's wishes, Adam's temper began to fuel his words. "Sir, if you would hear me out—"

"I'm a busy man, MacGreggor."

"I appreciate that. However—"

"And the answer would still be no."

"You must give me the opportunity to explain—"

"I 'must' give you nothing of the sort."

"Mr. Milton—"

"Good day, MacGreggor."

"Sir!" Adam's voice rang out strong and clear as a church bell.

"Enough!" Milton glowered and pointed the stem of his pipe at Adam. "I warn you. If you approach my daughter with anything other than the most professional of intentions, I will not hesitate to send you packing. Without references."

The air crackled between them. Adam was sorely pressed to remain calm. But finally, he steadied himself. With dignity, he nodded. "Very well, sir. I must admit I hope you change your mind . . ."

Milton glared.

"But I respect your position as Violet's father and my employer."

"Good." Milton put the pipe back in his mouth. "Now, leave. We both have work to do."

• ● •

While Adam was speaking with Mr. Milton, Violet was upstairs in her room, mulling over her prospects yet again.

Sitting in her feathery soft armchair, her feet resting on a stool, which bore a floral needlepoint pattern she herself had stitched, Violet peered at the list she had drawn up. Who among these possibilities was writing her those letters?

She glanced at the latest missive, propped up against the slender bud vase that held the fragrant rose that had accompanied it.

That letter did not contain a marriage proposal. However, it did hold something that made Violet even more sure that the author of the letters was her soul mate. With words that all but leaped off the page, Violet's suitor spoke of reaching out to poor families, not only at Christmas but throughout the year. He wrote of giving more than token assistance to parents in need. He spoke of holding close the children that seemed lost in the increasingly stupefying bustle of a Chicago rising up from the ashes of the great fire. Didn't that match exactly the work she felt God had also set before her? And he ended with such a turn of phrase that Violet's heart pounded even upon reading it many times over:

> Your care is unbounded, your spirit so pure as to be all
> in all. I feel honored to be allowed to be in your pres-
> ence and await only the Lord's will in speaking with

*you with all the joy in my soul. In anticipation of that
wonderful day, I remain,*

Your most affectionate admirer

Most affectionate admirer. He had gone from *humble
admirer* to that more endearing term. Oh, he was clearly
coming closer to revealing to her his identity and the full
flower of his intentions. And none too soon, for she could not
wait much longer. She had to know. She simply, utterly had
to know!

Violet went back to her list. There were several names
she recognized as belonging to young men who had expressed
a certain interest in her. Which of them had this deep desire
to help the unfortunate? Which of them knew it was her most
fervent wish also?

Ever since she was little, Violet's desire to be happily
wed had rested side by side a true burden for the less fortunate around her. Perhaps it was her desire to make everyone
around her happy, or perhaps it sprang out of her deep faith.
Whatever the reason, she seemed to have a special empathy
for the downtrodden, the destitute, especially the children
and, more to the point, children who had lost their parents.
She longed for the day when she and her beloved would be
able to work together among the needy.

Was there any young man on her list who shared
those feelings? Violet read the list again, then shook her
head. Sadly, she could not imagine any of them writing her
letters like those she had been receiving, let alone have
such a heightened interest in anything beyond the latest
fashion.

And what was more, Violet knew she was not in love with any of them.

Restless, Violet rose from her chair and went over to the thick curtains that covered her floor-to-ceiling windowpanes. She parted the drapery and gazed out at the awakening day through sleet-spattered glass. The world took on a dreamlike haze through such a prism.

Violet sighed. What if she were to dream? What if she were to throw her list aside and open her mind to other possibilities? Could there be a total stranger, someone she'd never met, admiring her from afar?

The thought made her heart flutter with a tinge of fear. Even if he were Sir Galahad himself, Violet knew she would not be able to marry a complete stranger on such short notice. She would need to have more than a passing acquaintance with the man to whom she gave her heart and life.

So, if not a stranger and if not someone in her own social circle, then who? Someone she already knew, but who wasn't a part of her regular life? Gazing through the ill-focused glass, Violet tried to think of whom she might be forgetting.

At that moment, Adam MacGreggor left the house, his head bowed and his hands shoved deep into the pockets of his long overcoat. Violet watched as he crossed the path leading away from the house and headed toward the stables. As always, she was struck by his tall, strong presence, even through the prism of her sleet-streaked window. There was always something comforting about him, a feeling of warmth and protection, of genuine friendship that glowed warmly from his wide, gray green eyes.

She turned from the window.

Adam was a trusted friend. She had come to know him well, especially as they often worked on charitable projects together. And he was present the evening before when she had bid farewell to Fern and found the latest letter.

Of course, he could not have written the letters, but might he know something about the messenger? Or might he know something about the author himself?

Violet gathered her letters and tucked them carefully under the feather mattress of her bed. It would do no good to wonder all day. Violet hastened outside in search of her answers.

Chapter Three

Adam was sitting cleaning an already shiny bridle in the tack room at the end of the stables' long central corridor when he heard light footsteps on the hay-strewn walkway. Looking up, he found himself unable to speak at the sight of Violet framed in the soft glow of the stable lamps, her light pink wrap setting off the glow in her cheeks and the burnished bronze color of her hair.

She smiled at him and her heart-shaped face lit up like a radiant candle, the dimples dancing on either side of her rosy mouth. Adam's breath caught in his throat. His head was still reeling from his conversation with her father. He knew he should behave like the elder brother or friend he had always been. But this was the woman he loved, the woman he had been courting with letters for months.

Had her father already spoken to her of his interest? He would be mortified if she had come to merely reinforce what her father had ordered. His hands fumbled and the bridle clattered to the floor. Flustered, he bent to retrieve it as Violet walked into the room.

Violet stood before him, a little breathless and with a flush rising in her cheeks. "Adam, there is something I must ask, and you are the only person who might know the answer."

Adam looked at Violet and was lost in her deep blue eyes. How was he to honor her father's words, with feelings so strong, with knowing he loved her? He looked away. "I will b-be happy to help in whatever w-w-way I can, Miss Violet."

Violet stepped nearer and Adam was compelled to meet her gaze. The flush increased in her cheeks, and her voice held a slight tremor that made him ache to enfold her in his arms. "Is there something wrong, Adam? You seem a bit pale."

Her words took him aback. Surely he did not appear as distraught as she? Eager to reassure her, he worked at the bridle more swiftly, succeeding in tangling his shaking fingers in the slender leather straps.

"I assure you I've never been better, Miss Violet." In a way, it was true. In spite of his discomfort at the conversation with her father, in Violet's presence he always felt as though he were walking on a cloud. Finally extricating his fingers from the bridle, he rested the contraption on his knees and bestowed a smile upon his beloved. "What is it you would like to ask me?"

Violet glanced at the open door, then back at Adam. "Do you promise not to tell anyone I've asked you this?"

It was an innocent question. They had held some confidences before, when Violet wanted to hide a gift for her father in the far reaches of the stables, or when she wanted to surprise her grandmother with a visit.

But somehow the familiarity that was once common-place between them seemed too personal now that he had spoken up about his feelings and been rejected by her father. And he certainly did not feel comfortable with her dainty hand resting lightly on his arm, a frown on her lovely face.

"I do think there's something wrong," Violet said, lean-ing forward. "Are you sure you are not ill, Adam?"

Adam stood and moved away from her. "Perhaps I might have caught a touch of something, Miss Violet. Best to leave me be. You mustn't take ill so c-close to Chr-Christmas, what with your w-w-wedding and all."

He could have sunk into the ground for mentioning the ever-looming time when Violet would be married away. He knew the other servants were talking of nothing else, but he would have preferred to think he'd never heard of it at all.

She seemed less cheerful as she replied, "Yes, Christmas is coming rapidly." Violet tilted her head and looked into Adam's eyes. "You were present last evening when my friend Miss Lafferty visited, weren't you?"

"I was, Miss Violet. I trust nothing was the matter with her carriage or horse?"

"No, nothing like that." Violet took a deep breath. "But did you happen to see anyone leave anything on the front steps? A . . . a flower, perhaps? Or an envelope? I was wondering if you did, if you could tell me who the messenger was? A description, at least, or a name?"

Violet's eyes searched his as if they could see straight through to the thoughts running wildly in his head. She was so close, he could feel her feathery breath on his face, smell the faint touch of lavender that rose from her and mixed with the earthier smells of the stables.

If he were in Scotland, if he didn't have this problem of speech, he would shout from the rooftops that he was the messenger and the author all rolled into one. And she, knowing fully who he was, would laugh and fall into his arms.

But he wasn't in Scotland. As kind and good as Miss Violet was, her father had made it quite clear that she was also a member of the elite. Adam couldn't expect her to think of him in any way but as an employee of her father. And he, for his part, could not approach her without defying her father, which he, in all his honor, would not do. There were too many others depending on him and he would not let them down.

"Adam?" Violet moved closer.

The scent of lavender became stronger. He backed away. "Really, Miss Violet, you should not get near me." He sank onto the bench. What he was about to say cut through his heart, but he had to do it, had to send her on her way once and for all. "Now that you mention it, I do believe I saw a young man that evening."

"You did." She hurried to him and sat down next to him. "Tell me, did you recognize him? What did he look like?"

Keeping his eyes fixed on the tangle of leather in his lap, Adam said, "I can't say that I knew him for certain, but he looked like one of your friends."

Violet's eyes sparkled. She gripped Adam's arm. "Please, tell me anything, any detail you remember!"

It was agony for him to continue this way, but he knew he had no choice. He had to keep himself above reproach. "It was d-dusk, Miss Violet, and snowing, if I recall. Very difficult to s-s-see. The man was . . . young. Tall. Well . . . well dressed in a . . . a blue greatcoat, I believe, with brass buttons. And s-s-smiling. He was s-smiling."

Now Violet's eyes were like deep pools of ocean water. "Smiling? I knew he had a good disposition. And well dressed, too? In a blue coat? That should eliminate some of the choices, for some do not dress in that color at all. And tall? That will help, too. Oh, Adam . . . ."

She squeezed his arm again, and a tremor of warmth rippled through him even as his heart ached. "Thank you so much!"

Violet jumped up from the bench and fluttered to the tack room door. "If you think of anything else or see anything else, or anyone, you'll let me know, won't you? And remember, please don't tell anyone I asked. I'll be able to positively shout about it soon, I'm sure!" Smiling, she twirled around on her delicate heels. "Adam, you are wonderful!"

Her cheeks were as rosy as her lips. The lavender scent wafted about the room and settled into his heart. Adam could no longer look at her; the pain cut too deep within him. He turned away and did not look up until she was gone.

Sighing, Adam set aside the bridle and cleaning cloth. Well, he had kept his promise to her father, that much was certain. His precious honor was intact, and he could be assured the sale of the farm would be completed soon. But he was sure to lose Violet, putting those ideas of blue coats and smiling faces in her head. How could she know that he himself possessed such a coat? that he smiled each time he left a letter for her to find? that the person he'd described was himself?

She would never guess. His description, though specific to him, was vague to her. It had to match at least one of her suitors.

And the letters? With a prize like her in the balance, any man would lie about writing the letters. She would never know who the true author was.

Violet would have her Christmas wedding. Without him.

Adam kicked at a cluster of hay. *Lord, is this what being honorable brings me? Is this where all my hard work leads? I know I am conducting myself as you would want. But what about this pain in my heart? What do I do about it?*

There were many chores that could keep him busy, and he had a myriad of details to take care of regarding the purchase of his farm. But there was only one thing he truly wanted to do.

Adam retreated to the small square room in a corner of the stable building where he slept. Drawing a leather pouch from under his bed, he took out a sheet of paper, a pen, and some ink.

"Dear Love," he wrote, "*I fear that you will never know me, that we will never speak . . .*"

Chapter Four

As Violet left the stables that morning and headed for the orphanage to help sew garments for the children, she was confounded by a feeling that Adam was not telling her all he knew. This disquieted her, for she had always believed she could trust him, as a valued friend, to tell her the whole truth of whatever she asked.

Oh, she still trusted him; Adam's friendship had proven more than completely honorable time and again. But the tinge of sadness in his voice and the way he edged away from her made her wonder.

Why wouldn't Adam tell her more? Why did he seem so reluctant to be near her? And why did her own heart quicken with his every word?

She did not want to wrestle with these questions for long. Time was running out. She decided she would insist that Adam accompany her on a ride the next afternoon. Away from his work and the other stable staff, perhaps he would be more forthcoming.

Her worry somewhat eased, Violet cheerfully worked at the orphanage, visited one of the poor families in a nearby neighborhood, and that night, slept dreamlessly. She woke with even more resolve to find the answers to her questions and, when the afternoon arrived, donned her riding clothes and proceeded resolutely downstairs.

However, on her way out the front door, her mother stopped her. "Have you forgotten, Violet, that you promised to accompany me on a call to the Darvishes? As I told you, Filbert Darvish has recently returned from his travels and has expressed an interest in seeing you. You were very agreeable when I mentioned it, but I see you are not at all ready to make a social call."

"Perhaps another time," Violet replied. "I feel a bit low today."

Mrs. Milton looked at Violet with a very serious expression. "Well, dear, you realize that Mr. Darvish will be calling upon all the suitable young ladies in the area?"

"Yes, Mother."

"I had thought . . . that is, your father and I had hoped that perhaps he might be the one . . ."

Violet stood on tiptoe and pressed her lips to her mother's forehead. Drawing back, she smiled. "I am sure Mr. Darvish is an exemplary young man, Mama. But I know he isn't the one for me."

Mrs. Milton sighed heavily and frowned. "I do not understand how you can be so sure, yet not tell your father and me who you have your heart set on."

"Don't worry, Mother. The Lord has it all worked out for me. Please tell Papa not to fret, either. You will both be so delighted when I tell you . . ." Her voice trailed off as she kept her secret close to her heart.

Mrs. Milton shook her head. "You know we have given you an unusually great amount of freedom because we have always trusted your good sense. But remember, dear, the wedding you are planning is only four weeks away. I know how you young people thrive on romantic notions, but we should like to meet our future son-in-law well before the precious day itself."

Violet smiled in relief. Her mother was a wonderful lady, and Violet loved her with all her heart, but sometimes she could worry more than a whole room full of debutantes just before their presentations. "You shall meet him soon, Mother. You and Papa. And you'll both love him as I do."

"Love him?" exclaimed Mrs. Milton. "Love takes much time to develop between a man and a woman. This must be someone you have known for a very long time."

"Indeed, Mother." Violet thought of all the months of letters, of words of encouragement and praise from her dear love.

Mrs. Milton's eyes brightened and her face relaxed a bit. "Someone whose family is known to us all?"

It could be; it had to be, Violet reasoned. Else how would the letter writer know her so completely, inside and out? "Of that, too, I am more than certain," Violet replied.

"There should be no problem in bringing him round to speak with your father and me, then?"

Violet's heart thudded in her chest. She would like nothing more, but without knowing her dear love's identity herself, she could not promise this to her mother. At least, not just yet. "I should like to, Mother. And I shall as soon as possible."

Violet took a deep breath, and her knees grew weak. *Lord,* she prayed silently, *please let "soon" be today, for I do not think I shall be able to withstand more of this waiting!*

"I am delighted to hear that, dear." Mrs. Milton patted Violet's arm. "Now, I believe you should rest. You do look a bit pale all of a sudden."

Violet remembered her afternoon's mission. "I rather thought I should go for a ride. It is such a lovely day, and the fresh air would do wonders for my complexion."

A faint frown crossed Mrs. Milton's face. "I'm afraid it is late notice to ask one of your friends to accompany you."

"It's quite all right, Mother. Adam can go with me. We've ridden together often, and I'm sure he'd appreciate the distraction."

"I don't know if that's a good idea. Your father—"

"Oh, Mother, you know I'd be perfectly safe with Adam. Why, he's as trustworthy as any of our oldest friends."

Mrs. Milton looked doubtful, but finally gave in. "Yes. Well, I was thinking of the work Adam must complete before Christmas. But I suppose it would not hurt to give him a respite from that." She smiled softly. "Have a good time, dear. But be sure to be home by suppertime."

•　●　•

Hurrying into the warm, low-lit stables, Violet found Adam sitting in his accustomed place in the tack room, the fabric of his blue cotton shirt stretching over his broad shoulders as he bent over a saddle that needed repair.

She stood before him, a little breathless. "Adam, let's go riding."

He nearly dropped the saddle that was draped across his arms. "I b-b-beg your pardon, Miss Violet?"

"It's a glorious day, and Mother said it would be all right if you had a break from your work and we took a nice, long ride."

"Y-your m-m-mother said that?"

Adam ran a hand through his thick dark hair. "Are you sure, Miss Violet?" Adam's burr disappeared for a moment and was replaced by wariness.

"Quite sure, Adam." Violet walked over to him and knelt beside the hay bale he was sitting on. She looked up at him, and her heart seemed to leap to her throat, making her shiver from warmth rather than cold. Violet put her hand to her breast, hoping to calm herself. But when she heard her voice, it sounded more breathless than steady. "She wanted me to pay a call on someone, but I . . . I did not want to waste this lovely day."

A spark leaped to his eyes as he looked upon her. "Wouldn't you rather ride with one of your friends? Perhaps Miss Fern?"

"Fern has a cold, poor thing. And anyway, I thought you and I could . . ." Her voice trailed off as she realized she was feeling very much the same emotion as when she read one of the letters! How unexpected!

"I have much to do here, Miss Violet." Adam edged away from her.

"Do you not wish to go riding?" Disappointment mingled with her excitement.

"It is not that."

"What, then? Do you have another pressing engagement?"

"No."

"The horses are ill?"

"No."

"Are you angry with me?"

Adam's eyes held hers for a long, deep moment. "No."

Violet's heart raced. "Then you have no excuse. Saddle the horses and come riding with me."

Adam's gaze was unwavering. "Is that an order, Miss Violet?"

She blinked in surprise. Never in the course of their friendship had she considered herself one to give orders. But if that would get him to accompany her, so be it.

"Why yes, if you like."

"Very well, then." Adam stood and took a firm hold of the bulky saddle. "Give me but a few moments to prepare the horses and we will be off."

"Thank you, Adam." Violet beamed at him. "And won't you be ever so happy to go out into this glorious day?"

"Indeed I shall, Miss Violet." Adam returned her smile.

Her head and heart felt light. Truly, she did need this time in the fresh air! She'd feared she might be falling ill!

Moments later, Violet's horse, Winsome, and Adam's horse, Lomond, stood ready in the stable courtyard. A groom held Winsome's reins while Adam stood beside Violet to assist her into the saddle. As he gazed upon her with his deep, gray green eyes, she was struck by how tall and handsome he seemed, and the way the cut of his chin gave him an air of nobility.

Her mouth suddenly went dry. It was only Adam, she told herself. But being so close to him was suddenly both exhilarating and frightening.

"Up you go, then, Miss Violet."

With his strong hands circling her waist, Violet felt a fresh jolt of warmth that traveled through her veins and rested in her heart. As Adam lifted her to the saddle and made sure she was settled there, a sense of peace spread through her, too.

How good to have a friend such as Adam, Violet thought. True, she had never had feelings quite like these with any other friend. But with Adam, she knew she had a unique bond.

She watched as he expertly mounted his horse and gathered the reins in his gloved hands. Strong hands. Hands that could calm the most skittish mount or lift the heaviest piece of saddlery.

"Miss Violet, is there something the matter?" Adam's voice broke into her reverie.

"Not at all, Adam. I am quite fine. In fact—" she smiled playfully, patting Winsome's neck—"I believe this will be a wonderful ride. Very wonderful, indeed." She urged her horse forward, trotting briskly out of the protective courtyard and onto one of the paths leading toward a wide, flat meadow.

Adam pushed his hat low over his brow and came up beside her. "The horses will appreciate the exercise, I'm sure. A pleasant jaunt along the paths will do them a world of good. We mustn't go faster than that, of course, Miss Violet. Yesterday's snow has made the ground somewhat slippery in places."

"I will mind the terrain." Violet lifted her chin. "Surely you don't doubt my capabilities as a horsewoman?"

"In truth, Miss Violet, I have never doubted your capabilities in any regard. You are a very accomplished lady, all in all."

Violet cast a sidelong glance at her riding companion. If she didn't know better, she would have thought that Adam's words were plucked directly from one of her recent letters. Time to find out what more he knew of them. "Adam, tell me again of the person who delivered the letter."

"I believe I told you everything I c-c-can, Miss."

"Ah, Adam. I've known you far too long to allow you to behave this way."

"What way, Miss?"

"You are not telling me something. Something about the letters."

Adam frowned.

Violet pressed him. "From your very silence, I see I am correct."

As if laboring under a great burden, Adam turned to her. "As I said, Miss, I've told you all I can." There was pain in his eyes, and something akin to regret. These emotions touched her, nearly bringing her to tears.

Oh, why did he have to be so difficult when she knew she was so close to finding out the identity of her true love?

"My apologies that I cannot tell you more," Adam said. "Rest assured that I only have your best interests at heart."

It was something her parents would say, and it rankled that Adam, her friend, would resort to such words. "Well, then . . ." There was a clear field before her, and she suddenly had the urge to gallop. "Hah!"

Leaning forward, she spurred her horse. Winsome took the bit and changed gaits to a smooth canter and then, just as swiftly, began a gallop. The horse's hooves pounded. Violet's curls dislodged from her cap and streamed into the wind.

Adam called out, "Careful, Miss Violet! Mind the ground!"

But Violet was too intent upon losing some of her ill humor in the exhilaration of a breakneck ride. "Come along, Adam! Don't be so slow!" she cried.

"Miss Violet! You might fall! Your horse could stumble!"

His voice grew louder and Violet knew he had spurred Lomond to follow. The chase was on over the uneven, solid ground that seemed to stretch for miles.

Chapter Five

The wind in Violet's face and the heady feeling of freedom were delicious. Violet's horse seemed to relish the release after being confined to the stables during the recent storm. Winsome arched her neck and flew across the packed, hard earth dusted with new-fallen snow toward a wide pasture.

"Come along, Adam!" Violet cried, forgetting her earlier irritation. An expert rider, Violet gripped the reins with just enough pressure to secure control while allowing Winsome to have her head on the rousing gallop.

As they approached the pasture, a deep pounding reached Violet's ears. Adam was galloping after them, gaining ground on his fleet gelding. Violet's hair was billowing behind her quite freely now, and her heart was lighter than her hold on Winsome's reins. This was just what she needed!

"Ah!" Violet mouthed the wordless sound as if to let escape the pent-up emotions inside her. The crisp air tingled against her teeth and she smiled. "Onward, Winsome!"

Yes, this was just what she needed!

The mare, ever eager to participate in a good race, burst forth with fresh energy. Turning slightly, she homed in on a plain slatted fence that was the only barrier between her, her rider, and another enticing pasture beyond. Violet eyed the fence with an expert eye. It was not too high for them, although she knew the ground beyond could be uneven and unstable after the recent bad weather.

Behind her, Adam was coming up fast. He was as good a rider as she; Violet knew he could take the fence with no trouble. There was still the problem of the landing, but before she could check her mount, she felt Winsome gather her hindquarters for the mighty lunge over the wood slats.

"Miss Milton!" Adam's voice carried a stern warning, but Violet did not even turn her head to heed him. Leaning forward over Winsome's neck, she loosed the reins ever so slightly. "Now, girl!" she yelled, and the mare sailed over the fence neatly, just past a rather rough-looking patch of bramble and slush.

Violet let Winsome find her footing before pulling on the reins. She turned the horse around and saw Adam approaching the jump just as she had, his handsome face set in complete concentration, his hands steady on the reins.

Lomond was a much taller horse than Winsome and so had a longer stride. Adam placed the gelding at exactly the right spot and leaned forward in his saddle, his face clouded momentarily by the horse's streaming dark mane.

Violet stood her mount to one side, several paces from the fence. She watched, fascinated, as Adam and his mount sailed over the fence. It was as if they were suspended in the air. Adam moved as one with his horse as expertly as any of the men in her social circle, even those who rode for show or racing.

She watched in awe as the skillful rider and his mount landed neatly on the other side, light as a feather. As he slowed Lomond, his eyes met hers and he smiled, a free and joyful expression that mirrored her own sudden burst of feeling.

Adam turned his horse to come alongside her, and Violet felt her heart beating in excitement.

"A wonderful day for a ride, isn't it, Miss Violet?" Adam's cheery voice gently interrupted her thoughts. She noticed he did not stutter, and the absence of the impediment made him sound all the more attractive.

Adam did not seem to notice her silent contemplation. He doffed his cap to her, then patted Lomond's neck. "Although I daresay I will never tell your father about how fast you took that fence. One of the stablehands must have put extra oats in old Winsome's grain bucket today." His gaze met hers again, and this time his eyes were twinkling with mischief. "Or did you do that yourself, Miss Violet? Just to have good fun of it?"

Violet lifted her chin and said tartly, "Certainly not. You know yourself that Winsome is not even five years old and is quite capable of matching any horse in Father's stables when it comes to running. Or jumping."

"Indeed?" Lomond began to prance, and Adam held him with a firmer hand. His gray green eyes flashed with a bit of gold as he rose to Violet's good humor. "Well, since my horse just had a bit of a warm-up and since you were so bold as to start the last race unfairly, . . ."

"Unfairly?!" Violet felt her face color in defense of her mount and her enjoyment in the banter. "Why, even if we had started evenly, Winsome would have taken the fence well in advance of Lomond!"

"Really?" Adam swiftly gathered his reins and turned Lomond to face the expansive pasture. "Then, let's have a rematch, shall we?"

He spurred his horse, which needed little prodding to reach a full gallop. It took Violet only a hairsbreadth longer to urge Winsome to follow after them. And the race was on again.

•　●　•

As his horse ate up the ground beneath him, Adam knew in his heart that he didn't care a whit whether he won the race or not. He didn't even know where or how it should end. He only knew that at this time and in this way he could be with Violet and enjoy her company without the prying eyes of her parents or other staff and without fear that he would break the promise he'd made to her father.

How could he, flying along with the wind in his face? There would be no improper moments, no slips of the tongue. Merely good amusement between two . . . friends.

Lomond's ears pricked forward as they approached a gently sloping hill. Behind them, but not very far, Winsome and Violet sped. Adam smiled as he heard Violet let out a cry of exhilaration.

And then he saw the ditch.

Just beyond the crest of the hill was a wide gash in the

earth that had been carved by the late fall rains. The water in it was frozen over, making the surface glisten in the afternoon sun. Its reflection made judging the exact depth and length of the ditch nearly impossible.

They were racing too fast to risk a sudden stop. It would be dangerous to gallop over the obstacle. They must jump.

Adam quickly calculated the distance, then prepared for the take-off. "Heads up, Miss Violet! There's a ditch five yards beyond the hill!"

"What?" Violet's confused voice let him know she hadn't heard. But he trusted her to be more alert as she approached the hill.

Violet was not one of those simpering girls he'd known in Scotland and then in his uncle's church. She was a superb rider and intelligent. He loved that about her, too.

There was no more time for thought or warning as Lomond tensed for the jump ahead. Adam readied himself in the saddle, allowing more rein than usual for the athletic feat his horse was about to perform. Then they were in the air, the deep gash of earth beneath them.

Lomond cleared the jump, but his hindquarters slid on the bank of the ditch. He stumbled, but Adam coaxed him to keep his footing, breathing in relief as the horse settled on all fours on the solid ground. Then he turned around to watch Violet approach the same jump.

Alas, she had not been as ready for the ditch as he had. Her eyes widened in surprise as she took stock of the obstacle. Adam's heart was in his throat as Winsome galloped the last few paces before the take-off point. Violet looked so small and fragile on the horse, and her hands were so slender.

Could she hold her own over such a treacherous jump? He'd never forgive himself if something happened, never be able to laugh, smile, live . . .

How he regretted making the promise to her father now. Violet, his precious Violet, might never know how he loved her!

Violet set herself squarely behind Winsome's arched neck. By the expression on her face, Adam could tell that the jump had come up quickly for her, and that it was more forbidding than she'd expected. But there was no turning back. They were at the point of departure. He said a prayer for her safety as Violet gathered the reins and leaned over her horse's neck.

"Ha!" she cried, giving herself and Winsome an added boost of encouragement. Violet and her horse flew over the ditch and headed for the bank beyond. It seemed to take forever for them to clear the obstacle. Adam prayed again as he saw horse and rider airborne, with nothing grounding them to safety.

Finally, Winsome's legs unfolded toward the slippery ground beyond the ditch. Adam's eyes were fixed upon Violet, sending her all his strength, his courage, and his love.

And they landed firmly, all four of Winsome's hooves connecting squarely with the ground.

Violet patted her horse's neck. "Good girl."

In a flash, Adam raced up beside her. "Miss Violet, if I had known th-th-that gully was there, I would n-n-never . . ."

Violet put her gloved hand on Adam's arm. "It's all right, Adam. Really. There was no harm done. And, as a matter of fact, it was great fun."

With a rush of relief, Adam allowed himself to smile. "Indeed it was, Miss Violet, if I may say so. And never again will I call Winsome 'old.'"

Winsome nickered and shook her head, and Lomond followed suit. Violet laughed, and Adam joined her. Her smile—courageous, impish, and genuinely kind—was all he needed to replace his fear with happiness. For a moment, he forgot about the promise made to her father, forgot about the vast social ditch that separated them. They had sailed over this particular one, after all. And they were none the worse for it.

Adam knew she had not removed her hand from his arm. It warmed him like a welcoming fire, and he did not move away. Her eyes met his, and they seemed to shine with admiration . . . and questions.

Aye, she must have all sorts of questions. Such as what is a fellow like me doing standing here with her like this, allowing her touch upon my arm. If only I could say . . .

"Adam?" Violet's voice trembled slightly. He didn't dare respond, but kept looking into her eyes as if he were speaking eloquently. "We don't have to . . . even though it went well, you won't tell Father about this . . . this jump? He might not . . . I don't want him to worry."

There was much more to her words than fear of letting her father know about the gully jump, Adam was sure of it. And her lips were shaking as she spoke, as if they wanted to say something else but couldn't.

Stunned, he turned his head and forced his eyes upon the path they had just taken. Was she developing feelings for him? Could he dare hope that his affections were returned? Despite his promise to her father, it would be a glorious answer to prayer if it were so. He couldn't ask for more. That is, at least he shouldn't . . .

On impulse, Adam's hand came to rest upon hers and enveloped her slender fingers in a warm grip. "A time such as this would be best enjoyed between the two people who partake of it," he said. It was a sentiment he had expressed in a recent letter, but he didn't think she would recognize it so out of context.

To his amazement, Violet leaned toward him and sighed.

Adam thought his heart would sing and break all at once. There was hope, if Violet felt as he did! For it would mean that the Lord was smiling upon them both, giving them both this marvelous gift of love.

Yes, there was more than hope! And, seeing her respond like this made Adam want to speak his mind, no matter what the consequences. "Miss Violet?"

"Yes, Adam?"

"I should tell you . . . I must tell you . . ."

"Yes?"

"I—"

"Miss Milton!"

Another man's voice called out to them, like an intruder into a most precious moment. The words between them remained unspoken. Adam wheeled around, looking toward the far end of the field.

A tall, broad-shouldered man on a dappled horse was racing toward them. The man's dark blue coattails were flapping behind him like a banner.

Violet watched the man approach. Her full lips parted as if she were greatly surprised. "I believe it's Frederick

Hallsworth, the son of one of Father's business associates. Whatever is he doing here now?"

Frederick reached them in a flurry of coattails and clods of earth kicked up by his horse's hooves. "Miss Milton! Are you all right? I saw you go over that ditch." Frederick pulled up roughly on the reins, causing the horse to lunge back on his hindquarters before settling on all fours.

Violet half smiled. "Mr. Hallsworth, truly I am quite well."

But he seemed not to even notice her. Instead, he whirled upon Adam. "You!" Frederick glared at Adam. "Letting her take that kind of risk. Such total disregard for Miss Milton. Good thing I came along, or who knows what might have happened."

"She's an expert horsewoman," Adam said stoutly. He was used to the harsh behavior of the social elite toward servants, but in this instance he took it more to heart. "More competent than many men. She needs her freedom every now and then, and who can blame her?"

Frederick snorted. "What a thing to say about a lady." He turned to Violet. "If you are too tired to ride back, Miss Milton, I would be honored to lead your horse myself. In fact, I would not be surprised if your horse sustained some injury, from the angle and the depth of the jump it took."

Frederick's eyes rested upon the sight of Violet's hand still enveloped in Adam's. "Miss Violet, I insist that you allow me to escort you back to your home. And you—" he glared at Adam—"should return to the stables posthaste and await the consequences of your actions."

Adam sensed reluctance in Violet's expression as she

removed her hand. On his part, he felt as though all warmth and light had gone with the simple gesture. But he knew his place, knew that he had jeopardized his future plans with his recklessness. He nodded in agreement.

Violet frowned. "Frederick, please don't be alarmed. It was great fun, really. There is no need to burden my parents or yourself with worry. Adam was only doing what I asked of him." Her voice had the very tone of the society in which she moved.

Adam stiffened in his saddle. What had she asked of him? Had she asked him to be in love with her? to write letters revealing his feelings, and to lead her to return his sentiments, even if she did not know the whole truth of it?

Of course she hadn't. But she had asked him to go for a ride, and like the dutiful employee, he had obliged. Perhaps he was mistaken in thinking she returned his feelings. Perhaps she was only being kind, as he knew she was, and nothing more.

Suddenly Adam was relieved that Hallsworth had come by. It meant that he had not broken his promise to Violet's father. And it meant that Violet need not know the double meaning of Adam's friendship with her. As much as he longed to tell her of his love, he knew she moved in such circles as to make the possibility of their union completely implausible.

Yes, she was different from all the other women in higher society. Yes, she had a heart of gold and a soul just as beautiful. But Violet had been born to a world where Adam did not belong. And he did not want to cause her unnecessary grief by trying to draw her out of it.

Adam knew he could never again come as close to revealing the truth as he had just moments before. He must rein in his feelings. And pray that Violet would be none the wiser.

"I have to admit I agree with Master Hallsworth's assessment of the situation, Miss Violet. I should never have suggested you take that jump. And I do believe that Winsome seems to be favoring her left hoof. Perhaps if Master Hallsworth will oblige, he could escort you back home on his mount, and I could take Winsome back to the stables at a more leisurely pace?"

Still frowning, Violet nodded. "Very well, then."

Frederick lumbered off his mount, and Adam watched with inward regret as he saw the lad help Violet down from her mount. To see another man's hands circle her waist and hold her light frame, even for a moment, was beyond painful. But he could do nothing else. After dismounting from Lomond's back, Adam wordlessly removed Winsome's saddle and started to undo his mount's as well.

"Ho, there, MacGreggor," Frederick intervened. "I don't think that horse of yours can be trusted with a lady such as Miss Violet. Put her saddle on my mount. Patsy's a much more docile horse, much more suited to the lady."

Adam glanced sideways and saw Violet suppress a smile. That silent communication made him a bit less saddened, and he complied with Frederick's request with all due haste.

Soon, Violet was sitting atop Patsy, and Frederick was struggling to control Lomond. "Are you sure that you are satisfied with Lomond?" Violet asked Frederick as his horse pranced sideways.

"Quite sure, Miss Violet." Frederick tapped his heels against the horse's side, and Lomond was off like a shot.

Violet looked over at Adam and smiled broadly. Her eyes had recovered their shine, and her face was rosy and cheerful. "I'll see to it that he does no harm," she said. Then more softly, "I am certain he meant nothing by what he said. He was only concerned for me. Please don't take offense, Adam." She sighed. "I do so wish we could continue as we were, but, well, perhaps some other time? We still have something to discuss."

Adam gazed at her, still not daring to speak.

As if disappointed by his silence, the smile faded from Violet's face. "Do take care to get back before night falls. It will be cold this evening," she said. "And my thanks, Adam, for a wonderful ride."

Violet gathered Patsy's reins and cantered off. Adam doffed his cap as they rode away, then clucked to Winsome to follow him home.

Chapter Six

The moment she set foot on the path between the stables and the main house, Violet's father appeared, his face a study in thunder. "Whatever were you doing, riding away with MacGreggor?"

Then Milton saw Frederick ambling up behind Violet, and his face broke into a bright grin. "Hallsworth!" He looked from Frederick to Violet and back to Frederick. Then Milton winked at Violet's mother, who also appeared on the path. "I believe I understand now. Mrs. Milton mentioned Violet said we might soon have a visitor. I am delighted that she should have found such a suitable escort."

Milton extended his hand and Frederick grasped it.

"Thank you, sir. And might I say that I, too, was quite relieved to come along just as I did. Why, if I hadn't, there's no telling what MacGreggor would have allowed . . ."

"It wasn't like that at all," Violet protested. She looked from her father to her mother, searching for their approval, as they all walked toward the main house. "I was so intent upon riding in the fresh air that I took a very fast course along the lower pasture and then into the upper one. In truth, Adam urged me to slow down, but Winsome was in fine form."

"Please, Miss Violet, I am sorry to interrupt your tale, but I must say that your horse looked quite the worse for wear after taking the ditch," Frederick said.

"A ditch!" Milton's face clouded. Just then, Adam arrived on Winsome. Violet couldn't make out the expression on his face, but her heart went out to him as she considered her father's mounting anger toward him.

Milton whirled on Adam, who had dismounted and was leading Winsome their way. "Have you lost your mind completely? What did you mean, allowing Violet to jump over a ditch?"

Adam glanced at Violet, and it was then she saw a flash of pain in his eyes, as though her father's anger had cut him deeply. Violet felt her face flush. "It wasn't Adam who suggested . . . oh, I began the racing in the first place."

"Racing!" Now Violet's father was a study in purple rage. "You had no business being allowed to race! Mac-Greggor—"

"There was never a question of being allowed, Father. It was I who initiated it."

"Now, Violet," Mrs. Milton said, taking Violet's arm. "Your father and I understand that there was a good reason for your wanting to ride so quickly, don't we, dear?" Mrs. Milton smiled at her husband.

Mr. Milton looked at Frederick again. "I suppose so. Ah, you young people . . ."

Mrs. Milton spoke to Frederick, "You are welcome to stay for supper, Mr. Hallsworth. In fact, we insist."

"Thank you, Mrs. Milton. I would be honored."

"Of course you would be." Mr. Milton clapped Frederick on the back. He turned to Adam. "As for you, MacGreggor, I will see you in my study as soon as we have finished supper."

"Yes, sir, Mr. Milton."

As he turned away, Adam shot a glance at Violet that contained something she recognized as disappointment, even sorrow. Her heart leaped within her. She longed to reach out to him, to assure him that she would make the situation right for him, but her mother steered her toward the house. As they walked, she heard her father engage Frederick in conversation.

"Now, my boy, tell me how you are doing. I believe you have completed your studies and are about to join your father's business . . . ."

Violet tugged on her mother's arm. "Mother, I do hope Father isn't too harsh with Adam. He didn't do anything wrong on the ride. Really. I insisted on jumping the ditch, and in racing across the pastures, and—"

Violet's mother held up her hand. "Take this advice, Violet dear. Say nothing further about your ride with Adam, especially not to your father. For Adam's sake, if nothing else."

"Whatever do you mean by that, Mother? Adam is a valued friend, as you well know. Frederick just doesn't understand."

"Perhaps not," Mrs. Milton answered, her hands upon Violet's shoulders. "But we must be careful when speaking of Adam with your father."

Puzzled, Violet was about to ask her mother what she meant, but just then they reached the house.

"Now run along upstairs," Mrs. Milton said, "and get ready for supper. Your father will entertain your guest." Violet's mother shooed her upstairs with talk of dinner dresses and hair arrangements.

• • •

In the short time between when Violet returned from her ride and the hour supper began, the servants outdid themselves to put out the finest place settings and the most succulent of food, not to mention lend a hand with Violet's toilette.

In fact, Violet did not think her maid, Bridget, had ever giggled so much or fussed so over a simple dinner gown as she did this evening. Finally, after Bridget tried without success for the third time to tie the slender velvet ribbons that fell from the shoulders of the blue silk gown, Violet had to ask. "Bridget, please be still for one second while I ask why you and the rest of the household are in such a fine mood this evening?"

"Why, because we all know, Miss Violet."

"Know what?"

"Know who it is you're going to marry, if you don't mind my saying so."

"I do mind, because I don't know myself," Violet replied. Thoughts of Adam's handsome face swirled in her head along with passages from her letters. Did she imagine it, or had he quoted from one of the lines just before Frederick had interrupted them? It seemed impossible, because Adam was a stable manager, not a learned gentleman, and the letters were clearly written by someone who read poetry and knew literature and could pen a very elegant phrase. Still, Adam's speech was better than any of the other servants' . . .

If only she had enough time and privacy before dinner to take the letters from their hiding place and reread them, just to be sure! But as it was, she barely had enough time to repair the damage to her hair caused by the wild afternoon ride.

"I'm sorry, Miss."

Bridget's apology brought Violet back to the moment. "So, who is it you all think I'll be marrying?" she asked.

"Well, Miss, I don't know if I'm right to be saying." Bridget finally succeeded in tying one ribbon and started on another.

Violet smiled. "I didn't mean to be short with you before. Please, tell me what everyone's saying."

"Ever since you returned from your ride, there's been talk," Bridget said.

Once again, an image of Adam looking at her so warmly, speaking so eloquently, broke into Violet's thoughts. Again, she doubted he could be the writer of the letters. But clearly she had strong feelings for him, and she was beginning to wonder if they were only connected with friendship alone.

"Has there?"

"Master Hallsworth is a fine young gentleman," Bridget said, stepping back to survey her work. "And when he sees you all lovely like you are, he'll be foolish not to make his intentions known throughout the whole city."

Stunned, Violet stared at Bridget as though she were bereft of any intelligible thought. Frederick? Her husband?

True, he was well learned, well traveled, and a favorite of her parents. He came from a very respected family; his father was very involved in some business dealings with her father. Certainly Frederick had the manners and bearing that befitted a man of his standing. And he was wearing a blue coat, too, just like the man Adam described delivering her letter the other night. But could Frederick have possibly written that letter and all the others? Was he the one she was to marry?

Thinking back to Frederick's appearance in the pasture, Violet remembered how she had intended to ask Adam more about the letters and who had delivered them. She had been thrown off by his seeming to quote from one of them, and then Frederick had appeared.

Thinking of the conversation she'd had with her mother just before her ride and of the prayer she had uttered, Violet wondered even more. She had prayed that the Lord would bring the man of her dreams to her that day.

Was Frederick's appearance God's way of showing her, again by way of a sign, that she should cast her attention from Adam to Frederick? "Miss, if there's nothing else?" Bridget waited by the door.

"Thank you, Bridget. Please tell Mother I'll be down shortly."

"Very well, Miss. And might I say, congratulations?"

Bridget left, and Violet sank onto the soft armchair in a dimly lit corner of her room. Frederick was certainly acceptable, she thought. Her father all but called him "son," and her mother smiled upon him like a prize. And, too, everyone else in the household seemed to like Frederick.

Everyone except Adam.

Violet knew the moment he saw Frederick that Adam

did not approve of him. But if everyone else approved, could this be another way that the Lord was steering her toward Frederick?

Oh, instead of getting easier as her wedding day approached, things were becoming more and more unclear!

Gathering her skirts, Violet left her room and began the descent toward the lower level of the house. Frederick met her at the foot of the stairs and offered her his arm. She noticed that he had tidied his appearance and that his freshly washed face was pleasantly round and open, if not as strongly handsome as Adam's.

"May I have the pleasure of escorting you in to supper, Miss Milton?"

"Yes, Mr. Hallsworth." Violet rested her hand upon his proffered arm, and they walked slowly toward the dining room.

There was none of the warmth or energy from her contact with him that she'd felt with Adam. Still, Violet again noted how courteous Frederick was and how perfectly he went through the rituals of leading her to her place at the table, then seating her, settling her in her chair, and then sitting across from her.

Dinner, too, was a very polite, quiet event. With her father and mother presiding over an abundant repast, Frederick regaled them with tales of his travels the previous year, of the completion of his studies, and of his plans for going into business with his father.

Violet laughed quietly at one or two of his humorous, tasteful stories of faux pas committed in foreign lands. But she couldn't quite pair him with the man who wrote her lavish letters with such great emotion.

Rather, Frederick seemed to her to be a steady, well-meaning person. True, he had spoken gruffly to Adam. But it could be that he had only been worried for her safety. As Violet spent more time with him, she noted that Frederick seemed for all the world to be a very well-groomed, well-brought-up man. Not qualities to dismiss, Violet reasoned. But still, she could not imagine—

"Yes, the world is full of treasures, but the best are closest to home," Frederick said, smiling at Violet.

Violet began to cough so that she nearly choked on her cream of mushroom soup.

"Dear, are you all right?" Violet's mother half rose from her seat.

"Miss Milton, I trust I have not offended, or have spoken too personally?" Frederick looked concerned.

Violet dabbed her mouth lightly. The words he spoke sounded very like ones from a letter she'd received. Not exactly, to be sure. But close enough to make her wonder.

She decided to be bolder in her assessment of him. "That sounds very poetic. Are you a writer, Mr. Hallsworth?"

Frederick nodded. "I confess that that is a rather cherished pastime of mine, Miss Milton. Although I do not aspire to making it a professional pursuit, it is certainly useful for certain communications." He smiled again, and Violet looked deeply into his eyes to see if she could discern some other clue as to the true import of his words. But all she saw were his pleasant nature, his polite manner, and nothing more.

She tried to take another spoonful of soup, but it, too, lodged in her throat. She lifted her napkin to her lips and tried to control her reaction.

It was all such a puzzle!

"Perhaps we should change the subject," Frederick said, clearly concerned about Violet's cough.

Violet did not protest as the soup was cleared away and another course began. She weighed the possibility that Frederick was her secret admirer and tried to pay closer attention to his conversation. She even tried to picture herself sitting across the table from him every meal.

But all she could think of was Adam.

While they were inside enjoying a feast, he must be finishing his work with the horses for the night. Eating a simple dinner provided by the main house kitchens. Waiting for the meeting with her father.

But she should not even think such things if Frederick was the one for her!

"Don't you think, Miss Milton?"

Violet looked up from her roasted quail. She hadn't heard the question Frederick had posed. And now everyone at the table was waiting for her response.

"I'm sorry, Mr. Hallsworth," she said finally, "I was so intent upon the conversation I failed to fully contemplate your question."

Violet's parents exchanged glances and Frederick smiled at her. But his expression had not nearly the effect of Adam's smile upon her.

"That is quite all right, Miss Milton. I am flattered that you should be listening so closely. I was merely asking whether you might not wish to keep Patsy for a while, considering how ill suited your present mount is to you, as well as her current unsound condition?"

"I'm sure that Winsome is in fine form," Violet said. She wanted to continue, but saw her mother send her a warning look. Remembering her mother's admonition not to bring up the ride or especially Adam, Violet forced herself to back down. The last thing she wanted was to cause more trouble for Adam.

"But if you think that I could benefit from Patsy, well, Mr. Hallsworth, I would be very appreciative. She is a . . . a kindly horse."

"Excellent!" Frederick's smile widened. "And perhaps you would honor me with a ride tomorrow, Miss Violet? That is, if I have your parents' permission to accompany you?"

"Of course you have our permission!" Mr. Milton looked so happy he was almost leaping out of his seat. "Violet, what do you say?"

Violet felt her parents' eyes upon her. They seemed to be expecting something from her, some declaration of sorts. With their approval and the other signs she had received, it would be so easy to accept Frederick's attentions!

But was this God's plan?

She supposed she should act to find out.

"Thank you, Mr. Hallsworth. That would be lovely."

Violet tried to keep her thoughts firmly on the rest of the meal, if only to prevent herself from making any more faux pas or unintentional promises. But still her heart and mind wandered elsewhere, far away. In the pastures and riding beside a certain stable manager, perhaps, but not at this sparkling, rich table.

When dinner was over, Milton offered Frederick a fine cigar and the two retired to the library. Relieved that the evening was almost over, Violet started to go upstairs when her mother stopped her.

"Dear, I cannot tell you how happy I am for you."

"What do you mean, Mother?"

Mrs. Milton kissed Violet's forehead. "I understand, dear. You are waiting until tomorrow, when you can confirm the conversation Frederick is having with your father."

Violet gave her mother a quizzical look.

Mrs. Milton smiled. "Ah, don't fret, Violet. Your father is very exacting of those who have expressed interest in you, that is true. And he will be very demanding of any young man you might introduce as your intended. But Frederick Hallsworth is a very remarkable young man. I am sure he will get along famously with your father, and I'm sure your father will approve, just as I do."

"I don't know . . ." Violet's voice trailed off.

"Don't worry, dear," Mrs. Milton said. "You have made an excellent choice. Go upstairs now. And pleasant dreams. Your father will want to speak with you as soon as you are up, and then all will be wonderful."

Violet went upstairs to her room, wondering about her mother's words. The day had passed in such a blur. But at the end of it, had she made a choice? A choice about her dear love? Was all that had happened part of God's plan?

She couldn't tell. All she felt was confusion about Frederick. And as for Adam . . . Violet remembered that her father was to speak with Adam that evening.

She knew she would not be able to sleep without knowing the outcome of their meeting.

When she was sure Frederick was gone, she stole downstairs. A raised voice came from the library. She tiptoed toward the door and found it to be open a slit. She pressed her ear to the door.

"I warned you, MacGreggor, and you gave me your word. I should dismiss you on the spot. However, given the extra work that will come with this wedding, you are to stay. But not a moment beyond the wedding day. Then you are to leave. And I never want to hear from you again."

Violet was horrified. What did her father mean when he said he'd warned Adam before? And how could he dismiss him over such a silly thing as an afternoon ride? As much as she knew Adam respected her father, surely he would try to speak reason?

"Mr. Milton, I am grievously sorry at the trouble I have caused you. I will abide by your orders, sir. And in the meanwhile, I will do my best to prevent contact between myself and Miss Violet."

"See that you do," Milton said. "Now go. You can let yourself out."

Violet was so astonished that she couldn't move from the door fast enough. Adam hurried through, and the force of the door opening and closing knocked her off balance, sending her tumbling to the floor.

"Oh!"

Instinctively, she put a hand over her mouth. It would not do for her father to find her out in the hallway, especially not with Adam.

"Miss Violet, are you all right?"

Adam's voice was low, but his concern for her was obvious. He reached out and with his strong arms scooped her up and set her on her feet. For a moment, he held her there, inches from his face. Violet caught her breath. The surprise in his dark eyes became joy, and suddenly she felt happiness, too. Happiness and comfort, as though being in Adam's arms was the most natural thing in all the world.

But then Adam's expression closed against her. Gently but firmly, he set her from him. "Forgive me, Miss Violet. I didn't realize you were there."

"No matter, Adam. I . . . I heard what my father said, and I am so sorry for what just occurred." Holding one hand over her heart for fear it would jump out of her very body, she said, "I will speak with Father this very moment—"

Adam took a step near her. For a second, Violet thought he would sweep her into his arms again. But then he stopped and fixed his arms firmly by his sides.

"Miss Violet, I ask you with all the r-r-respect that is within me, please say nothing to your f-father. It is best for all c-c-concerned."

A stab of disappointment shot through her. Violet felt tears spring to her eyes. "But you don't want to leave, do you?"

Adam sighed. In an almost whisper, he replied, "You need to think of your wedding, Miss Violet. That's what you should be thinking of."

He turned from her and opened the front door. Cold air swept into the house as he stood for a second, looking back at her. Then he was gone.

Upstairs, Violet read her Bible and said her evening prayers. But it was hard to concentrate on the lesson before her as the events of the day swirled in her mind. Her father had sounded so angry during his conversation with Adam that Violet doubted his meeting with Frederick could have gone well, or else he would have been in a better mood. This could complicate her thoughts that Frederick was the man the Lord intended for her to marry; Violet could not see herself wed to anyone who did not meet with her father's approval.

And then there were her novel, jumbled feelings for Adam.

Until now, she had considered him a friend, someone she could trust and rely upon, someone whose company she enjoyed. But after this afternoon's ride, more feelings, deeper and warmer, seemed to have blossomed in her heart.

Frederick had the education, the demeanor to be the author of the letters. Adam, with his lack of education, could not be.

But Violet's feelings did not seem to concur with the facts before her.

"Oh, Lord, please make me see your will for me," she prayed. "For that is what I most want to do. Only your will."

Finally, after tossing and turning for hours, Violet fell asleep, wondering if things would be clearer when she spoke with her father in the morning.

Chapter Seven

Violet stood waiting for her father to fill his pipe, light it, and send the first fragrant curls wafting to the ceiling of his office. The anger she had heard from him the night before seemed to have faded and, despite his formal manner, he sounded quite cheerful.

"Did you enjoy yourself yesterday, child?"

Milton's first question caught her off guard. Did he mean to ask her about her ride? About Adam's part in it? Or did he mean Frederick's presence at dinner?

"It was a lovely day, Father," Violet answered, remembering the crisp weather, the exhilarating ride, and Adam's wide smile.

"Indeed." Milton regarded her kindly, then sent another plume of smoke upward. "Hallsworth thinks a great deal of you."

Thoughts of Frederick's concern for her flashed in her mind. His words at supper, too, resonated there. He did sound poetic.

"I am . . . pleased to hear that."

"More than that, in fact, as you must know." Milton swung around from behind the desk and came to stand beside his daughter. He helped her sit in an armchair, then took his place in another chair across from her and held both her hands in his.

"Violet, I have been puzzling over your conduct these past months. You planned to be married at Christmastime, but you waited so very long to tell your mother and me the identity of the man whom you will wed."

Violet set her back firmly against the chair. She prayed that somehow her father's words would lead her to where God wanted her to go.

"I wanted to press the issue and choose someone suitable myself, if you had not already done so. However, your mother assured me that you have certain romantic notions, and we should not interfere with those." He smiled. "I am very pleased I listened to your mother. When you appeared yesterday with Hallsworth, I was delighted. I couldn't have thought of a better match."

"You couldn't?" Violet blinked in surprise. He was usually so demanding of anyone who expressed interest in her. But now his words confirmed what she had surmised the night before: Frederick met with her father's approval!

Could it be another of God's signs? If her mother and father approved of Frederick, could she continue to have her doubts?

"My dear daughter, as you know, Hallsworth's father and I have extensive business interests together. It seems a natural progression of our association that our two children should unite in marriage, thus making ever stronger our relationship." Mr. Milton winked at her. "And I don't have to tell you that Hallsworth is a handsome young man, with more good qualities than I could hope to have in a son-in-law."

Violet let her father's words sink in. She had no idea of the extent of her father's business dealings; he very seldom shared any information about his professional work with her. But it made sense that he would smile upon Frederick, now that he had explained more fully the reason for his approval.

Was this the final sign that she should marry Frederick Hallsworth?

Her father continued, "Now Hallsworth was a bit flustered when I spoke with him last evening, but that is only natural. I told him not to worry, of course, and that I could not have thought of a better choice for my daughter. Then I gave him permission to engage in an abbreviated courtship, followed up with a quickly assembled engagement party so that we can abide by your desire to wed at Christmastime."

Her father was smiling in a way she hadn't seen for years. Violet already knew her mother would be overjoyed, too, at such a good match.

Violet was still unsure, but she felt herself bending to the outpouring of her parents' encouragement. "Father, I must say that this is . . . overwhelming."

"Well, of course it is. I imagine all young women of delicate constitutions feel just the same way when faced with a life-changing occasion such as their wedding. But with a man such as Hallsworth to be your husband, Violet, you really have nothing to fear."

That much she knew. Violet was certain that Frederick would be an exemplary husband and father.

She could not say she loved him yet, but she did love whoever wrote her the letters. And if she was discerning her situation clearly, she should come to the conclusion that Frederick was the author of them. If he was being led by the Lord as she was, then the only thing for her to do was agree to the courtship. She trusted God's hand in this, as in all things, and was sure he would bring the right sentiments to her heart. The love she wanted to feel would, Violet believed, come with time and proximity.

"I suppose then, Father, that I agree with what you have just proposed."

"Excellent! That is just the thing I was hoping to hear!" Milton jumped up from his chair. "Mrs. Milton!" he cried. "Mrs. Milton! Come here!"

Violet's mother came running in from the arboretum, where she kept a veritable jungle of tropical plants. Her arms were full of white winter lilies as she bustled in.

"What is it? What's wrong?"

"Violet's agreed! We're going to have a son-in-law. Frederick Hallsworth."

Mrs. Milton dropped the flowers and lifted her daughter from her chair in a fervent embrace.

"My little girl! Oh, dear, you are going to be so happy."

As her mother wiped tears from her cheeks, Violet had the feeling that she was watching her parents as if from a distance. None of this seemed real, nor did it fit with what she had imagined such a moment would be.

"Have you nothing else to say, girl?" Milton said, puffing out his chest with pride.

"Oh, she's just being shy, as all brides are." Mrs. Milton continued to cry and dab her cheeks. "Now, come along. We have plans to make for your engagement party next week."

"Engagement party next week?"

Milton laughed. "Well, we can't very well have one after the wedding, can we? It'll have to be no later than next Tuesday. We have to keep some semblance of propriety, as fast as you young people want to do things. Now you two ladies make all the plans you want. I'm going to pay a call on Hallsworth Sr. and tell him the good news." Milton hurried into the hall. "Someone tell Adam I need the carriage! Be quick about it!"

•   •   •

Adam could tell by the spring in Milton's step that Violet had agreed to marry Hallsworth. And as much as it tore at his heart and soul, he had to admit it was a good match. The two families were well known in business circles, and this union would no doubt bring them even more fortune. Violet would be cared for in luxury all her days, and her children would inherit tremendous estates.

It was more than Adam ever could have hoped to promise her, with his humble plans of a horse farm and orphan refuge.

Still, all the rationalizing in the world did nothing to assuage the pain that burned within him. Violet, his Violet,

DEAR LOVE

would be another man's wife. The thought lodged in his heart, causing a pain he knew would linger for years to come. He tried to soften it by looking over some of the paperwork the bankers had given him in anticipation of his acquiring the farm he'd dreamed of. But it was a hollow victory when he thought of the years ahead without the woman of his heart beside him.

Shortly after Milton left, Frederick arrived. He ordered Adam to saddle Patsy and went to the main house to collect his betrothed.

Silently, Adam prepared the mount, and silently he watched as Frederick helped Violet onto the horse.

Adam thought she appeared a bit unsure as Frederick adjusted Patsy's bridle and bit to his approval. And when she turned to follow Frederick, he thought she gave him a forlorn smile, not at all like a happy bride-to-be.

But it must all be his imagination, he decided. For Violet was making a good match, and that was what every young woman of her circle wanted to do, wasn't it? And as for happiness, he should be happy for her and for himself that both their futures were so secure. Shouldn't he?

He watched them ride off and knew all the rationalizing in the world would not turn him from what he knew was the truth: Adam would go through the rest of his days keeping Violet in his heart without ever being honored with her by his side.

•　●　•

"Now, Fern, we've gone over this a thousand times." Violet's patience was wearing thin. It was the day before her engagement party and there was still much to be decided. "I insist that you, as my dearest friend and maid of honor, sit to Frederick's left at the engagement party."

Violet shivered. They were sitting in the parlor, and a bright fire was blazing in the hearth, but to her it felt as though a wave of cold air was perpetually surrounding her. How different she felt now that her betrothal was going to be announced. How different from the day when she confided in Fern about the letters.

"I don't know if that is quite correct," Fern said. She looked long into her friend's eyes. "But if that is what you want, then so be it."

"Thank you," Violet said, making a note on her list. She put down her pen and massaged the back of her neck.

Fern set down her embroidery. "Do you mind if I ask a question, Violet?"

"Of course not."

"Please know that I am asking you because I love you and care for your happiness and future."

"What is it, Fern?" Violet asked more warily.

"Are you completely sure Frederick is the man you are to marry?"

Violet stared into the fire. She wished she could warm up, but even more she wished she knew the answer to Fern's question.

In the days following her conversation with her father, Violet had ridden with Frederick, had gone into the city with him, had spent time with his family. But she had detected none of the eloquence, none of the emotion from the letters, those precious letters that had won her heart.

Oh, Frederick was still polite, still concerned for her welfare. And at times, he quoted this or that piece of literature. But she couldn't help but feel as though he was acting more out of societal duty than head-over-heels love. He spoke of nothing more personal than what an honor she was to his family, and how their fathers approved of the marriage.

Violet turned back to her best friend and sighed. "Oh, Fern, I am not so sure. It is a good match, and one that seems to bring such happiness to both our families, indeed to everyone. But I do not feel the joy of spirit that I expected. And I fear Frederick does not, either."

Fern listened, a serious expression on her heart-shaped face. "Could it be that you are both becoming nervous as the wedding day approaches? I have heard that happens in some cases."

"It is possible." Violet nodded. "I know I am praying more often for calm and peace than for anything else."

"Well, that tells the story then," Fern said, picking up her embroidery again. "You and Frederick are simply edgy. You'll calm down, by and by."

"There is one other thing," Violet said.

A log sizzled and fell farther into the fire. Violet watched the sparks flit up the chimney. "It is this: I cannot be certain that Frederick is the one who wrote me the letters."

Pausing in midstitch, Fern eyed Violet with surprise. "I thought you said he quoted from them at supper."

"He quoted something like them. And at the time, I was led to believe he had written them. But now . . . now I doubt that."

"Why?"

"Because he does not mention any of the contents. Not

one line, not one word. And his regular speech is not as, well, as fluid as that in the letters."

"People often speak differently from the way they write."

"True. But I fear there is another reason here. I fear that Frederick never wrote me the letters that have won my heart. I fear that my heart belongs to another."

Seized by her emotions, Violet rose from her chair and knelt by Fern's side. "Oh, Fern, if I am wrong to marry Frederick, it is a graver offense than if I squandered my parents' money in planning an imagined wedding. Will you help me now, as you always have, dear friend?"

"Of course." Fern smoothed Violet's hair. "What can I do?"

"It is the reason why I want you to sit beside Frederick, why I want you to spend much time with him tomorrow evening."

Violet took a deep breath.

"You have read the letters. You know how they sound. Talk with Frederick. Try to discern whether he could have written them. If you like, hint at some of the passages, too. He won't think anything untoward of you. He will only think you are being a romantically minded friend of mine."

"I like the idea," Fern said, a bright twinkle in her eyes. "It reminds me of one of those mystery stories people speak of. But won't he consider it forward of me to pry?"

"Frederick is a very sociable person," Violet assured her. "There should be no harm in engaging him in conversation."

Fern smiled. "Very well, Violet. Tomorrow I shall test your gentleman and see if he is worthy of you."

Violet blushed. "Oh, not quite like that. Only see if he is my love. For it is he, my dear love, who is the only one I wish to marry."

Chapter Eight

The balmy weather of the week before had turned to cold by the time the hour of the party arrived. As the partygoers began to arrive in their elaborate carriages, Violet and Fern watched from the parlor window.

Adam directed the other staff in the chill and managed to keep all but himself out of the inclement weather. Violet longed to take an extra scarf to him, or perhaps a mug of Cook's hot apple cider. But she knew her place had to be inside.

"My, but I never realized how handsome your stable manager is," Fern exclaimed.

Violet felt her face flush. "Oh?" she asked, although she had been thinking exactly the same thing.

"Yes," Fern said, enthusiastically. "Now, he's the sort I would imagine writing secret love letters. He has that dark, mysterious air about him. And strength. See how he keeps Mrs. Tippleton from falling over her ostrich feathers!"

Violet chuckled along with her friend as they watched the portly lady simper at Adam, who helped her firmly onto the sheltered front porch. But in her heart, Violet felt not joy but fear.

"Well, Fern, he is a stable manager and not a professor of letters," Violet said. "I doubt very much that he would put pen to paper to woo any lady."

Fern looked at Violet closely, until Violet's flush felt positively hot. "I see. Well. If you say so . . ." Her words trailed off and left a myriad of unanswered questions between them.

But there was no time to address those questions. Soon Mrs. Tippleton and her niece arrived, and Frederick's carriage pulled into the drive.

"He's here!" Violet said, pulling Fern toward the door. "Remember what you said you would do, Fern."

"How could I forget?" Fern giggled. "Only I wish I had one of those peculiar hats and long pipes to complete my ensemble."

The door opened and Frederick came in. He handed his tall hat and cloak to one of the servants, then came immediately over to Violet and Fern. "Ah, Miss Milton, you are looking lovely this evening."

"Thank you, Mr. Hallsworth." She edged Fern forward. "And may I introduce you to my dearest, oldest friend, Miss Fern Lafferty?"

"Not so old, I see," Frederick smiled and bent over Fern's hand, grazing it with a kiss. "Delighted to meet you, Miss Lafferty. I've heard much about you."

"Oh, dear. As bad as that?"

"Not to worry, Miss Lafferty. To the contrary."

"Oh, that reminds me," Violet said suddenly. "I promised Mother that I would see to the final preparations for the cake. Fern, would you please be a dear and help Mr. Hallsworth get settled? One of us, at least, should be present to greet the other guests."

"I would be honored, Miss Lafferty."

"Very well, Mr. Hallsworth. This way."

Violet watched her friend and her fiancé walk away, then bustled away to the dining room, where the servants were fussing over the proper folding of napkins. As she surveyed the dinner table, Violet heard a fierce noise and realized the wind had begun with a vengeance. Her thoughts went to Adam immediately. No doubt he would send all his staff to shelter while he stayed outside to take care of the remaining latecomers.

Violet glanced at the gilt clock on the mantel. If she hurried, she could take him some of Cook's hot apple cider before she was expected in the parlor.

In the kitchen, Violet tucked a warm cloth around a piping mug and wrapped herself in a cloak that hung on a peg by the side door. Ignoring Cook's remonstrations, she stepped out into the cold. The wind blew back the hood of the cloak and stung her face. Violet knew her cheeks would be beyond rosy by the time she returned to her guests, but she was intent upon her errand.

True to what she'd thought, Adam was by himself in the curved drive. One carriage had just come, and another had just passed through the gate far down the path. As her slippers crunched on the gravel, he turned.

There was that same look of surprise and joy she remembered from the night outside her father's office.

Heartened, Violet approached him. "It is far too chilly for you to be outside in this weather, Adam."

"I was going to say the same of you, Miss Violet," he replied. "Shouldn't you be inside with your—your g-g-guests? What brings you out here?"

Violet noticed he did not say "with your betrothed." She felt herself warm, despite the chill wind. "I've brought you some of Cook's cider," she said, offering him her bundle.

Adam seemed even more surprised than when he first saw her. "You came out here to bring me cider?"

Violet nodded. "I couldn't bear thinking of . . . of anyone out on a night like this."

"Truly, you are too kind, Miss Violet," Adam said. His hands grazed hers as he reached for the cider. "A rare jewel."

The wind seemed to catch his last words, but Violet thought she heard them plainly. They sounded familiar. As if, again, they came from one of the letters.

She was about to ask him about it when her mother called from the front door. "Violet! There you are! Come inside this instant!"

"I had better go," Violet said reluctantly.

"Yes, Miss." Adam's eyes lingered upon her. "And thank you again."

"Keep well, Adam."

Her feet felt heavy as she tripped up the stairs and entered the warm house. And her thoughts lingered on Adam, working outside on this blustery night.

• • •

It was a long while before the dinner was eaten and the guests were sent home in their carriages. True to her promise, Fern had engaged Frederick in the most lively of conversation before, during, and after dinner. Violet was certainly relieved that she did not have to worry about entertaining her betrothed, on top of all the well-meaning friends and family in attendance.

But she was beside herself with wondering what Fern's estimation of Frederick would be. Finally, the two friends managed to meet in the arboretum, where, amid the plant fronds and flowers, they whispered about the evening.

"It was a great success, Violet," Fern said, pressing her friend's hand warmly. "Now the wedding should be no worry at all for you, for you have proven yourself in planning this soiree."

"Thank you, Fern," Violet replied. "But you know I am not as anxious about the plans themselves as I am about the person with whom I am celebrating the occasion. I noticed that you were able to converse with Frederick quite a lot. Did you discern anything?"

Fern looked at some camellias blooming nearby. "Yes, Violet. Quite a lot, in fact." She turned and smiled, and Violet noted there was a fresh brightness to her eyes. "He is a marvel in every respect. He is courteous, intelligent, very compassionate, and even good-humored. I could easily imagine him penning letters—no, volumes—to the lady of his heart."

Somehow, this was not what Violet expected to hear. "Truly?"

"Truly."

"We are speaking of Frederick Hallsworth, are we not?"

"The one and same," Fern replied. "And you, my friend, are not to worry that he is less than what you have imagined your true love to be. He is all of that, and more."

"Hmm . . ." Violet twirled a curl of her hair. "Did he speak of writing me letters?"

"He did not have to. He spoke of finding you that day in the pasture and of his father's joy at the news of your marriage. But, more than that, he spoke of his travels and work and life and, oh, Violet, you are indeed a blessed bride! I only pray that I may one day be as fortunate."

Fern embraced Violet with a fierceness that seemed a bit overmuch, even for the occasion. For the second time that night, she wondered at the suitability of Fern for Frederick, rather than herself.

But all the signs had pointed to Violet's becoming Frederick's wife. And now that Fern had given her assessment of him, Violet could really not do anything but continue on her path to marriage with him.

Frederick Hallsworth.

Violet wriggled out of her friend's embrace and stood.

In less than two weeks, she would become Mrs. Frederick Hallsworth. Well, there was much to be done between now and then, not the least of which would be to recognize in him what Fern saw so plainly—to find in him the man of her letters and her dreams.

"Thank you, Fern, for your help. And now it's time to retire. For I fear there is much still to be done before my wedding day dawns!"

Chapter Nine

The whirlwind of final wedding preparations left Violet little time to ponder anything deeply. Moreover, because of the social obligations pertinent to a wedding of such stature in the community, Violet had no opportunity to be alone with Frederick to set her heart at ease about the matter of the letters and his love for her.

At every turn, Fern assured her that she was making the right choice and that Frederick was indeed the very gallant gentleman. But Violet still could not see it, nor did she detect from him anything but the utmost respect and admiration.

Two days before the wedding, Violet had had her fill of frenzy. It wasn't how she had expected to feel. When she had first planned her wedding, she thought she would be giddy with excitement and anticipation, even up to the time she would walk down the aisle of the stately brick church. But now she felt only confined, restricted, and altogether unhappy. Why, she hadn't been able to visit the orphanage since the day before her ride with Adam, and all of the family's charitable activities had been canceled because of her wedding.

Finally, she could take no more. Gathering her wool cloak and heavy leather gloves, she headed for the front door.

"Dear, where are you going?" Her mother stopped her in the hall. "There are floral arrangements to consider, and a last dress fitting. There are place cards to write and your entire trousseau to bring together."

"I know, Mother. But I must go out."

"Out? It's cold. You don't want to become ill for your wedding day."

"Mother, I must."

And Violet left without another word and headed straight to the one place she knew that was warm and unconfining and full of comfort.

The stable.

She walked past Patsy's stall. She was tired of riding the slow, steady mare. Instead, she headed for her beloved Winsome, who seemed glad to see her.

The horse nickered in welcome as she slipped through the stall door. Violet picked up a curry comb and began to brush Winsome's glossy coat. Immediately, her nerves began to calm.

That must be the problem, Violet thought. *Not that my choice is a bad one, but that my nerves are on edge. After the wedding, I will no doubt settle into life with a much better outlook. After the wedding, when Frederick and I are in our own home . . .*

Suddenly, she realized she had not fully comprehended

the consequences of marrying Frederick. He had told her that he was looking forward to sharing all of his life with her. That she need not bring anything other than her clothing and "lovely self" to live with him at his home.

But she had not fully thought . . . two days from now, Violet would be living in Frederick's home, living his life. She would have a socially high position, but as his wife. All of the things she knew as familiar—from Winsome to the comfortable armchair in her bedroom—would no longer be with her.

Nor would her mother or father.

And nor would Adam.

Suddenly, Violet felt a sharp pain in her heart. She buried her face in Winsome's mane and let out a sob that had been building up for weeks.

●　●　●

Adam heard Violet come into the stables, but he tried to block out the sound of her dainty footsteps on the walk. It had taken all his resolve to avoid her these past few days, and it would only take a little more. For tomorrow, on the morning of the rehearsal for her wedding, Adam would close the deal on his farm and the next day, Violet's wedding day, he would be gone from the Miltons' world forever.

He supposed it was always meant to be that way. He should never have hoped for anything more. He should wish he could take back all the letters he had written Violet, all the promises of a life and love beyond all others.

But he couldn't. Because in his heart his love still

remained, and that was something he knew no amount of resolve could make him deny.

As if that knowledge propelled him, Adam rounded the corner just as Violet entered Winsome's stall. He heard her crooning to the horse as she brushed her coat, and imagined her talking about all the beautiful things she was preparing for her wedding.

But then he heard her sob. The sound tore at his heart. No bride-to-be should be in such pain, but for Violet—his Violet—to cry thus was too much for him to bear. Adam slipped into the stall beside her and silently, gently took her into his arms and cradled her as she wept.

"Oh, Adam, I don't know what I'm to do. I don't know if this is the right thing or if I'm overlooking something else. I don't know! I don't know!"

"Shh . . ." Adam breathed into her hair. Her scent, that lavender scent, drifted around him and mingled with the spicier aroma of horse and leather. "What's all this about, Miss Violet?"

Violet's sobs subsided, and she rested her head on Adam's shoulder. "It's about the wedding. I don't know if Frederick is the one I should marry. I've tried to discern . . . oh, how I've tried. But I can't tell."

"What do you mean?" Adam was loathe to break his embrace, but was still intent upon keeping his promise to her father that he not approach her. He was so close to achieving his goal that he dared not ruin his chances now. He led Violet to a hay bale, handed her his clean handkerchief, and sat beside her there.

"Well, first there is my role in society."

"Which will undoubtedly increase with your stature as Master Hallsworth's wife."

"But I need to do more than be a wife, Adam. I have my work at the church, at the orphanage. I feel as though Frederick means for me to stop those activities, but I know I can't."

"He will be your husband and he loves you. Surely he wouldn't prevent you from doing what is in your heart to do."

"There is something else, actually."

"What is it?"

"The letters." Violet dabbed her eyes. "I can't imagine Frederick writing them now. I thought I could, but I can't."

Adam's tone betrayed his skepticism. "Did he tell you he wrote them?"

Violet shook her head. "Not in so many words. Some of the things he said were like the letters and I assumed . . . that is, I thought . . . oh, Adam, I am in a terrible state!"

Fresh tears began to flow. Adam longed to take Violet back into his arms, but refrained. The thought that Frederick might have somehow misled Violet was a serious one, and one that made him angry toward the gentleman. But still, if Violet were to marry Frederick, he would be Violet's gentleman after all.

Oh, it was a fine mess!

"What should I do, Adam?" Violet's eyes studied him with liquid worry. "Tell me."

Adam lifted a silent prayer that the Lord would guide his words. Then he took Violet's hand. "Miss Violet, the first thing I believe you should do is pray."

"But I do. Although lately, I don't seem to get any signs at all."

"Signs?"

"Signs of the Lord's intent for me. Such as the letters, my parents' approval of Frederick, the businesses our fathers have together, his appearance when we were riding."

"You took those as signs?"

"Why, yes. What else could they be?"

A dawning realization struck Adam. Violet was embarking upon a marriage based upon things she saw as signs from the Lord. But he was beginning to believe that the Lord was not leading her in this direction at all. He dare not tell her so; he must rely on God to sort it out for her. For only then would it be decided in the right way.

"Well, Miss Violet, here's what I think you should do. I think you should pray some more, and rely on Scripture, too, to give you some clarity. There are many who love you dearly, Miss Violet, and who wish only the very best of all life's and the Lord's blessings for you. Always. What you must do is find within yourself the way the Lord intends for you to go."

Violet had stopped crying and was regarding him with frank surprise.

"What is it, Miss Violet?"

"Your words. They sound familiar, Adam. Have you told me this before?"

Adam realized too late that he had quoted from one of his letters. He released Violet's hand and stood, the stutter returning to his voice. "I'm s-s-sorry, Miss V-V-Violet. It was none of my business to intrude l-l-like that. No d-d-doubt you are distraught over all the arrangements you must make for your wedding day. N-nothing more, I'm sure. I bid you all the h-h-happiness you so greatly deserve."

Adam left the stall, hurrying away before she could say anything more.

• ● •

Violet stared after Adam for a long time. There was something familiar in what he said. And something true, too. Perhaps she had been putting too much stock in outward signs, and not so much in what she heard the Lord tell her inside.

Violet returned to the house and, feigning a headache, retreated to her bedroom and locked the door. She turned to her Bible. At first, she found its words stern. "Take heed therefore that the light which is in thee be not darkness" she read in Luke 11:35.

Somehow these words rang true. She had been feeling so unhappy lately that it was as though she had been running from the light instead of toward it. She had been taking her new status as Frederick's bride to be the better way, even though she was not sure that she could carry her "light," her faith, and her work with her.

Adam had assumed that Frederick loved her enough to let her continue with her work. But Violet did not believe that. That he admired her, respected her was true. But love her? In fact, more than ever, Violet could say that she knew she didn't love Frederick, either. But what did that mean?

Leafing through her Bible, she found a verse in 1 Corinthians 13: "Though I speak with the tongues of men and of angels, and have not charity, I am become as sounding brass, or a tinkling cymbal." The words leaped from the page.

Everyone was speaking about the wedding, about Frederick being perfect for her. But the one word absent from all the talk was *love*.

Violet reread the passage, letting the words sink into her heart. The Bible was saying that one shouldn't even speak without charity, which she knew meant love. How could she possibly marry without it?

Whoever wrote her the letters loved her, and she him. If Frederick was not the author of the letters, she could not marry him. For as sure as she put all her trust in the Lord, she could only marry for love. Not for all the trappings of a good, socially acceptable match, nor because outward pressures and duties required it. Nor even because she felt it was time to wed.

No, not for any of these "signs."

She must marry out of love—and love alone.

Moreover, not only must she marry someone she loved, but she must marry someone who supported her work with the less fortunate—work she had always felt sure was the Lord's will for her. She must be sure that Frederick would allow her to continue this work.

Violet dropped to her knees and clasped her hands tightly.

"Dear Father, please show me the right way. Let me hear it even through all the other sights and sounds that I may come upon. You know what is in my heart to do, even if I have lost sight of it for a time. You know that I carry a burden for those less fortunate and wish to continue my work among them. You know that I only want to do what is right and marry someone whom I love. Please give me the strength to follow your will and no other, in all things. In Jesus' name. Amen."

Getting up from the floor, Violet retrieved her letter box and drew out all the carefully folded missives she had received over the past seven months. Beginning with the first letter, she pored over them until each word of love, each mark of true devotion, rested in her mind and heart.

Then she set her sights on what she must talk about with Frederick, and what answers she must find before she made the mistake of her life.

Chapter Ten

The day of Violet's wedding rehearsal, three days before Christmas, dawned crisp and clear. There was no sign of storm, and the wind had calmed. It was exactly what Violet felt in her heart, too. This day, she was sure, she would know her love for certain. And she would know, too, if her dreams of a Yuletide wedding would come true at last.

Midmorning, Violet arrived with her parents at the stately brick church where the ceremony would be held the next day. As soon as she spied Frederick walking into the church, she hurried over to him.

"Frederick, I must speak with you."

Frederick looked at her, puzzled. "Well, Miss Violet, I . . ."

Mr. Milton coughed, and Mr. Hallsworth chuckled.

Violet's mother laughed, too, and said, "You know, dear, there's time enough for talking when you two are wed. We need to get on with the rehearsal."

But Violet's resolve did not waver. "Really, Mother. I must speak with him. The matter is most urgent." She turned to the minister, who was standing close by. "Reverend Williams, you don't mind, do you?"

"I suppose not, dear," replied the minister. "But please don't be long. I have a baptism scheduled in one hour."

"I understand." Violet smiled at Frederick. "Frederick?"

"Very well, Miss Violet." Frederick offered Violet his arm and they walked to the front of the church, just near the door. When she stopped and turned toward him, Frederick asked, "Is anything the matter?"

Violet hesitated, then prayed for the right words to form her questions. This was her opportunity to know, once and for all. She needed to be absolutely sure.

"Frederick, I know we have not had the opportunity to speak much privately because of the precipitous nature of our courtship."

"It has been rather hasty," Frederick said. "I myself have been somewhat surprised at the pace."

Violet took a deep breath, steeling herself for what she needed to say next. "There are things that are very important to me, and that I must have understood between us."

"Very well, Miss Violet. What are they?"

"You know of my work with the poor?"

"Yes. Admirable activities, Miss Violet."

"When we are wed, I hope that you and I will work together to bring about an even better life for those less fortunate."

Frederick's eyes grew round. "Well, actually, Miss Violet, I had thought that you would be quite busy being my, er, my wife. You know, running the household and bringing up our children while I, er, work to secure the future fortunes for them. Especially for our eldest son. At least, that is what I had thought to do, and I'm sure your father and mine will concur."

"Oh."

There was the answer to one of her questions. Frederick did not intend for her to continue the work of her heart once they were married. But Violet was certain the Lord intended for her to continue her work.

The answer to her next question could make her even less unsure she was to marry Frederick. "Tell me, then, for I must know before we are wed, have you sent me any love letters?"

"Love letters?"

"Or poetry?"

"Poetry?!"

"Yes," Violet said patiently. "Please, Frederick, have you?"

"Miss Violet." Frederick's voice rose. "To talk of poetry or love letters, well, I don't think this is the time or the place—"

Violet's own voice rose, too. "Frederick, I must know."

Frederick looked suddenly uncomfortable. He walked to the door, opened it, and breathed in some of the cool air.

"Miss Milton, I admire you a great deal, and our families are firmly behind our wedding. And I have even thought . . . ."

"Go on."

Mrs. Milton called out, "Dear, we're waiting. You have a whole life ahead of you to speak with Frederick."

Violet held up her hand. "Please, Mother. Only a minute more." She turned back to her betrothed. "You thought . . . ?"

Frederick's face went pale. "Once or twice, I thought we might wed one day. But I never seriously considered what it would be like to be here, like this, our families gathered . . . and now you talk of love letters and poetry . . ."

Violet glanced at her mother and father and saw them conferring quietly while Mr. and Mrs. Hallsworth and the others looked on.

"Violet, enough." Mr. Milton began to walk toward them. "You're rattling the poor boy."

Frederick stammered, "Believe me when I say that I admire you and respect you. But I am a man of business and far from a poet."

"*Admire* and *respect*?"

"Aren't those two highly important sentiments?"

"What about other sentiments, Frederick? What about *love*?"

"Love?"

"Violet, daughter, you are stepping over the bounds of propriety!"

"Father, please."

"Miss Violet, I'm sure I don't know what to say."

"Tell me if you love me."

"This isn't the time or place to—," her father began.

"Father!"

"Violet!"

"Miss Milton, I—"

The door to the church opened wide. Another voice

broke into the confusion, speaking strongly and clearly. "I do not know if you experience half the joy upon seeing me that I do upon seeing you, but believe me, mine encompasses the stars and the moon and the very breeze itself when you are near, dear love."

Everyone turned around to face the door. There, to Violet's amazement, was Adam. He wore a new, finely tailored suit and hat and looked even more the gentleman than any of the other men in the church.

Violet's heart leaped for joy. "Adam!" She beamed at him.

Gone was the desolate expression she had seen on his face before. Instead, he was smiling back at her. He strode toward her, but Mr. Milton barred the way.

"What did I tell you, MacGreggor?"

"That I was to leave your employ on the day of your daughter's wedding, sir. And leave it, I shall. But I will speak my piece beforehand. I shall no longer be afraid to tell her what has been in my heart for oh, so long. It would not be right, it would not be fitting, to squander what the Lord has so graciously and abundantly given."

"Oh!" Mrs. Milton swooned. Fern caught hold of her and helped her to a chair.

"I say, MacGreggor," Frederick started to speak, then looked at Fern. "Well, I . . ."

Mr. Milton clenched his fists. "See here, MacGreggor, you are my employee."

"No, sir. I am my own man." Adam drew a packet from his coat pocket. "I own the Morning Light Farms, free and clear. As of today."

"You what?"

"The papers are all in order, sir," Adam said, offering the packet to Mr. Milton. "Signed by your partner at the bank, I might add. Upon this farm, I shall start my own life and, I hope, provide shelter for those who've fallen upon hard times, too. Outcasts, much as I myself was when I first came to this country. And orphans, as well. Any and all who need a good home and a new start."

Mr. Milton opened the packet and started to read the papers.

Violet clapped her hands. "Oh, Adam, that's wonderful! What a great thing you will do. And it's what you've always wanted."

"Part of it, at any rate."

He dropped to one knee before her. "The other thing is more dear to my heart. Miss Violet, I have loved you from afar, and I hope that my intentions were always clear to you in the letters that I wrote."

"Letters?" Mr. Milton looked up from the papers. "What letters?"

"Shhh," said Mrs. Milton, recovered from her swoon.

Violet felt as though she were being transported on a cloud. "Oh, they were, Adam. Truly, they were."

"But I dare not presume to know your heart, Miss Violet. Nor can I know what you have discerned as the Lord's will for your life. So, I kneel before you to ask, in all truth, do you love Frederick Hallsworth?"

Violet glanced at Frederick and noticed he was still quite pale, but somehow she knew what she was about to say would make him relieved more than distraught. "Oh, Adam, we are friends. But there can be nothing more between us."

"Then, can I dare to believe that perhaps you love another?" The glint in Adam's eyes was unmistakable, as was the slight smile that Adam had on his lips.

Violet smiled back at him. "Correct again, Adam."

"And who—"

"Dear man!" Violet clasped his hands to her face. "Let us not be so circumspect now. It is you that I love and always has been."

"Then may I ask for your hand in marriage, Miss Violet? For now I have the means. A humble farm, to be sure, but a way to provide a good life for you, and a spirit that is willing to embrace all that you are and wish to become."

Violet was beside herself with joy. Her Christmas wedding uniting her with the man of her dreams and her heart would truly come to pass! "Oh, Adam. My dear man! My dear love! Of course I'll marry you!"

"What? What is this?" Mr. Milton asked.

Mrs. Milton smiled. "Hush, dear, and tell the minister there will be a wedding, only with a different groom. Finally, our daughter's found her love."

"Whatever are you talking about?"

Adam stood and clasped Violet's hand in his. "But only, sir, if we have your blessing. You see, sir, during all the time I was in your employ, I intended to make my own fortune in this wonderful place. My family is very well placed in Scotland and elsewhere in this country, and my upbringing was that of privilege. But for many reasons, I have determined to forge an honorable life for myself. My farm, and my intention for it, is a modest beginning, but one that I am mightily sure of. Rest assured that your daughter will always be provided for, and her happiness will be ever first on my mind."

Milton looked from his daughter to his former stable manager. Then he looked at Frederick. "My boy, I don't know what to say. This is a turn of events."

"Just the thing, actually," Frederick said, letting out a great breath of air. "For, no offense to you, Miss Violet, but I was beginning to realize that you and I, while the best of friends, were not necessarily meant to live in wedded bliss." Frederick clapped Adam on the back. "Well done, Mac-Greggor. I suspected there was more to you than what one could see on the surface."

Violet turned to her father, her heart in her throat. Surely he could see how honorable, how blessed Adam was— and how right for her! She smiled sweetly. "So, Father? May we have your blessing?"

Her father did not return Violet's smile right off. He looked at Adam, as if seeing him for the first time. "I seem to have misjudged you, MacGreggor. And for that, I am sorry." He turned to Violet. "Will you be happy, daughter?"

"Oh, I shall be, Father." She smiled up at Adam. "Very, very happy."

"Then, you have our blessing." Mr. Milton took Mrs. Milton's hand and returned Violet's smile.

"Er, excuse me?" Reverend Williams walked up to them. "But am I to understand that there is a new groom?"

"Yes, there is," Violet said, standing proudly beside Adam.

"Oh, er . . . ." Reverend Williams looked at Frederick.

"Quite all right," Frederick said.

"Don't they look wonderful together?" Mrs. Milton asked.

"I'll be your best man, MacGreggor, if you need me," said Frederick.

"I'd be honored," said Adam.

And the wedding party moved to the front of the church for the delayed but very happy rehearsal.

• • •

The next day dawned even lovelier than the previous one. Violet and Fern arrived at the church early. Together, they drank in the marvels around them. With its festoons of pine boughs, white roses, and sprinklings of red ribbons and garland, the inside of the church looked spectacular. All of Violet's plans had gone into creating an atmosphere of joy and love.

But for all the beauty of the surroundings, to Violet the most wondrous part of the day was the knowledge that she was finally going to marry the man of her dreams. The author of the letters.

Her dear love.

"Oh, Violet," Fern said, her voice hushed in the thick, candle-scented air. "Isn't this grand?"

"Better than that," Violet said, a tear of joy trickling down her cheek. "It's just as I always imagined. And more."

Soon, Mrs. Milton and Fern helped Violet change into her lace-and-corded-silk gown, fastening white roses in her hair.

"I have never seen a more beautiful bride," Fern said, dabbing a tissue at the corners of her eyes.

"And I have never seen a more beautiful maid of honor," said Violet, giving her friend a hug. "I believe a certain best man is going to find you very fetching, Fern."

"Oh, my." The blush on Fern's face made Violet smile even more.

Soon organ music wafted into the small room at the back of the church, where Violet awaited her cue. She peeked through the door. The church was filled with people and, standing tall and handsome at the altar was Adam. Violet's heart sang. He was smiling and waiting.

Waiting for her.

And moments later, when they stood before the minister in the festively decorated church, Adam's voice was clear and strong as he spoke his vows of a forever love, and Violet's trembled with happiness and joy.

A NOTE FROM THE AUTHOR

My dear friend,

The art of letter writing and the joy of receiving heartfelt correspondence are two delicious aspects of life that are, alas, threatened by the instant and sometimes impersonal means by which we communicate with one another today. What a delight, then, that we can settle down with a steaming cup of tea and read of times gone by when people opened their hearts to each other through carefully crafted missives on crisp, ivory paper sealed with wax and ribbons and care.

The theme of loving communication inspired me to write "Dear Love." There is the love exhibited by Adam as he pens his affection for Violet and the delight with which Violet reads Adam's letters to his "dear love." All through that, and above the human correspondence between Violet and Adam, there are God's words manifest in Scripture. His love for his children is so brilliantly clear that in many ways the Bible reads like a long love letter to humanity, meant to be taken to heart and shared.

This day, as your heart fills with the wonder of God's love and the wisdom of his Word, perhaps you might continue the gentle tradition of expressing yourself to a loved one through the written word. Settle in a comfortable nook and take your pen to paper, writing of the miracles and mysteries in your heart and touching another with the gift—your gift—that is at once personal and universal.

Blessings and peace to you and your family,
Maureen Pratt

ABOUT THE AUTHOR

 MAUREEN PRATT is from Illinois, but she currently lives in Southern California. She has written numerous plays for children and adults, as well as articles on business and writing that have appeared in newspapers and national publications. Her first nonfiction book, about coping with lupus, is due out later in 2002. In addition to her writing, Maureen is a music minister at her church, and conducts and sings with a gospel choir.

Maureen welcomes letters written to her in care of Tyndale House Author Relations, P.O. Box 80, Wheaton, IL 60189-0080.

FOR
VARINA'S
HEART

Lyn Cote

Dedicated to the warm memory
of Therese "Rose" Sifler, our Staramama

• ● •

Also to Judy L. Harford, my longtime critique partner.
Thanks for all your help and encouragement.
And keep that red pen handy!

Chapter One

*People judge by outward
appearance, but the Lord looks
at a person's thoughts and
intentions.*
1 SAMUEL 16:7

WISCONSIN · APRIL 1898

Gannon looked up. The fragrance of lavender wafted around
the slender young woman as she navigated down the narrow
passenger-car aisle toward him. Her high cheekbones gave
her face an exotic cast.

The train rumbled into motion again. She lurched
against his shoulder, then straightened. "Pardon, sir," she
said with an accent. He felt her grip the back of his bench,
obviously trying to become accustomed to the rocking motion
of the train.

His gaze took in her white shirtwaist and black skirt, her
raven hair and straw hat. Her stylish outfit didn't fit with the
modest old-fashioned valise she carried in one hand and the
worn violin case tucked under her arm. Under eyebrows
arched like a swallow's wings, her deep brown eyes looked
intelligent but cautious, just like Annie's so often had. He

made himself smile and nod, but that sad drawing-down
sensation, which thoughts of his sister always brought,
dragged at his insides.

A child two rows in front of Gannon shrieked again and
began crying. The noise set Gannon's teeth on edge. Since
the train trip started, the little pair, brother and sister, had
fought, howled, and whined. All the while, the mother had
rocked a discontented baby.

Usually he'd have moved to another car, but the train
had become crowded; in addition, on this trip everything
seemed to hit him harder, stronger than usual. He wasn't just
riding the train back to the university in Chicago as he had so
many times in the past three years. Today he was beginning
his venture beyond everyday life. His destination could
change—or even end—his life.

Glancing back over her shoulder the way she'd come,
the young woman reversed course and went forward to the
two long bench seats which faced each other. Her back to
Gannon, she took the vacant seat facing the distracted
mother. *Brave woman!* Gannon thought.

"Hello," she greeted the mother. "What lovely boy and
girl you have. They are yours, yes?"

The frazzled mother looked ready to disown the pair, but
managed to nod. The baby in her arms began squalling again.

Reaching across the space between them, the young
woman stroked the little girl's blonde hair. "What sunny hair
you have."

The youngster stopped shoving her brother and stared
up at the woman. "What's that?" The child pointed at the
violin case the young woman held on her lap.

"This is violin. You like music?"

Both children nodded vigorously.

"I play music for you?"

Both children bobbed their heads again.

"I play if you lay head on your mother's lap." Looking to their mother for approval, she motioned the little boy to lie next to his mother. "And you, little girl, lay head on my lap." After receiving her mother's nod, the girl came to her.

Unbelievably, the ragamuffins obeyed. Chatting softly in what Gannon thought must be a Slavic accent, the young woman lifted out her violin, plucked strings, tightened knobs, then rested the instrument on her shoulder. Mellow strains of what sounded like a lullaby floated over the rattling of the train. The melody sounded familiar. Was it Hungarian or Russian? Soon, the two children napped, the infant stilled, and the distracted mother sighed.

The older man beside Gannon breathed, "Thank heaven." Gannon suspected most of the other passengers agreed with this sentiment. *What a thoughtful girl, kind just like our Annie.*

But the violin player's suntanned face and gloveless hands marked her as less than well-to-do—despite the fashionable cut of her clothing. Perhaps the outfit had been a gift from a friend? No doubt this young woman was an immigrant, one of the many flocking to America. In Gannon's mind, his mother's voice decried this influx of foreigners: *"Uneducated Slavs with no background in democracy have no place in America!"* He wished his mother could have witnessed this young woman's style, sensitivity, and kindness. He frowned. Where was she headed all by herself?

The train rattled and shook as it picked up more speed. Gannon closed his eyes. The young woman's music continued, soulful and melodic. She had a gift. But her music did more than soothe and entertain. It gave him something to concentrate on, something to push away the thoughts of the future he didn't want to deal with right now.

•   •   •

Startled back to consciousness on the hard bench, Gannon wondered what had awakened him in the murky darkness of night.

A woman's shriek, though muffled, gave him his answer. "No! Please!"

By the moonlight flickering through the train windows, Gannon glimpsed a large man sitting ahead on one of the forward benches. He had trapped a poor woman beside him in an awkward embrace.

"Girlie, just give us a little kiss," the man coaxed.

"Help!" she gasped.

It was the young woman with the violin! Gannon sprang to his feet and lunged down the aisle to her. He grabbed the man's shoulder. But the ox shook him off. Gannon stumbled, righted himself. He threw his arms around the man's thick neck and hauled up on his windpipe from behind.

The man tried to twist and break Gannon's hold. Exerting all his strength, Gannon managed to drag him off the bench and toward the door at the end of the car.

The conductor opened the door from outside. "What's the problem?"

"Masher," Gannon gritted out. "Accosting a young woman."

"Bring him out here. We're slowing down—"

"Let me go!" the ox growled. "Let me go!"

"We certainly will," the conductor agreed in an amiable tone. "Step outside. We'll let you go right here."

Gannon wrestled the man out onto the small walkway between the cars. The train had slowed on its way through a town. Cool wind in his face, Gannon saw the glimmer of town lights.

"Now!" the conductor yelled over the clacking of wheels on the rails. "Let him go!"

Gannon obeyed and the big man rattled down the metal steps and staggered onto the wooden platform. Landing hard, he roared a curse after them.

"Here's his bag." The man who'd been sitting beside Gannon came from behind. Gannon took the bag and tossed it onto the platform as the train sped up, leaving the town lights behind.

The conductor led them into the car back to the young woman. She sat alone now. The mother and children had gotten off at a stop before dark. "Are you all right, miss?"

She wept into her handkerchief without looking up.

The older man who'd brought the suitcase passed around Gannon and returned to his seat.

"Miss?" The conductor bent forward. "We've put that lout off the train. You have nothing to fear now."

Though she nodded, she didn't stop crying.

The conductor looked to Gannon. "Why don't you sit beside her for a moment until she can calm herself? I have to go through the other cars again, make sure everything's all right there, too."

Gannon nodded and sat down beside the young woman, ransacking his mind for a way to soothe her. Maybe if he distracted her? He dug into his pocket for his watch. Pulling it out by its chain, he snapped open the watchcase, revealing a miniature photograph inside. He offered it to her. "My sister."

Reaching into his other pocket, he took out a match, struck it, and held it over the miniature so she could see it better.

She accepted the watch and held it. "Your sister?"

"Yes, Annie. She died seven months ago. You remind me of her." Why had he said that?

"I'm so sorry you lost sister." She still sniffled into the handkerchief.

He nodded and took the pocket watch back.

"You have just one sister?"

"No, here's my whole family." He flipped a catch at the watch rim and displayed another photograph.

Looking at the faces of his father, mother, and two younger brothers, Gannon recalled his father's prayer over him at the train station: *"Protect our son and let him bring honor to our country, to you. . . ."* Each word stung like a yellow jacket. Would he bring honor . . . or more sorrow? He blocked this thought from his mind.

"You're safe now," he told the young woman beside him. "No one will hurt you."

"May I ask question?"

"Certainly." He slipped his watch back into his pocket.

"You dress like rich man, but you are strong." She touched his arm. "You have muscles."

He chuckled. "I'm an upperclassman at the University of Chicago during the school term, but my father, a lumberman, has me work as a lumberjack in the summers. He says it's good for a young man."

"He is right. I glad you are strong. I thank you very much. That man frightened me."

"I'm sorry. Anyone could see you are a decent girl."

She drew in breath. "Some men don't . . . respect women."

He moved to stand.

She touched his sleeve. "You sit beside Varina? We talk, yes?"

How could he say no? Besides, comforting her steadied him, gave him someone other than himself to consider. He settled back into the seat. "You're Varina? I'm Gannon, Gannon Moore."

"Varina Theresa Schiffler. Please to meet you, Mr. Moore," she whispered. "Tell me about family please?"

He understood she didn't want to sit quietly with her thoughts any more than he did. Her soft voice pricked his sympathy, too. An innocent girl, she probably felt more jittery than he did after tussling with that ox. "There's not much to say really. Tell me about yours, Varina."

"We come from old country when I am a girl. Here my papa works on farm, cow farm . . . dairy," she whispered back.

Trying to sound sympathetic, he asked, "Do you have any brothers or sisters?"

"I have two sisters from my mother and four brothers from my second mother."

"You mean your stepmother?" The creaking train swayed around a curve in the rails. He wondered if he would get any more sleep tonight.

"Yes, I forget word. Stepmother."

The moonlight reflected on her large, luminous eyes. She was a woman men would notice. Why was she traveling alone? "So they are your stepbrothers then?"

She nodded.

"I enjoyed your music earlier. What were you playing?"

"Some Smetana. Brahms's 'Hungarian Dances.' A little Tchaikovsky."

Gannon stared at her. "You're trained? You don't play by ear?"

"No. No. My mother's family has been musicians in Ljubljana for generations. This is my grandfather's violin."

Gannon wondered what his mother would say to this revelation. Having a Slavic accent didn't mean as much as his mother might think. "Where is Ljubljana?"

"It's in Slovenia in the Austro-Hungarian Empire, near northern Italy." Varina smiled. "I read music better than English."

He gave her a smile in return. "I definitely read English better than music. My mother made me take a year of piano. Torture."

Lowering her chin, she shook her head at him. The moonlight flashed on and off her face, giving him a flickering view of her. In spite of her gentle humor, her face looked shadowed, sad.

He couldn't keep from asking, "Where are you headed so far from home, Varina?"

"I go to Chicago." She clenched her hands in her lap.

"Are you going to visit relatives?"

"No." She pursed her lips.

Wondering at her suddenly stiff tone, he waited, then asked, "Are you going for a job?"

She shook her head, her chin drooping. She sighed. "I go to be married."

Why did her reply bring back that drawing-down feeling inside him again? Something occurred to him as peculiar. She was going to be married? All by herself? "Why didn't your family come with you?"

"Papa can't leave work. Mother can't leave children. I go alone." She looked away.

"What's your husband-to-be's name?"

"Mr. Paul Ramos."

Her sudden terseness baffled Gannon. He wondered why this young woman didn't add any information to her intended's name. Even though her circumstances were more modest, all the brides he'd ever talked to couldn't stop describing their wedding dress, the flowers, the groom, and on and on. "How did you meet Mr. Ramos?"

Varina gazed down at her hands folded in her lap. She took a deep breath. "I never meet Mr. Paul Ramos."

Chapter Two

At her own words, Varina felt her heart pound in her ears.
Did anyone else hear it? No. Only soft snores in different
keys, the clacking of wheels, the creaking of wood, joint
rubbing joint, sounded in the dusky stillness around her.

"You've never met Mr. Ramos?"

The American gentleman's voice came low, meant only
for her, but the shock she heard in it forced a hot blush to
Varina's face. *I should have given him a polite lie, not an
honest answer!* She pressed both hands to her cheeks, willing
their telltale warmth to ebb.

"Is it . . . is this a family arrangement?" the gentleman
demanded, but in a whisper.

She repeated, careful of her pronunciation, "Family
arrangement? What is that, please?"

"I mean, did your family promise you to someone when
you were very young . . . or something like that?"

In spite of her mortification, she half smiled and shook

her head with rueful amusement. "No. I am poor girl. Not a princess."

"Then what . . . I mean . . . how?"

She wished she'd remained silent about her future. This American gentleman, this Gannon Moore, didn't know when to be discreet, to respect a person's privacy. But she had opened herself up to this by telling him the bald truth. And she couldn't have withheld it from this sympathetic gentleman any more than she could hold back the rich melodies that daily flowed through her mind.

With resignation, she sighed. "I told you already. My papa is poor. He works hard, but we are large family. It is time I should marry and leave home—"

"Why didn't you just get a job?"

How little he knew about women who didn't wear butter-soft kid gloves and elegant silk gowns like the ones she'd seen in discarded magazines given to her. There were no good jobs for a girl with a foreign accent. She tried to explain a little. "If I go to work as maid or cook, maybe someone treat me like . . . like that awful man just now. Papa says I am safer married." *That's how it is for poor immigrant girls like me, Mr. Gannon Moore.*

From under her lashes, she glanced at the American gentleman in the flickering light. His handsome face and fair hair made her feel plain and dowdy—even though she'd done her best to sew her outfit in the mode of the day. That wasn't enough. Americans, like well-born Europeans, prized white skin and pampered hands. She had neither. Oh, for a simple pair of gloves to hide her callused hands! Now that she had answered him honestly, would he end their conversation and say good night?

Leaning forward with his elbows on his knees, he propped his chin on his folded hands. "I see. But if you haven't met Mr. Ramos, how . . . ?"

Her gaze lingered on his hands, brown from his summer spent as a lumberjack—good hands, large, but with slender aristocratic fingers. She pushed these foolish thoughts aside. "The Slovenian newspaper. Papa gets it every Friday." *And I read it to him because he needs spectacles we can't afford.* "It has news of old country and . . . notes about people who try to find friends and family here—"

The American dropped his hands and turned toward her. "And wives?"

"Yes, Papa and Mr. Ramos write letters back and forth until it is all arranged. Mr. Ramos sends money for my ticket. Papa gives me cloth for new dresses and I sew." She patted her suitcase at her feet.

"But no one could come with you?" His eyes examined her intently.

She shook her head no. Why did he study her so? His gaze made her skin prickle with inexplicable excitement.

He sat back. "I'm sorry for intruding. I just thought that this close to the twentieth century, arranged marriages were a thing of the past, an anachronism."

"Ana . . . ," she echoed. "What is that?"

"An anachronism is something from out of the past that is out of place in a modern setting."

She didn't pay close attention to his explanation. He obviously was a learned man. Her own education was limited to her native language and to music, which was the same in any language. Someone behind them moaned in his sleep, reminding her that they weren't alone.

"I wish I could help you," he murmured.

She noted the honesty in his voice. "You did." Thinking of what she'd just been through made it difficult to speak. That awful man's hot breath had made her feel sick. "You push that man off train."

He touched her sleeve.

She felt his fingertips through the broadcloth of her sleeve. At his touch, she shivered and felt her windpipe nearly close. With difficulty, she drew in breath, then averted her face. What would it feel like to have this American gentleman hold her hand with affection?

His urgent voice whispered into her ear, "I wish I could find you another way, a job for you, something. But there's no time. I'm only going to Chicago for two days, then I'll leave to join the army in Florida—"

Startled, she swung back to face him. "The war? You go to fight?"

He nodded.

What must he be feeling on his way to war? Her own situation paled in comparison. "I hear there is a war." She edged closer to him. "Do you have to go?"

"I had to volunteer. Cuba is an island dominated by cruel Spain. General Valeriano Weyler has dragged the Cuban peasants from their homes and put them into recon-centration camps where they—men, women, and children—are starving!" His voice, though still low, shook with his passion. "America can't stand idly by while a tyrant does what he will in our hemisphere. I can do nothing but follow the cause of liberty and humanity."

"Oh, my." This gentleman could soon face death for the sake of others who suffered! What a brave, good man! His words flared warm in her roiling emotions. She drew his hand up and kissed it. "God be with you."

For one moment, her hands and his entwined, then she released his, flustered by her own audacious response to his sacrifice. She closed her eyes, willing away any further show of emotion.

The gentleman cleared his throat and straightened his collar. "I don't think you should be forced to marry a stranger. I wish I could help—"

"I will be fine. My papa knew Mr. Ramos's family in Slovenia." She blushed again when speaking aloud her husband-to-be's name. "They are good family. I will be fine."

The American's jawline stiffened as though her words caused him pain.

But that couldn't be true. She gazed at him. The moon had risen, rippling brighter through the windows. His troubled expression said much to her. They were strangers—very different strangers—yet maybe only she could understand how uncertain the future had suddenly become for both of them. She looked down to her hands folded in her lap. *We both have to face the future, whatever it brings.*

She silently began reciting a prayer she'd been taught by her mother and had repeated all her life. But the familiar words brought no comfort. How did one ask the Holy God to bless one with a marriage born of love? Did the Holy God care what happened to little Varina or to the man beside her?

"I'm not going to let you go alone to meet Mr. Ramos." The American said the quiet words with resolute determination.

She glanced at him from under her lashes. His fair hair gleamed in the moonlight, contrasting with his stark voice. "What?" she whispered.

"I insist on accompanying you. What if you meet him and know it's not going to work out? What could you do all alone?" His words came faster. "It would be different if your family had come with you. Then if you didn't want to go through with it, you could tell your papa and he would call it off."

"But I have no choice—"

"This is America." His voice stiffened. "You do have a choice. If you meet Mr. Ramos and decide you don't want to marry, you will refuse him. Then I'll help you find a job with a respectable person—"

His words uncapped a crazy hope in her, but she refused to give in to it. No matter what this man said, she would marry Mr. Ramos tomorrow. Protests bubbled from her lips, "But you must leave for war. You—"

"I refuse to leave you to face him alone." He laid his hand over hers with infinite regard. "I insist."

His concern and her reaction to his gentle touch caught her around her throat. She could not reply, so she nodded. All the fear she'd been pushing to the rear of her mind came rushing out, flooding her, making her tremble inside. She swallowed tears. Maybe God did care. He'd sent Gannon Moore, a young American gentleman, to help her.

The gentleman withdrew his hand. "It's settled then. Now close your eyes and try to sleep," he said in a compassionate tone. "We reach Chicago's Union Station in the morning."

Bereft of his touch, she obeyed, squeezing her eyes shut against threatening tears. One errant tear slid down her cheek, but she didn't wipe it away. She didn't want to acknowledge it. She'd been all alone. Now she wasn't. *Hvala vi, Bog. Thank you, Holy God.*

· ● ·

Varina listened to passengers waking with loud yawns, clearing their throats and bemoaning the lack of hot coffee. She tried to smooth her hair and the wrinkles in her black cotton skirt. What would Mr. Ramos think of her? But she would have no way to freshen herself before they met.

The American gentleman stirred beside her, then sat up straighter. "We're slowing down. We must be in Chicago."

She nodded. By the morning light, she'd been watching the rickety houses and small train depots pass by her window, each mile bringing her closer to a life she hadn't chosen. She pulled herself together. In daylight, the stranger beside her might regret his offer to stay with her when she met her fiancé. And perhaps Mr. Ramos would not like such a fine gentleman accompanying her.

Taking a deep breath, she began, "I thank you for your offer, but I will be fine. You don't need to come with me."

"I won't hear of it. So let's not have any more discussion. I intend to meet Mr. Ramos." The American's blue eyes stared into hers. "And you will let me know if you have second thoughts about going with him."

"Second thoughts?" She wrinkled her brow. "I don't understand."

"I mean if you don't want to go through with it, you will tell me."

In the face of his stalwart gallantry, how could she oppose him? Especially since his support was the only thing that made her circumstances bearable. The tightness inside her unfurled, letting her breathe more easily. *Mr. Ramos, I could face you alone, but please understand.*

With earsplitting whistling and screeching of brakes, the train lurched into Union Station. She let Mr. Moore take her valise and lead her down the metal steps and onto the platform. People rushed around them, calling, "Porter! Porter!" White steam billowed into the cool morning air. A conductor bellowed, "All aboard!"

In the midst of the noise, rush, and bustle, Varina couldn't stop herself. She clung to the American gentleman's strong, reassuring arm. He piloted her into the huge cavernous train station. She'd been here once before as a little girl. Her family had arrived in America, taken a train to Chicago, and then traveled on to Wisconsin, where her father had had a job waiting for him. Now she was happy to let Mr. Moore guide her out of the flow of people to a corner beside a newspaper stand. "Where are you to meet Mr. Ramos?"

"I am to wait near the ticket windows." She glanced around her.

"This way." He nodded and once again led her into the fray. She avoided looking into faces. What would they be thinking of her—a poor girl on the arm of a gentleman? They reached the ticket windows and settled on the first wooden bench across from them and waited.

And waited.

The large round clock above the gates to the train platforms ticked off the minutes relentlessly. The American pulled out his gold pocket watch and checked it, then rose to buy them coffee and doughnuts.

After thanking him, she sipped the steaming liquid and felt herself revive. She'd meet Mr. Ramos calmly, thank Mr. Moore for his help, and leave to start her new life. An edgy shiver vibrated through her. She spilled a few drops of coffee on her dark skirt.

Out of the corner of her eye, she glimpsed what appeared to be an immigrant family. Huddled together and looking out of place, they all wore tags pinned to their coats that told their names and the town where they were headed. Oh, how Varina remembered the humiliation of wearing those tags!

Without thinking further, she put down her cup, rose, and walked toward them. *"Dobre Dan,"* she greeted them. "Good day."

The man walked eagerly toward her. Shaking her hand, he greeted her in what she recognized as Hungarian.

"Do you know these people?" Mr. Moore asked, appearing at her elbow.

"No, Mr. . . . . Moore," she stammered, "I ask if they need help."

With a hesitant nod, Mr. Moore walked back and sat down.

She turned back to the man and pointed to his tag. "You

go to Mil-wau-kee?" She sounded out Milwaukee so he
would understand her.

The man nodded and said, "Ticket?" He pulled out
a wallet from his pocket.

With an encouraging smile, she gestured to the ticket
counter. "Come."

She spoke to the ticket agent, "Please, sir, this man
needs tickets to Milwaukee. What time next train?"

With only a glance, the agent issued tickets and gave
change. "Milwaukee—10:45 A.M. at gate four."

Varina motioned the family toward their gate, then
unpinned the demeaning tag from the man and handed it to
him. She wished him luck.

Looking relieved, the rest of the family shed their tags.
With waves and smiles, they walked away toward gate four.

With a smile on her face she couldn't quell, Varina
returned to the bench where Mr. Moore sat.

"It was kind of you to help them," Mr. Moore said.

Something inside her wanted this American to know
what it felt like to be someone like her. Varina chose her
words carefully. "I remember what I feel when we come to
America. We speak little English." Her smiled dimmed.
"Did you see the tags on their coats?"

He nodded.

"In New York, they put those tags on us." She looked
into Mr. Moore's eyes, willing him to understand her embarrassment. "It was so . . . shaming."

"The train officials probably didn't want you to get lost."

She struggled with her emotions. "Could they not speak
to us? We knew our names and what city we needed to go to."

Mr. Moore studied her for a long moment. "I never even noticed those tags until you asked about them."

"Did anyone make you wear a tag?"

He shook his head. "But I'm sure they meant no disrespect."

She couldn't agree. "If you will not speak to someone, do you respect them?"

Mr. Moore studied her. Then looking over her shoulder, he touched her arm. "Could that be Mr. Ramos?"

She turned, but the tall man in a dark suit walked past her and greeted another traveler. She sank back down on the bench. *Please come soon, Mr. Ramos.*

One hour.

Two hours.

Two and one half hours passed, reducing her tenuous poise with each moment. Her tension came out in waves of trembling. Could the man beside her see her nervousness? *Mr. Ramos, why aren't you here? What is Mr. Moore thinking of this?*

She cleared her throat. "I am keeping you from what you need to do before you leave. Please, you have waited with me long enough." She forced herself to smile.

"Something's wrong." His voice revealed no annoyance over Mr. Ramos's delay, only concern. "Are you sure today is the date he is expecting you?"

She opened her purse and took out Mr. Ramos's last letter. "I read what he wrote." She ran her finger down the wrinkled page, then translated from Slovenian, "I will meet Varina at the ticket windows in Union Station on the morning of April 30."

"Then something has kept Mr. Ramos from coming."
He stood up. "Is that his home address on the envelope?"

Staring at him, she nodded.

"Then we'll go find him."

"But—"

He drew her to her feet and picked up both their valises.
"He's over two hours late. That's more than just missing a
trolley. We'll catch a trolley ourselves and go to Mr. Ramos."

Uneasiness quivered through her, but she hurried to
catch up. What else could she do? *Mr. Ramos, what will I do
if you've changed your mind?*

Chapter Three

The sleek, green electric trolley carried Varina and Gannon to the West Side around Halstead, where the streets grew narrower and became clogged with people arguing and shouting in foreign tongues. The smells of exotic spices, the mud-puddled streets, the rows of two-flats in desperate need of paint crowded close together—all made it clear. This wasn't Gannon's Chicago.

His muscles tense, Gannon carried both valises while Varina gripped his arm. He repeatedly tried to relax his jaw without success. His anger at the careless bridegroom grew with each step.

Varina glanced up at him, worry etched on her pretty face. "I can go by myself—"

"We've come this far. We'll find Mr. Paul Ramos together." He nodded forward. "There's his street." At last, the elusive Mr. Ramos was near.

"I so sorry. Mr. Ramos live so far from train station."

Gannon smiled to reassure her. This wasn't her fault. What kind of man offers marriage to a young innocent, then leaves her at the station without any escort? Anything could happen to a young farm girl alone in a big city! *I have a few choice things to say to you, Mr. Paul Ramos—but privately!*

"This is the house number!" Varina said with evident relief as she started up the steps. "I will not take more of your time."

Gannon glanced up at the modest house, then froze. "Look!"

"Oh no." Varina stumbled back and bumped his shoulder.

Dread and disbelief tightening inside him, Gannon read the sign aloud, "Quarantined by the Chicago Health Department—CHOLERA." It was spring, the season for cholera, that deadly, wasting disease. Ramos can't be in there!

Gannon dropped the valises and started to reach for Varina.

"Hey! Mister!" a woman hailed him from a window in the house next door. "They got the cholera there! Didn't ya see?"

Gannon dropped his arm and looked over at her. "We're looking for Mr. Paul Ramos, who is supposed to live at this address—"

"He don't live there anymore!" the rotund woman proclaimed. "They just buried him yesterday."

Gannon heard Varina gasp. He reached out to catch her, but she didn't faint. Her mouth opened and closed. No words sounded. She stood, petrified.

He swung back to the woman. "Are you certain? This is Miss Schiffler, who was to marry him—"

"Oh, my! His landlady told me about him writing to get a wife. I'm real sorry for ya. That Mr. Ramos would have made you a good husband. Sorry."

Still Varina neither moved nor spoke.

Gannon tucked her hand into the fold of his arm and grabbed up the suitcases and violin, pulling her along with him. He didn't know exactly what her thoughts might be, but he'd been ready to give Mr. Ramos a piece of his mind. And now the poor man had been dead before they'd even boarded the train. His sister Annie's pretty face flashed in his memory. How could life slip away so quickly? And leave behind such pain, such heart-wrenching sorrow?

Gannon gently urged Varina onto the next trolley. Obviously in shock, she remained silent as he guided her to a seat. When he collapsed onto the horsehair seat beside her, she took out a handkerchief, which she twisted between her two hands. Not knowing how to comfort her, he stared out the window, letting the passing housefronts mesmerize him. The trolley would take them back toward the part of Chicago he knew best, Hyde Park, the area around the university. Maybe he could make sense of this there.

When they disembarked wearily from the final trolley, Gannon realized he was heading right for his own boarding-house. He halted. He couldn't take Varina to his room! What was he thinking? His landlady might write his mother about Varina; he shouldn't upset his mother with gossip when she'd already borne losing Annie and his leaving for war. "I need to find you somewhere to stay."

Varina gazed around at the imposing brick homes, small groomed lawns, and the newest electric streetlamps. Red and yellow tulips waved in the breeze. "This street is too fine for me," she observed.

Her words goaded him and shamed him at the same time. Just as he had been out of place in Mr. Ramos's neighborhood, now Varina in her modest clothing and inexpensive straw hat stood out in Gannon's. Though her appearance was neat and in the latest Gibson Girl style, the low quality of her cotton fabric was evident even to his untrained eye. In truth, his mother would turn up her nose at Varina's suntanned face and foreign appearance. And most likely the landladies in this neighborhood would agree.

All except Mrs. Amberly. She didn't seem to care about such things; she'd even rented a room to a young Chinese student last year.

He propelled Varina the few blocks to Mrs. Amberly's boardinghouse, where it perched on the edge of the university neighborhood. Mrs. Amberly presided over a large three-story house with a turret. Since a few of his good friends had boarded with her, Gannon knew he'd get a warm welcome. He led Varina around to the familiar kitchen door.

The landlady's distinctive clipped Yankee voice came through loud and clear, dropping her *r*s as she gathered momentum. "I hope you told the butchah if he gave me rotten beef again we'd take our custom elseweh!"

"I did, and I din't mince my words," Opal, the gaunt, large-boned black cook, replied in her deep, raspy voice.

Hearing this homey exchange steadied Gannon. Grinning, he pushed his way through the screen door into the kitchen. "He must have had a weak moment."

"Oh! It's you, is it?" Silver-haired and stylish, Mrs.

Amberly put her hands on her hips, making a show of teasing him. "I didn't know if we'd see you again. I take it you haven't enlisted like most of my boardahs."

"I have enlisted," he replied. The woman's words added another layer of concern to him. He had so much to do before he left tomorrow evening. Time had been short enough, but now with Varina to care for . . .

He performed the introductions.

"My girl, you look bushed! Come in and sit down." Mrs. Amberly clucked over Varina while Gannon set both valises down. Soon he and Varina were sipping hot, black coffee as Gannon explained the young woman's predicament. "Could you rent Varina a room?" he asked. "I would take her to Mrs. Evens at my place, but—"

"But Mrs. Evens has always prided herself on the exclusivity of her boardahs," Mrs. Amberly said the words with asperity and a prissy lift of her nose, all the while grinning.

Varina blushed. "Your house is too fine for me. I can't afford—"

"Varina, you have to stay somewhere tonight and this is where you will stay." Fatigue hit Gannon in a strong wave, making him speak more sharply than he wished. "I'm sor—"

"You ride de train all night and don't sleep." Opal shook her wooden spoon at him. "Then you walk all over Chicago. It's time you went to your own boardin'house and took a bath and rest. You come back later and take this pretty young lady out for a bite to eat. No back talk. Go." The cook waved her flour-dusted red apron at him. "Shoo, now."

Varina half rose. "But I can't . . ."

"You set yourself back down." Opal turned to her with

273

a smile. "The Lord provided Mr. Moore when you needed him, so don't you argue with Jesus!"

. . .

Gannon sat across from Varina in the discreet little café downtown, where he knew he wouldn't run into many of his college friends. He'd chosen a table in the rear so they could speak without being overheard. He wasn't ashamed of being seen with Varina, but he saw no point in starting rumors.

As he gazed at Varina, he marveled at her resilience. She'd gone through so much in twenty-four hours! Yet, she made no complaint and asked for nothing. He noted she'd brushed her hair and pressed her shirtwaist and added a few sprigs of Mrs. Amberly's lily of the valley in the black ribbon on her hat. He'd been very aware of the appreciative male glances she'd garnered on their way to their table. But Varina was so much more than a pretty face. She'd more than proven herself worthy of anyone's respect!

"Varina, I'll buy your ticket home and take you to the train station tomorrow." To comfort her, he moved his hand over the tablecloth, but stopped just short of touching hers. As he recalled the soft touch of her lips on his hand the night before, his hand tingled. He let it lay next to hers on the starched cotton tablecloth.

Varina didn't lift her eyes to him. The low light from the wall sconce highlighted the richness of her black hair. "No."

A lady's laughter from another table nearly masked Varina's response. "What?" Gannon asked.

"No." Varina shook her head. "I stay in Chicago."

"What? But—"

She wouldn't meet his eyes, but traced a pattern of circles on the white tablecloth with her slender index finger. "There is no place for me in Plover Station. No job. No room at home. I stay in Chicago."

"But you're alone." *I can't leave you here by yourself!*

Varina raised her chin a fraction. "Mrs. Amberly says I can work for her a little, and she will find me other cleaning or laundry to do. I will pay her for my room."

He didn't want to mar Varina's innocence, but there was a red-light district—not far from where they sat now. A young immigrant woman without family was easy prey for some unscrupulous men. His voice tightened. "You would be safer at home."

"I will be safe staying with Mrs. Amberly and Opal. She says she lost all but one boarder because of men going to the war. She is glad I am come to stay with her. You must not worry about me. I will be fine."

"But—"

She touched the cuff of his sleeve. "You are good man, very good man. But this is my chance. Before I meet you, I say a prayer on train that God open another way for me. I sorry it was Mr. Ramos's time to die, but now I live here. In this city, there is music." She paused as if struggling to find words. "There is hope. I get a second chance to find a man who will love me."

Very aware of her innocent touch, he tried to come up with an argument. Leaving her without family, without male protection in the big city, was unthinkable. What could he say to change her mind? When she withdrew her hand, he fought the urge to reach for her. They were strangers—they had nothing in common except the events of the past day.

•　•　•

Later, Gannon stood beside Varina on Mrs. Amberly's porch, still trying to persuade her. "I haven't given up, Varina. You need family—"

"I will be fine." She lowered her thickly lashed eyes. "You leave tomorrow?"

"Yes, my train leaves at 5:48 P.M."

"Will I . . . ? Will you . . . ?" she stammered.

"I'll come to say farewell, of course. In the morning, I'll take care of last-minute business, then I'll stop to see you."

She pursed her lips and frowned. Did she want to say more? She offered him her hand. "Good night, Mr. Moore."

"Good night, Varina." He squeezed her hand, then left her.

All the way home through the darkened streets, he thought of nothing but the young immigrant girl and her predicament. Maybe he should write his father and have him contact her family? Again, he decided not to let his family know of his acquaintance with Varina. Their meeting was just circumstance, not romance! But people jumped so easily to wrong conclusions! Gabblers!

He'd danced twice with a girl at a spring ball last year. Some gossip must have written his mother because she'd sent a letter, urging him to finish his education before forming a lasting relationship. She'd impressed on him how important it was to take time before making one of the most important decisions of his life and that she hoped he'd find a woman of good family who would be worthy of him. It had all been so unnecessary. Gossips!

At his boardinghouse, he went upstairs and slowly undressed for bed. Mrs. Evens's big house echoed with the strange quiet of empty rooms. The war had sucked out all the lively voices and camaraderie of university life. He sat a long time on the side of his familiar bed, praying earnestly, trying to come up with an idea for what to do with Varina, a new course of action, but nothing suggested itself. Exhausted, he finally lay down and closed his eyes.

⁕ ⁕ ⁕

Annie stood beside his bed. "Gannon, I need you. Please come home."

He tried to rise to go to her, but he felt bound as though steel bands pressed him down on his bed.

"Brother, I'm sick. Won't you come and help Mother? She nurses me day and night. I try to speak to her, but no words come. The fever consumes me like flames. Help me, Gannon! Please come! I need you!"

The piteous cries of his sister wrung his heart. "Annie, I can't come. I can't reach you!" His pulse pounded, and he heard himself moaning as though he were far away from himself.

The scene changed. He found himself in the silent mortuary. Annie's coffin stood open in front of him. Her eyes were closed and her lips—so pale. Her soft brown hair would never come undone again as it had when they'd played tag around the old oak behind their house. "Annie, I should have been there. I should have come home sooner. Forgive me, Annie!"

The face in the coffin changed. Varina's beautiful dark hair flowed on the white satin pillow, her evocative nutmeg eyes gazed at him. Her rose red lips parted. "Gannon, I needed you. Why did you leave me?"

Gannon sat up with a shout. Sweat drenched his pajamas. The parallel of Annie and Varina had been startling. It was a dream—just a dream. Nevertheless, he couldn't shake the conviction that he couldn't leave Varina alone in Chicago. *But I can't stay. I've enlisted!*

Then a new, startling thought flashed through him like electric current. *Now I know what to do. Don't worry, Annie. I won't leave her alone. I won't fail again!*

Chapter Four

The next morning Gannon sipped coffee as he sat in Professor Trevor's walnut-wainscoted dining room, awaiting breakfast. Gannon made himself appear poised and unhurried while he listened to the professor expand on his idea for improving Gannon's future master's thesis topic. This tedious appointment with his academic advisor couldn't be put off if he hoped to receive credit for the past semester and be welcomed back to the university after the war.

After the war. These three short words sliced his world in two.

Tonight he'd leave his normal life behind.

He'd dispatched a note earlier to Varina, telling her to expect him at one o'clock for a late lunch. His plan for them had crystallized with the dawn. He'd written, *"And please wear your wedding dress."* He wanted her to be prepared for the day, and he knew a woman of her class wouldn't wear the yards of white satin and lace his sister would have worn—

A crash of breaking china came from behind the kitchen door. A foreign voice, much like Varina's, spoke rapidly in another language, sounding as if in apology.

The crack of a sharp slap.

Then silence.

Gannon moved uneasily in his chair.

"You should concentrate on Scottish poetry," the professor droned on as though he hadn't heard the unpleasant sounds from the kitchen.

Tantalizing aromas of coffee and fried bacon following her, Mrs. Trevor walked in from the kitchen and took her seat across from Gannon. She interrupted her husband, "I'm so sorry for the delay, Mr. Moore. Breakfast will be served now. I've had a terrible time replacing my last maid when she left to marry."

A young woman, dressed in a black uniform, stepped cautiously through the kitchen door, carrying a large tray.

Gannon flushed with temper when he noted the red mark on her cheek. The contentious Mrs. Trevor dropped even lower in Gannon's regard.

Grimacing, Mrs. Trevor stared hard at the poor girl as she painstakingly placed each dish in its proper place on the lace tablecloth. Gannon suffered right along with the trembling maid. Finally, she finished, curtseyed, and escaped to the kitchen.

While her husband continued his argument point by point, Mrs. Trevor smiled at Gannon. "That Miss Jane Addams always wants contributions for her Hull House, but in my opinion, she just coddles the lower class. I employed this girl on her recommendation." His hostess gave a huff of displeasure. "I may start going back to an agency for my help."

LYN COTE

Caught between husband and wife monologues, Gannon tried to follow both speakers, but ended up listening to the lady since he wanted to hear her justification for how she treated her staff.

"It seems that I'm always training maids for other people." She sniffed. "You'd think the girls would have some loyalty." She huffed again. "But these Slavs are so inferior to good Anglo-Saxon stock or even Celtic. If only I could get and keep a good Irish girl like my mother always had."

You'd have to learn how to treat them like human beings first, Mrs. Trevor. He thought of the immigrant family Varina had helped yesterday. He hadn't even noticed them. Was he as guilty as Mrs. Trevor in his attitudes toward people who were not just like him? It was an unpleasant thought. Certainly his father hadn't raised him to be blind to others—no matter who they were.

"What do you think of that point about Robert Burns, Gannon?" the professor asked.

"I'll think about it." Gannon hadn't heard a word of his teacher's highly intellectual opinion.

But he had thought enough about what was uppermost in his mind—Varina's future. His dream last night had given him strength and purpose. *I'm not leaving Varina here to be demeaned by someone like Mrs. Trevor,* he resolved. *She'll just have to agree to my plan. I won't take no for an answer.*

• • •

After finishing all his errands and having lunch with Varina, Gannon had suggested a walk to Jackson Park on Lake Mich-

281

igan. Unsure of how to broach his idea, Gannon offered Varina his arm and led her along the deserted sandy beach.

Varina looked charming in her wedding dress in practical navy. Knowing it was home-sewn, he'd been surprised by its distinctive touches, the extravagant, puffed bell sleeves, and the delicate mother-of-pearl buttons. Evidently, Varina's artistry didn't limit itself to music.

Over her shoulder, she smiled at him. "The lake is very beautiful, so big."

Out of politeness, Gannon nodded. *I guess there is no easy way to begin.* "Look. I don't have much time, and there are some matters we need to take care of before I leave at five."

Varina gazed at him solemnly. How could she look like that? Like both a child and an attractive woman at the same time? It was disconcerting.

He sucked in a deep breath. "Last night I had a dream. I think it was from God."

"Yes?" She looked soberly bewildered.

Glancing away, he continued, "I saw my sister, Annie, may she rest in peace. You two are close in age . . . you bring her to mind."

"I so sorry."

His sorrow over Annie's passing threatened to break open afresh and pour through him like burning acid. His guilty mistake gripped him around the chest, making speech difficult. *How do I say it to her?* He cleared his throat. "We've met in unusual circumstances."

"Yes." She held her large hat in place with one hand on its crown while she gazed upward at the swooping, squawking gulls overhead.

Her so-feminine pose distracted him from what he wanted—had—to say. He forced the words out in one rush. "We weren't thrown together at random. I don't believe in chance. We met for a reason."

"I never think . . . I don't know." She concentrated on the gulls. They squawked and keened to one another, making his nerves spike.

His head hurt from thinking so hard. Delay had been his mistake with his sister. He wouldn't make it again. "Varina, you came to Chicago to marry a stranger. Why don't you marry me?"

She let out a soft exclamation in her mother tongue. "I could not marry you! You are gentleman. I am poor girl! I am not the daughter your mother would wish for you."

He hurried to reassure her. "The marriage would be in name only. I leave at five today." He caught her eye, letting the meaning of his words sink in. He started again, "When I come back . . . from the war, you and I would merely get a quiet annulment. This is only to help you. Our families need never know."

He hated to do anything that might be construed as deception, but to tell his mother about his marrying an immigrant girl would only add to her worry. Why tell her something—which she really didn't need to know—if it would only cause her pain? And it would be a marriage in name only, not a real one.

Varina frowned. "Secrets get . . . told. I don't think I should do something your family and my family would not like."

"This is just between you and me. No one else."

"No, I could—"

He urged her over to a park bench and pulled her down to sit beside him. "You need someone to take care of you—"

"But you are leaving today!"

"Yes, but as my wife you would receive my military pay—"

"No! I will earn my own way. I can work as maid or laundress. I'm not afraid to work hard—"

He strained to keep his voice even. "If I provide for you, you'll have a chance to become more than someone's maid."

He left out "or someone's paramour." That possibility bothered him in a way he hadn't experienced before. Of course, he wouldn't want any girl abused. But he especially didn't want any man to touch Varina.

He tore his mind from this worry. He wouldn't mention this, just as he wouldn't tell her that if he didn't return from Cuba, as his wife she'd also receive death benefits. Why shouldn't that money go to someone who needed the money? His family certainly didn't!

"My dream—"

"Not all dreams are from God," she cut him off, her hands twisting in her lap.

"I know this one is," he insisted. *Listen to me, Varina!*

She shook her head. "We both leave home yesterday. We both make big changes in our lives. That can give us dreams, bad dreams."

"Whether you believe the dream is from God or not, please believe that what I want to do is for your good—your protection—"

"I know!" She clutched one of his hands in hers. "But we are strangers!"

"So was Mr. Ramos!"

"You have done so much for me! You need do nothing more—"

He edged closer to her, willing her to agree. "I won't take no for your answer, Varina. Ever since I heard you play your violin on the train, I've known that you have talent. You deserve a chance to develop yourself, get more education—"

"I am too old for school."

He'd anticipated this. "Have you heard of Jane Addams's Hull House?"

"No."

"It is a private free school . . . no, it's hard to describe. Miss Addams has set up a settlement house where she offers classes for all ages, including adults, to teach newcomers how to read and write English, to learn new trades. Oh, and so much more. You could go there and learn more. I want to give you a chance to be more than a maid, don't you see?"

She gazed at him, her eyes soulful. "You are very good man. That I know already. But I am not your problem. You have enough to do to get ready to go to war," she begged. "You should not think of me."

• ● •

For more than an hour, Gannon and Varina talked and paced in the park. With each step, he renewed his arguments to persuade her to marry him. His arguments made Varina think of her butter churn at home. Now she felt as though she were the cream under the relentless churn, pounded and beaten to butter.

Her certainty weakening, over and over she'd tried to tell this good man that she didn't need his help, that she would be very careful. Mrs. Amberly had already warned her about not going out alone after dark and about certain parts of Chicago where Varina must not go under any circumstances. Her bad experience on the train gave her every reason to take Mrs. Amberly's warnings seriously. Papa had been right. She would be safer married. But Mr. Moore paid no attention to her arguments.

Now she watched his handsome, earnest face as he implored her to think of the benefit to her whole family if she got more education and could help them.

"But you owe me nothing. I owe you!" she objected.

"Hear me out." He drew her hands into his. She tried to ignore the instant warmth his touch imparted. "This is something I'm supposed to do. The dream was so real. I just lost my sister. Helping you will give me a chance to make up for Annie." He paused. "I made a terrible mistake."

Hearing the somber shift in his voice, she searched his grave face. "Tell me."

Cold sweat dotted Gannon's forehead. "My parents telegraphed me that Annie was ill, very ill. But I delayed going to see her. I was in the middle of final exams. I waited too long." His father had met him at the station, Gannon continued. Before Gannon could ask about Annie, his father said, "We lost her an hour ago." An hour! One hour too late!

"I hear . . . sorrow in your voice. I so sorry. But . . ." Her voice trickled into silence. *What a good man. He only thinks to help me. He's going away to war and I deny him the only thing he has asked of me. Am I right to refuse him?*

She studied Mr. Moore. His flaxen hair gleamed in the sunshine. His blue, blue eyes matched the lake and sky behind him. So handsome. So kind. So good. Was he a man or an angel? As a child, she had heard stories of angels who visited and looked like people, and one didn't know they were angels until they had performed a miracle or done their good deed.

Varina closed her eyes, wishing she'd never heard of Chicago and that there was no war. *Holy God, should I marry this man who leaves for war today?* She sighed. It was not for the likes of her to hear from God. She was just poor little Varina, nobody important.

She opened her eyes. The man beside her sat, leaning forward, his elbows on his knees, his hands folded together. He looked lost inside himself. How could she deny this brave, good man what he wanted her to do? Marrying him didn't seem right, but certainly this American knew his country and its ways better than she.

Then one thought made everything clear. *He might not return.*

"Mr. Moore, I will marry you."

He looked up, startled, then joyful. "You won't regret this!"

She hoped he was right. She only knew she could no longer withhold agreement from this man who'd done so much for her. Over the past two days, what would she have done without him?

"We marry . . . where?" She hoped he wouldn't say a church. She'd never been to a church in Chicago. She'd feel even more out of place if he took her to a fine cathedral in this daunting city.

"We'll go to the courthouse and get a license and a justice of the peace will marry us."

She nodded. When she'd sat on the train the first day of her journey, she'd felt the steel locomotive wrenching her away from the people and places she knew toward a shadowy, unknown place called Chicago. Once she'd boarded that train, she'd been powerless to turn aside.

Now this man's proposal was carrying her forward—like a lost feather swirling and spinning atop a rushing spring river. She could not draw back now.

•   •   •

"Do you have the ring, young man?" The justice of the peace glared at them.

Gannon dropped Varina's hand. "I forgot the ring."

The older man's disapproving, florid face deepened to scarlet. "Then you shouldn't be getting married, young man—"

"I have ring." Varina pulled a small, worn, navy blue velvet pouch from her purse. She unfolded it and revealed a small gold-and-ruby ring. "It was my *staramama*'s, my grandmother's." She handed it to Gannon.

Her possessing a fine piece of jewelry surprised Gannon. But he accepted it without question.

The ceremony went on without further delay—though Gannon was acutely aware that the justice of the peace disapproved of their union. He hoped Varina hadn't noticed.

"You may kiss the bride."

Gannon leaned down and pressed his lips to Varina's. His breath caught in his throat.

Varina's soft, pliant lips under his tempted him to linger. *I've wanted to kiss you, Varina, since the first moment I saw you.* This self-revelation shocked him. He pulled away from her and hurried her from the high-ceilinged room.

"Is something wrong?" She tried to catch his eye as he guided her into the hallway.

"Nothing," he lied. The magnitude of what they'd just done, what he'd just felt for this woman, blasted through him like a cannonball. *I know what I've done is right!*

"Have you?" his conscience chided. *"What would your parents say about your hasty marriage?"*

He offered her his arm; in the other he carried his valise. They need never be bothered about this marriage in name only. He was doing this for Varina, to help Varina. Someday, he'd have a proper wedding with a young woman his mother would adore. He'd make certain of that.

They shuffled quickly down the marble steps and out the double doors into the spring sunshine. His heart beating from his unexpected reaction to kissing Varina, he masked it by pulling out his pocket watch to check his time. "It's almost four o'clock."

"So little time." She laid her hand on his coat sleeve.

Again, her touch charged through him. He wanted to draw her hand to his lips to kiss. Instead, he glanced away. Why hadn't he realized how attracted he was to this lovely woman?

After a tense trolley ride, he, with Varina close beside him, walked into crowded Union Station for the second time in two short days. Feeling upended, he didn't know what to say to her. Evidently, going through a marriage ceremony, even one which wasn't intended to last, changed forever a person's perception of the other party. Now each step distanced him from her, taking him closer to departure. Had he done right? Would she be safe here?

"I will be fine," she murmured.

He glanced up, a crease furrowing his forehead. Had he spoken aloud?

"I worry about you. You worry about me," she explained shyly. "So much happens in short time." She made a gesture of bringing her hands together, leaving just inches between them.

Her practical words steadied him. How could he have expected to marry a stranger and leave for a war all in one day and feel normal? He cleared his throat. "You're right. I can't believe we met only two days ago."

She nodded, looking grave. "I will pray for you, Mr. Moore. I wish you will be careful."

He yearned to pull her close and absorb her steadiness. "I will. Promise me you'll go to Hull House and not work." He stared at her, waiting for assent.

She nodded.

Relieved, he looked up at the chalked board listing scheduled departures and purchased his ticket. Then with Varina by his side, he walked to his gate. An odd sensation overtook him. He wasn't simply getting on a train. He was one man in a great army of Americans being drawn apart from their everyday lives. Was this what it felt to be part of history?

The huffing of the locomotive building up steam overwhelmed the silence between them. Other young men hustled around them, calling to each other. How many of them were headed south to join the army? Gannon watched them, startled by their exuberance. Did they think they were going on a vacation? Was he the odd man, feeling the strain of leaving?

Finally he halted beside the train. The commotion swelled in his ears. He put down his valise. The moment had come. Impulsively, he pulled Varina's slender form into his arms.

She gasped into his ear. He felt the tiny burst of air against his skin, but she didn't draw away. The scent of lavender clung to her, blending with her own distinctive scent. He'd never forget it. Turning his head, he kissed her soft lips. "Write me, Varina. I'll send a letter to Mrs. Amberly's house. Stay there. Don't go anywhere else."

"I won't," she whispered into his ear.

In the crescendo of noise bombarding them from all sides, he squeezed her once, then released her. Quickly, he pushed some bills from his pocket into her hand; then, picking up his case, he vaulted onto the train. *Chug. Chug. Chug!*

Varina raised her pretty face, showing him her concern, her sense of loss. He knew what loss felt like. Annie was beyond his reach, but no matter what the future brought, he'd done all he could for Varina. He waved farewell to his new wife. *God protect you.*

Varina felt tears spring to her eyes as she tried to memorize her brand-new husband's face. The large metal wheels began to revolve, filling her ears with their clacking. She hurried along, keeping pace with the quickening locomotive. Tears streamed down the sides of her face as she ran. Finally, the train sped away from her. She lifted her arm in farewell and sobbed, *"Zbogom!* Good-bye!" *God go with you, Mr. Moore, and keep you safe!*

Chapter Five

Tampa, Florida, should have been a tropical paradise.
Instead, it was a sandy quagmire of unwashed men and
horses under clouds of mosquitoes.

Sitting under a live oak with its veils of Spanish moss,
Gannon slapped the back of his neck for the millionth time
and wished he could curse. A woven palm fan in one hand, he
continued his letter in the notebook on his bent knee.

> *Dear Father,*
> *I'm sending this letter to your office because I don't*
> *want to worry Mother. In Tampa for over a week, I've*
> *done nothing but lounge around in irritating idleness!*
> *No rifle! Not enough drill sergeants to train us!*
> *Thank you for teaching me how to handle a rifle. Our*
> *country has called for volunteers but made no proper*
> *provision for us. You'd fire everyone here!*

Only officers have uniforms, and they are the heavy blue wool winter ones for use in a tropical summer war! I'm glad I'm not an officer! I won't die of heat prostration!

Gannon paused. He couldn't write these facts to Varina; they would only worry her. She had such a tender heart. Who else had taken pity on that poor mother on the train and the immigrant family at Union Station? How he wished he could ask his father to check on Varina. She was so young, so innocent. He'd received a letter from Varina, which she'd dictated to Mrs. Amberly. Since the landlady would read his response to Varina, he'd written back a polite note. If only they'd had more than two frantic days together, he could have said so much more! As he had written his formal reply, he'd composed quite a different message in his mind:

Dear Varina, my bride,
I think of you every morning, every night. I know you are being brave and facing all the challenges of your new life in Chicago. I see you in my mind all the time. I recall your slender form beside me, strolling the sand of Jackson Park Beach. I hear your sweet voice with that intriguing accent that makes each phrase poetry. I feel your soft lips under mine—

Gannon halted, swallowing deeply. That good-bye kiss warmed his blood each time he recalled it. That kiss had nothing to do with a marriage of convenience. How could he have missed how attracted he was to Varina?

• • •

MAY 20, 1898

At Hull House, Miss Jane Addams sat beside Varina at an oak desk by an upstairs window. "Now, Varina, here is pen and paper—"

"I don't know . . . I still don't write—"

"You said Mr. Moore is the one who wanted you to come here to learn better English. You must show him that you are indeed improving."

Though biting her lower lip, Varina nodded.

"Then show him what you've learned. He is preparing to fight for freedom in Cuba. He deserves our support. After you write your letter, will you come downstairs to help furbish up the used clothing again? I'm told you're an excellent needlewoman." After patting Varina's shoulder, Miss Addams rose and walked away.

Varina stared at the white paper, then picked up the smooth, cool fountain pen. Her hand trembled slightly, but she pursed her lips and wrote: *"D-e-a-r M-r. . . ."* She glanced at the page where Miss Addams had printed his name for her. *"M-o-o-r-e,"* she spelled each letter aloud as she wrote each one.

"I a-m w-e-l-l." She began to feel a bit more confident. *"I wish you ar well to. I help sew . . ."*

Frustrated by her halting progress, Varina stared out the window at the housetops so near. Writing in this new language held her back from saying what was in her heart:

Dear Mr. Moore,

My life is so different because of your kindness. You are with me every day. I feel you with me when I am learning. I feel your smile. Every day is a joy to me. Mrs. Amberly and Opal help me practice my English, and they make me spell the things on our table at each meal. When I have done that they make me have imaginary conversations with ladies and gentlemen of quality. They keep me laughing all the time—even when my heart is missing you so that I can't hold back the tears. I owe you so much. May God hear me when I pray for you, such a good man.

She pictured their wedding, his face as he'd leaned down to kiss her. "Oh, Mr. Moore, I can't forget your kiss," she whispered, touching her lips once more. Her breath caught in her throat and she swallowed, willing herself not to cry. Gannon Moore had done everything for her. Little Varina didn't deserve such notice and care. But how she wished she were worthy to kiss him in return! She pressed a cool hand to her flaming face. *He's not for the likes of you, Varina!*

• ● •

JUNE 2, 1898

The army cart carrying bodies to the Tampa cemetery trundled past. Gannon shivered in the hot sun. Following his father's advice, Gannon hadn't drunk anything that hadn't come out of a sealed bottle since leaving the train—even though he was sick of sarsaparilla and barley water.

Tragically, these young men had trusted Tampa water and they'd succumbed to typhus.

He recalled that April day in Chicago—the shock of seeing the quarantine sign for cholera. Once again, he pictured the way Varina had looked that morning with her fine raven hair and expressive eyes—so sad and fearful, so beautiful. Amid the disgusting conditions and stresses of army life, thinking of her had become the secret pleasure he savored.

He touched his inside breast pocket where he treasured Varina's first letter, scented with her own dried lavender. He knew each misspelled word and halting phrase by heart. He had written back an epistle, which would have disgusted his English professors with its short, simple sentences.

He hunkered down and began tracing her name in the white Florida sand—VARINA. His heart composed a letter which again he couldn't send:

> Varina, dearest treasure,
> You alone make each day bearable in this wasteland. When I eat, I imagine you sitting across from me. The candle glow casts shadows onto your lovely face. It's a portrait worthy of the greatest artist. When I march, I see your straight spine striding through Union Station, so undaunted. I play this game—because if you are near, I am content. So dearest Varina, you are wherever I am.

With a swipe of his arm, he wiped out the letters in the sand. *Varina, you're my bride, but we promised that our marriage would only last till I return. How can I let you go? How can I bridge the gap yawning between us?*

• • •

JUNE 10, 1898

A worn dictionary beside her paper, Varina wrote, seated at the same desk:

> *Dear Mr. Moore,*
> *I learn English quick—my teacher tells me so. Now I also teach children to play violin at Hull House. Many fine ladys come to teach and help cook for poor children. I buy cloth to make dresses for children. Mrs. Amberly lets me sew on her Singer sewing machine. I am happy, so happy! I go to church every Sunday with Mrs. Amberly and we pray for you. I pray for you every day. God be with you, dear Mr. Moore.*

Dear, dear Mr. Moore. She pressed a kiss to his name on the page, and then with her handkerchief wiped away a tear. If only she could express how much each letter from him meant to her, how much her feelings for him had grown. But he was beyond her, and she must expect nothing but friendship from him.

Later that day, holding her violin and bow in one hand, Varina paused outside the meeting room at Hull House. She peered in at the fashionable ladies around the tables. She'd seen dresses like theirs at Marshall Field's while shopping with Mrs. Amberly. How would it feel to wear taffeta, ostrich boas, and lace? With her eyes downcast, Varina waited for Miss Addams.

Arriving, the lady touched Varina's arm, urging her inside; then she walked to the front of the room. "Good afternoon, ladies. I'm pleased so many of you could attend today to discuss opportunities to volunteer here at Hull House. But first we will have our tea. And to entertain us, we have one of our English language students, Miss Varina Schiffler, on her violin."

Everyone's attention turned to her and Varina blushed. She curtseyed and lifted her violin to her shoulder. She began a Strauss waltz. Other Hull House students entered to serve tea and cakes. Varina moved around the room as she played light happy selections. But thoughts of Mr. Moore flowed through her mind, and soon she played a darker rhapsody. *Mr. Moore, how I long to play my music for you again. You have the heart of a poet. You understand the creative heart.*

Miss Addams caught her attention, and Varina finished with a flourish and curtseyed. As she moved to the fringe of the room, a lady rose and approached her. "Miss Schiffler, you play beautifully. I wonder if you would play at my church some Sunday."

The question caught Varina off guard.

"I'm Mrs. Ryerson. I'll talk to you again soon." Handing Varina a gilt-edged card, the woman swished back to her seat.

Varina walked away, beginning a new letter in her mind: *Dear Mr. Moore, Something wonderful happened to me. A lady has asked me to play my violin at a church. . . .*

• ● •

JUNE 24, 1898

In the midnight darkness, Gannon lay on a scratchy wool army blanket—all that separated him from the hard Cuban soil. The U.S. Army had left Santiago de Cuba just a day ago. In the hot night, land crabs' claws clicked as they raced sideways unseen.

He wondered what Varina was doing at this moment. *Will I ever see her again? Will I have a chance to tell her how my feelings for her have grown? Could she ever care for me?* Her latest letter repeated in his memory:

> *Dear Mr. Moore,*
> *A kind lady invited me to a church class. We study the book of Romans in the Holy Bible. Yesterday I memorized a verse, Romans 6:4: "Therefore we are buried with him by baptism into death: that like as Christ was raised up from the dead by the glory of the Father, even so we also should walk in newness of life." I feel that I know what this newness of life means—it is like coming to Chicago and starting a new Varina, but even better! I also read another verse, 8:15: "Ye have received the Spirit of adoption, whereby we cry, Abba, Father." I never knew this! I knew God loves everyone, but not that he loves me like my own papa does. I have always thought of him as Holy God, far away, but now I begin to see he loves even me, little Varina. I think of how he brought you to me to take care of me, and I begin to believe he cares about my little life.*

He considered her words: "a new Varina." *And I am a new Gannon.* Tampa had robbed him of what little optimism he'd had when he set off from Chicago. And in only two days, Cuba had opened his eyes even more. He'd seen the suffering tyranny could cause.

Surrounded by dark jungle, Gannon gazed at the canopy of

night. Palm fronds rustled with the breeze. He'd described the beauty of this island—its lush green mountains and white sand beaches—to Varina in his last letter. How he wished they could walk barefoot together, splashing through the tide pools and wiggling their toes in the sand. Varina wasn't the kind of girl who'd worry about saltwater spots and sand in her hems. But he'd withheld the truth from her, that coming here had been a mistake.

Gannon had come to help the Cubans secure their independence. But the Cubans, the outraged peasant guerillas, had been shunned by his commanding officers. Cubans weren't going to be allowed to fight alongside the American force. Why? Because they weren't lily white and didn't speak perfect English?

He recalled his own first impression of Varina—a poor immigrant girl. It shamed him now. God didn't judge by outward appearance. *Lord, Varina feels like a new creation. I feel you working in me, too. Meeting Varina and coming here has made me face my own prejudices. Thank you, Lord, for opening my eyes.* If his mother met Varina, wouldn't she realize what a wonderful woman she was? Would he have a chance to change his mother's mind? Would Varina ever want him as more than a friend?

Gannon let out a long draught of air. *God, take care of my family. And keep your hand on Varina, my bride. Give us a chance to have a future together!*

•   ●   •

JUNE 30, 1898

"Varina, you must stop thanking me. I just wanted to see what you could do with some really good fabric." Mrs.

Ryerson and Varina sat, sorting donated clothing at Hull House. Over the past weeks, Varina had sewn dresses for little girls. Making new clothing gave her something to do during the long, lonely, hot evenings. Then Mrs. Ryerson had surprised her with a bolt of high-quality cotton twill, which she'd insisted Varina sew up for herself. Varina had finished the forest green dress last night at Mrs. Amberly's Singer sewing machine and was wearing it now.

The lady rose and walked around Varina, examining the dress, which sported the newer flounced skirt and wide, capped sleeves with tight cuffs. "Who designed it?"

"Designed it?"

"Yes, who thought up the style?"

"I." Varina blushed at the woman's scrutiny, though she was pleased with the way her new dress made her look. Wearing her new creation, she didn't feel like a poor immigrant girl. She'd described it in this morning's letter to Mr. Moore. If only he could see her in it!

Mrs. Ryerson studied Varina. "You play the violin and design your own clothing. God's given you wonderful gifts."

Varina didn't know how to respond. This good woman taught the Bible study that Varina attended weekly. Now Varina lowered her eyes, inspecting a still usable man's plaid shirt to see if it needed any buttons. "I am not special," she uttered quietly.

The lady shook her head. "Why don't you let God decide that? The talents he has given you, you must employ to serve him. Life holds great possibilities for you, Varina. And I mean to help you use them!"

• ● •

JULY 1, 1898

The U.S. rear artillery streaked reverberating volleys over-head. Clutching his rifle to his chest and crouching low, Gannon inched up the incline of San Juan Hill. The lush greenness of the hillside mocked the raging blasts. The objective was the crest of the hill where the Spanish garrison perched. The return fire from the fort above whistled down through the heavy undergrowth and the few palm trees, the only cover.

Their vanguard, Roosevelt's Rough Riders, charged upward in front of them—in the face of Spanish gunfire. Bullets slammed into the ground around Gannon. Rifles blasted. Men screamed. Horses reared, trumpeting panic.

"Dear God, dear God," Gannon repeated, a litany. A bullet creased his scalp, stinging. Blood trickled over his right eye. He dashed it aside, but it clouded his vision. *God, whatever happens to me, keep Varina safe.*

His captain shouted, "Advance! Advance!"

Gannon reared up and raced for the next clump of huge ferns. He crouched over a lifeless soldier. Another bullet grazed his cheek, burning like liquid flame. He clenched his teeth against the pain. Then a bullet, a red-hot poker, plunged through his thigh. He went down, rolling beneath a scrub bush. He squeezed his thigh with his free hand. Crimson blood oozed between his fingers.

He reared up to start forward again. Yet another bullet thumped into his shoulder. His leg collapsed under him.

A vision of Varina's face flashed in his mind. "God!" he shouted, "God!"

Mayhem boomed around him. Soldiers stumbled and crawled over him. Fighting faintness—bursts of black and white exploding before his eyes—he ripped off his belt and looped it one-handed around his leg. He cinched it tight. A roaring in his ears drowned out the battle. He vomited. The sweltering, red-gold sun flickered and went black.

* ● *

Searing pain worked its way into his consciousness. He ached all over. His thigh and shoulder burned like red flame. Why? What had happened to him? His fuzzy brain gave him no explanations. His thoughts blew around like dandelion fluff.

He tried to pull himself up, but found he couldn't lift himself even a fraction of an inch. The reality shocked him. I'm helpless. How can I be so weak?

"*Senor.*" A Cuban woman knelt next to Gannon, pressed her cool hand to his forehead and murmured, "*Te estamos cuidando muy bien.*"

Understanding she meant to do him good, he managed to gasp, "*Gracias.*" He had to hold on, behave like a gentleman.

She nodded, then examined his shoulder and thigh. Though he could see she was touching him gently, the pressure of her slender fingers battered him like cudgels.

As his heart pumped blood through his battered body, it pulsed throbbing pain through him. He alternated between pain and oblivion. Only the face of a woman, a lovely woman with raven hair and nutmeg eyes flickered in his mind. *Dear God, please take care . . .*

   •   ●   •

Awakened at night, one in a string of agonizing nights where the pain and fever gnawed him without mercy, Gannon managed to pull the creased, soiled letter out of his pocket. Varina's last letter to him. With great effort, he pressed it to his heart. Her final phrases lingered in his mind: *"I know you are a soldier and soldiers live in danger. But please, please, be careful, dear Mr. Moore."* "Dear Mr. Moore"—*why didn't I insist she call me Gannon? Why didn't I tell her I loved her when I had the chance?*

But perhaps it was best that she never knew his true feelings. At lucid moments like these, he realized his chances of survival were slim. Fevered hallucinations had brought Annie, his parents, Varina, even angels to his bedside. His unnatural weakness didn't seem to be leaving him. How long had he lain here, dangling between life and death?

I might die here. He ached at the thought. *My mother, my father don't deserve such anguish, God. They're good people. They live Christian lives.* But good people died every day. Annie had been so sweet and kind and she'd died. Gannon closed his eyes. No hope glimmered. *I'm done for. Thank you, God, for opening my eyes to your love. Comfort my family and keep Varina safe. Thank you for letting me know her, for letting me love her.*

• • •

Varina paced in the moonlight, tears flowing down her face and onto the rose carpet of her bedroom. She pressed Mr. Moore's letters to her breast. How dear each of his words had become. Had she mistaken the change in the tone in his later letters? No, she couldn't have. Each eager question about her had revealed his tender regard. Each word of praise had been a gentle caress.

He'd even written: *"Dearest Varina, Your letters mean everything to me. You are always in my thoughts and prayers. How I long to see you again—"* A sob tore through her tear-raw throat. She pressed her hand to her trembling lips. He'd tried to shield her from the dreadful situation in Cuba, but she'd read the papers and had been able to piece together the awful truth. How he must have suffered there, but had said nothing to worry her. He'd written to her of vermilion sunsets and of water the color of clear turquoise—not of guns, suffering, and death.

When Mr. Moore's letters had stopped coming, her landlady had finally spoken to Mrs. Trevor, the wife of Gannon's professor. The woman had received news from Mr. Moore's family. He was missing in action after the Battle of San Juan Heights. Missing in action? What did that mean? Was he lying wounded or . . .

Her legs wouldn't hold her; she slipped down to the edge of her bed. Gannon's fair face, his deep voice, his strong arm around her, bolstering her that awful day on the steps of Mr. Ramos's house—memories appeared in Varina's mind, one after the other. Though they'd only had two days together, Mr. Moore had left his mark upon her life, upon her. He'd become the man in her dreams, her hero, brave and true.

She'd tried to express her gratitude to him in her letters. Had she also succeeded in letting him know how much she cared for him—without saying these words? She had no right to love him. She knew that! But because of him, her life had taken a turn into wonderful, unforeseen possibilities. *I don't deserve anything! He needs me and I can do nothing.*

Sweet Mrs. Ryerson had shown Varina that the Bible told her to take all her troubles to God. Tears streaming unchecked, Varina dropped to her knees and bent her face into her soft quilt. *Oh, Father, don't separate him from me for the rest of my life. I love him so—even if he never loves me! Let him live, so I can thank him, tell him the wonderful things happening to me. He deserves to live! He can't be dead!*

•   •   •

WISCONSIN · SEPTEMBER 1898

"Dear Varina, Varina," Gannon mumbled tossing on the sweat-drenched sheets of his bed. Varina in her wedding dress stood beside him, stretching her pale hand to his forehead. He reached up to grasp it.

His mother's voice called him from the fog that clung to him. "Gannon, you're home. Mother's here. We're all praying for you. Don't let go, Son."

The hand in his was Mother's. He stared at her face as it flickered in front of his eyes. He had to tell them. Varina would need them. "Take care of Varina. Take care . . ." His hand slid from his mother's grip.

"Oh, Tom, he's burning up. We're going to lose him. I know we are!"

Her husband put an arm around her. "He's a fighter. If he weren't, I wouldn't have made it home with him still alive."

"Who is this Varina he keeps calling for? Is it a Spanish name?" She began to weep into her hands. "I can't bear to lose him, too. I'd do anything to have him well again." She slid to her knees. "Oh, God, save our son!"

•　•　•

OCTOBER 1898

Muffled in a wool blanket, Gannon lay on a wicker chaise lounge on the porch of his parents' house. He watched his two brothers raking fall leaves into huge piles to be burned in the evening. The crisp autumn air braced him, his first day outside the house since he'd arrived home from Cuba. Where had the months gone? So many weeks he had no recollection of at all. His lingering weakness weighed him down. *Varina, Varina,* his mind chanted. The need to see her had become another ache inside him, a hunger he couldn't satisfy. *She needs me, Lord. Have you kept her safe for me?*

"Here's your tea, Son." His father walked out the front door.

"Thanks." Gannon accepted the warm mug and held it in his chilled hands. His father had insisted his mother go to a tea she'd been invited to that afternoon, assuring her he would take Gannon outside to get some restorative fresh air and sunshine. Now was Gannon's chance to do what he'd been fretting over for the last week. His mother would have asked too many questions. Dad wouldn't.

"Dad, I need to write a letter and send more money to my friend in Chicago."

"You mean Varina Schiffler?"

Gannon nodded his head.

"I've sent her money each week since you asked me to after you came home—though she sent me a note twice telling me she doesn't need any money."

"She's very independent," Gannon said with pride. He glanced at his father. "I appreciate your discretion in this matter, Dad. I don't think Mother would have understood that . . . I had merely befriended Varina. I—"

"Son, if you were a man to behave dishonorably with women, I would have been well aware of it by now. If you say that you befriended this Miss Schiffler, I have no reason to believe you have treated her as anything but an honest woman."

"She's a lady," Gannon stated. "I know Mother might not consider it possible for a young immigrant woman to be a lady, but Varina is in every respect."

His father studied him. "I believe you. I'll go get my portable writing desk for you." He set down his mug. Within minutes, he settled the wooden writing surface onto Gannon's lap.

Gannon picked up the pen, which felt foreign in his hand. It had been so long since he'd had the strength to hold a pen.

"I'll go make out another check for her."

Gannon drew a ragged breath. "Thank you, Father."

"Don't mention it. I'll go in now."

Alone at last, Gannon stared at the blank page on his lap. He penned, *"Dear Varina,"* then paused, tenderness and distress exploding inside him. *Varina, my sweet bride, I want you here beside me. Do you think I've forgotten my last letters to you? Maybe they no longer matter—has someone else come into your life?*

The last thought made him brace himself. Just walking down the stairs leaning on his father's arm today had exhausted him. His heart had pounded as though he'd just felled a tree. It would be weeks before he was strong enough to go to Chicago. His inner doubt took voice. *I'm not worthy of her! I'm barely a man. I look like I'm a hundred years old—thin and weak. What would she want with a husk of a man like me?*

He fingered the red gash where the bullet had creased his cheek. He still limped. Just a few days ago the fever had finally broken and he'd felt like a human being again, able to do more than try to bear the pain like a man. But he knew his days as a lumberjack were over. He'd didn't need the doctor to tell him that, while he'd survived, the strength he'd always taken for granted would never return in full force.

What would Varina feel when she saw him like this? He'd watched his mother's anguish over his extended illness take its toll on her. He'd wanted to tell her of Varina, but his mother's health had weakened and all because of worry and despair over him. Could he cause her more pain? And why? If Varina didn't return his love, what was the point of causing Mother more distress?

Chivalry demanded that he go to Varina and release her from their marriage of convenience. His heart constricted at the thought, twisting in his chest and making him gasp with pain. He bit his lower lip. Life without Varina—could he face it? He had pledged a marriage in name only and he must abide by that promise. A gentleman could take no other course.

They'd never talked of love. He had only dreamed that Varina might come to love him. He clutched the pen and whispered, "Varina, *could* you love me?" He couldn't write that in a letter. He must ask that in person.

Chapter Six

Surrounded by a few old friends and underclassmen he'd known before the war, Gannon walked in the winter twilight through the familiar streets of Chicago toward the brightly lit three-story house. November wind tautened his face and made him walk faster, even though twinges of pain shot through his weak leg.

Why am I doing this?

He'd arrived in Chicago very late in the afternoon. He'd stopped at his boardinghouse just to drop off his valise, planning to go directly to Mrs. Amberly's to speak to Varina and to settle matters between them. But his plans to seek her out had disintegrated.

Friends had spread the word that he was in town, and his room had filled up with well-wishers. The past two hours had been spent in the jovial camaraderie he'd missed so much. Before he could stop them, his friends had called the hostess of a dinner party everyone insisted he must attend. Of course, the prominent Mrs. Aldrich had said she would welcome any brave veteran of San Juan Heights! Then they'd literally helped him into his dinner jacket.

Tomorrow, bright and early, Varina, I'll come to see you and we will talk. . . .

He knew Varina would be happy to see him, but would it be the happiness of a friend or of a lover? His love for Varina, his bride, had grown to that of a man's love for his wife, the original relationship they had plunged into last spring. But what if her feelings had not grown? had remained at the starting gate? Could he persuade her not to end their marriage immediately? Would she give him a chance to win her heart? But as a gentleman, he had no right to leave her in a marriage she hadn't wanted and that he'd begged her to enter.

"Hey, stop frowning, Moore!" Jason Canty, one of the party, chided him with a poke in the arm. Gannon forced a smile. "Here we are!" Canty announced.

The group urged Gannon inside the mansion, where a butler received them and footmen relieved them of their coats and hats. Though Gannon's parents were wealthy, they didn't employ a butler and footmen. Thinking of the humble Cuban mother and child who'd saved his life, Gannon was uncomfortable with all this extravagance.

Mustering a polite smile, surrounded by his friends, he trooped into the fashionable maroon-and-gold drawing room to greet their hostess and other guests. Ostrich feathers, French perfumes, velvets, silks and sparkling diamonds, emeralds, and rubies decorated the pale, pampered ladies who lounged on jewel-toned love seats and sofas. If only Varina awaited him here! His chest tightened with longing. How beautiful she would look in dark rich velvet!

Mrs. Aldrich, their hostess, hailed them from a blue brocade chair near the green marble hearth. "I'm so glad you gentlemen were able to come. Chicago hasn't been the same since you left." The lady broke off, rose, and gestured toward the doorway. "Here they are, my last guests, Mrs. Ryerson and her protégé, the lovely Varina!"

• ● •

At the sight of Mr. Moore, Varina felt herself gasp for breath. Only then did she realize she'd stopped breathing. She gazed at Mr. Moore, noting the red gash along his cheek and feeling a sympathetic pain in her own cheek. *Gannon, you're well! You've come home to me!*

She took a step forward, then halted. He was in Chicago, but he hadn't come to see her. *I wasn't important enough for him to come to first!* The implications of this awful truth caught and lashed her heart into a tight wretched bundle.

"Varina?" Mrs. Ryerson touched Varina's elbow. "Is something wrong?"

"Yes, you look like you've seen a ghost!" Mrs. Aldrich trilled.

Varina would not—could not—acknowledge her husband! She'd agreed their marriage would remain secret. She pulled herself together, forcing her breath to come and go evenly again. "Nothing is wrong, ma'am. I was just surprised to see so many handsome young men in your drawing room."

Mrs. Aldrich chuckled and the other ladies joined in. "Too true, my dear. We have been a little thin of company with so many of our young men off to war. But the peace treaty is nearly done, and so we must adjust ourselves to this largesse."

Still hoping, Varina looked to Mr. Moore, willing him to step forward and say, "But we aren't strangers. Varina and I have met."

He said nothing.

Inside she winced at this blow. She lifted her shoulders to bear the crushing letdown. *Very well, Mr. Moore, you will not even acknowledge that you know me. I would not reveal our marriage, but you don't even want anyone to know we met on the train. That is your choice. I will abide by it.*

Summoning up a brilliant smile, Varina chuckled. "Getting accustomed to having many handsome gentlemen is not a difficult job, no? Will you introduce me, ma'am?" Along with Mrs. Ryerson, Varina walked as gracefully as she could to her hostess. Did Mr. Moore think she would behave like a clumsy milkmaid and embarrass him?

Mrs. Aldrich introduced her to a Mr. Canty, a Mr. Brown, and then, "And here is Mr. Moore."

Mrs. Ryerson glanced up at Varina. "Mr. Moore is the son of an old friend of mine. He left his studies this year for Cuba." She turned to address Gannon. "I've had a letter from your mother. You've just recovered from your ordeal. You're planning on reentering the university in January, aren't you, Gannon?"

"Yes, ma'am." Gannon bent and kissed Varina's kid-gloved hand.

Afraid to look into his eyes and find no love reflected there, Varina trembled at his touch—in spite of the thin layer of leather between them. For a second, she nearly lost her control and threw her arms around him in welcome.

But the moment passed. *He wants no one here to know about me, about us.* The pressure around her heart cinched tighter, but she refused to give in to it.

"Dinner is served," the butler announced from the doorway.

• ● •

Gannon still reeled from the shock of seeing Varina, his wife, here—dressed in a fashionable gown, accepted in society. Mrs. Aldrich had said she was Mrs. Ryerson's protégé. How? Had Chicago been turned upside down while he was gone? He hurried forward to be the first one to offer his arm to Varina. He must whisper his questions: *Why are you here? How?*

But so-suave Canty swooped to her side, cutting him off. When Varina accepted Canty's arm and let him lead her into the formal dining room, the man had the gall to smirk over his shoulder at Gannon. Canty had the look of a matinee idol—too smooth to be taken seriously.

Gannon was left fuming in their wake, watching Varina's graceful spine. Recovering himself, he claimed one of the debutantes, a Miss Armstrong, whom he vaguely remembered, and escorted her to the dining room.

"Oh, Mr. Moore, you're limping. Were you wounded in Cuba?" Miss Armstrong cooed as though he were a pet parakeet with a broken wing.

317

Varina glanced back at him, worry on her face.

He answered her with his expression. *Yes, I was wounded, Varina! Did you care?*

"Were you?" Miss Armstrong coaxed.

He nodded, feeling stiff and disgruntled. "Nothing serious," he said, skirting the truth.

He located the young lady's name card, then his own. He'd been placed directly across from Varina with Miss Armstrong at his left and another young lady on his right. According to etiquette, he'd be expected to entertain the ladies sitting beside him, not the lady across from him.

So he would be able to see Varina, but have no chance to whisper to her, ask questions throughout the long formal meal that could last for hours. Torture. *How can it be that you're here as a guest, Varina? When will we have time to speak?*

With a flurry of white linen napkins, the dinner commenced. Footmen served steaming consommé from silver tureens. Gannon caught himself staring at Varina. The maroon silk gown she wore contrasted vividly with her blue black hair and the natural rose red of her lips. He'd been prepared to see the Varina he'd left behind in April. He hadn't expected to find her as a confident beauty here in society!

The young lady beside him cleared her throat, reminding him of her existence, no doubt. Wrenching himself from Varina's sway, he made himself turn to Miss Armstrong. Out of politeness, he voiced one of the few phrases he'd learned that pleased women, "You're wearing a charming dress, Miss Armstrong."

"Oh, thank you! My mother was one of the first women to realize how talented Chicago's own modiste, Varina, is. I'm wearing one of her first designs!"

Gannon couldn't make any sense of this. "Designs?" he mumbled.

"Yes." The pretty debutante nodded toward Varina. "Mrs. Ryerson brought Varina to our notice. My mother agreed absolutely with Mrs. Ryerson. Why should we go to Paris for the latest designs when we have our own designer right here in America!"

"Varina sews clothing?" He couldn't be hearing right, could he?

"Of course not!" Miss Armstrong flashed him a superior smile. "She *designs*. Seamstresses sew her creations. She's an artist! And she's all the rage! Fortunately, since my mother was wise enough to view Varina's designs first, all my winter wardrobe has been designed exclusively by her."

The young woman on Gannon's other side leaned across him. "Can I help it if my mother is so dreadfully conservative? I tried to tell her that Varina was just the thing, but she didn't listen to me and now it's too late!"

Miss Armstrong sighed in sympathy. "Varina can only do so much. I've heard though, Janet," she lowered her voice, "if your mother would contribute to Hull House and perhaps volunteer, Varina might take time to do a consultation for you. She also knows how to add those little touches which make an average ensemble stand out."

"Really?" The debutante brightened.

Miss Armstrong nodded. "You see, Hull House is where Mrs. Ryerson first met Varina. Would you believe it—

she was sewing dresses for little girls! Miss Addams first noticed how talented Varina was."

"Ah," the debutante sighed. "I'll speak to my mother right away."

Gannon felt like cleaning out his ears. What he'd heard was preposterous. He'd sent Varina to Hull House to continue her education—not design clothes!

Across from him, Varina looked foreign, elusive— completely at ease seated between two gentlemen in dinner jackets! He, on the other hand, felt like popcorn being shaken over a fire. Where had his shy wife gone?

•   •   •

From her place, Varina couldn't help but overhear most of what the two young ladies had said. Every word they spoke about her transformation was true.

Did Mr. Moore believe them? She'd worried over him. She'd prayed for this moment of reunion. She'd imagined Mr. Moore's return a thousand times, but now she realized that she'd expected him to want her—if not as a wife, at least as a friend. But he hadn't even acknowledged her. How that stung! She stiffened herself against tears. *I thought, I hoped, you would be proud of me. And love me, at least a little.*

•   •   •

At the end of the interminable evening, Gannon tried to maneuver himself next to Varina in the entryway, where the footmen were helping the guests on with their wraps. He had to get to Varina to ask to escort her home. Mrs. Ryerson, an old friend of his parents, would notice, but he didn't care. He had to talk to Varina, to make sense of all that had happened to them since April. As he made his way to her side, a footman holding Gannon's hat and coat interrupted his progress.

Jason Canty cut in front of him, took Varina's pelisse from another footman, and draped it around her. "Do you recall, Varina, that I told you I was getting a new gig? I'd love for you to be the first lady to ride in it."

Gannon thrust himself toward them. The nerve of the young whelp!

Varina frowned. "But Mrs. Ryerson brought me—"

"Don't mind me, dear." Mrs. Ryerson gave a knowing smile. "Just don't take the long way home, Mr. Canty!" She wagged her finger at him.

Varina nodded at Canty. "I would love to ride in your gig. Mrs. Amberly's is not far—"

"I would drive you to the moon, Miss Varina, if that's where you wanted to go!" Canty offered her his arm.

Accepting his escort, Varina laughed. "No, not that far! Just Mrs. Amberly's, please!" Then she walked out, her hand through Canty's arm.

Gannon swallowed scalding words, holding his frayed temper by its ragged edges. What was she thinking? Canty was a dreadful flirt. Everyone knew that! *You'll talk to me soon, Varina! I won't stand for this!*

Chapter Seven

"Good morning, Mrs. Amberly." Gannon stood hat in hand at the door of the same kitchen where he'd brought Varina in late April—it seemed a lifetime ago. The change in him physically made him even more diffident. A glance in the mirror had reminded him too clearly that he wasn't the man he'd been last spring.

"Come in, Mr. Moore. It's a chilly morning." The landlady opened the door wide. "You could have come to the front door, you know."

"I wanted to speak to Varina without catching undue notice—"

"Why's that?" Opal, standing in front of the stove, objected. "She prayed and prayed you come through the fire safe, and now you don't want to be seen with her?"

The black woman's words pierced him like darts. "That's not true," he defended himself. "We're . . . I just don't want to excite any gossip."

Varina swept into the kitchen. A faint blush heightened her color and she didn't appear pleased to see him. "That is very kind of you, Mr. Moore. I saw you from my window and thought you might be here to speak with me. Yes?"

Her brisk frankness caught him by surprise. He spoke the first words that came to mind, "You speak English so well."

"That is what you wanted, isn't it?" The rose in her cheeks deepened and her eyes sparkled. "You are the one who suggested I go to Hull House for more education."

"Yes, I know. I just didn't . . ."

Her chin went up. "You did not think that I could learn to speak English well."

"No, not that. It's just being gone like I was . . . everything's gotten mixed up." Just being near her scattered his wits, and each word he said made him look worse. He wished the two older women would leave him alone to straighten matters out with Varina.

"Is that why we only heard from you once since early July?" Mrs. Amberly motioned for him to sit at the table. "Sit down. You look like you're in pain."

The mix of accusation and concern in the lady's voice disconcerted him. He remained on his feet. "My father contacted Varina." *I was too weak to hold a pen!* A man could not say that. Instead, he substituted, "I was wounded at San Juan Heights—"

"We didn't hear that from you first, did we?" Opal turned sizzling griddlecakes with quick twists of her wrist. "We found that out by Mrs. Amberly talking to that professor of yours, or I should say, his huffy wife."

The aroma of the pancakes and bacon distracted him.

After months of fasting, his body seemed hungry all the time now. "I was ill for many months. I couldn't write." Backed into a corner, he said it, but it cost him much to speak of it. He'd come here to make sense of things. Why were Mrs. Amberly and her cook challenging him? His empty stomach began to churn. How could he say, "I nearly died"? That would make him sound as though he were fishing for sympathy.

Very pale, Varina hung back from him to stand beside Opal. "Are you well, now? You were limping last night."

He heard the note of genuine concern in Varina's voice. If they'd been alone, he'd have drawn her close. Could Varina's touch soothe his pain? She was the balm he sought.

He cleared his throat. "I'm sure I'll be fine in time. Varina, can't we talk privately for just a moment?"

A knock came at the door. Mrs. Amberly opened it.

A delivery boy offered a cone-shaped brown-paper package. "Flowers for a Miss Varina?"

Mrs. Amberly stepped aside.

Blushing, Varina hurried to the door. "For me?"

The delivery boy nodded, handing her the package. "Thank you!" she exclaimed.

Gannon glared. Flowers? Who was sending his . . . Varina . . . flowers?

"Thank you, miss." The boy shifted from one foot to the other in the brisk chill.

Though fuming, Gannon read the boy's hesitance and handed him a dime.

"Thank you, sir!" The lad beamed, rattled down the back steps, and trotted to his cart.

• • •

Varina glanced at Mr. Moore shyly. Could it be? Had he sent her flowers? Did he regret disowning her last night? She held her breath as she read the card. "To a lovely lady. Jason Canty." Her spirits plummeted.

Mr. Moore took a step toward her. "Varina, we have things we must discuss—"

"I am very busy this morning," she interrupted him. Tears nipped at her eyes, begging to flow. He'd rejected her last night and again this morning. His regard for her hadn't grown as hers for him had. This realization jabbed her, a painful pressure in her heart.

She went on briskly, holding on to her composure. "I have to supervise two fittings for holiday dresses that the seamstresses have finished and give a fashion consultation." *Oh, Father, his rejection hurts so.* She lifted her chin. "After lunch I have a Bible class at Mrs. Ryerson's church and I am to play 'Hungarian Dances' at the Cathcart's musicale tomorrow night. I must take time to practice." Her excuses ran out. She turned and handed Mrs. Amberly her flowers.

"I'll put them in water for you, dear." The lady's expression showed such sympathy.

Varina stiffened herself against her disappointment. Hot tears were bubbling to the surface. She'd had such hopes!

"I would think," Mr. Moore raised his voice, "that taking time for an old friend who's just returned from war would supersede your routine."

"I am very sorry." *More sorry than I can say. But I am more than your friend, and you left me weeping and praying for so many nights without any word! It was unfeeling of you! Then I receive only civil notes from your father. Now you come back and I am to become little Varina again, nothing at all in your life? Your letters said so much more than the words on their pages. And though our marriage was in name only, as your wife, I think I deserved a little respect, a little consideration.*

Even in her sadness, she wondered fleetingly if she was behaving in a proud manner. But her emotions had become so strong and so intricate; she couldn't unravel her motives right now. "I don't think we need to discuss something which we already decided in April." *Before you left me,* she added inside. *Now you have come to tell me that you are going to annul our marriage. Go do it if that is what you wish.*

Gannon stalked to the door. "I'll leave you then." He paused with his hand on the knob. "But I must and I will speak to you."

In his chair at Cathcart's parlor, Gannon closed his eyes, letting the exquisite stringed melody Varina was playing spark his nerves and his heart. The mellow tones of her violin made him recall the beauty of the pink sunrise over Santiago Bay, the tropical afternoon cloudbursts of cooling rain, the white sand beaches meeting the crystal blue Gulf of Mexico. *Dear Lord, it wasn't all bad. I saw so much.*

"Why do you think you were called to see Cuba? Just to see the scenery?" His conscience pricked him. *"You made a promise. Will you keep it?"*

Galvanized as if by an electric current, he opened his eyes. Varina hit the final breathtaking note, then cut it off with a dramatic flourish of her bow. Eager applause exploded around him. Jason Canty stood up. "Bravo! Bravo!"

Professor Trevor's wife sat beside Gannon. Though she applauded, she frowned at Canty, shaking her head in disapproval. When the applause died down, she leaned over to Gannon and whispered, "She's cut quite a swathe through Chicago society—a girl out of Hull House—a Slav! Just because it amuses some people to pet her, to call her a modiste. Humph!"

Gannon paid scant attention to the petty, ill-tempered woman; trying to reason with her would be futile. No doubt if she'd deigned to notice someone, that would make it quite apropos. He watched Varina thread her way through her admirers and into another room.

This was the reason he'd come to this evening's musicale. After yesterday morning in Mrs. Amberly's kitchen, he'd been equally angry and confused. He'd tried to get a moment alone with Varina yesterday and today, but something or someone had always intruded. Tonight he'd get a moment alone with her if he had to lock her up with himself in the coat closet for privacy!

As another young woman swept forward to sit at the piano, he bowed to Mrs. Trevor and carefully made his way to the back of the room and out through a different door. Familiar with the house, he knew into which room Varina had disappeared. He found her alone by a window, looking out pensively. "Varina," he murmured just for her ears.

She gave a little start and turned around, swirling the skirts of her stylish royal blue velvet dress. The color of her gown brought out the glow in her white skin and the gleam in her warm brown eyes. How he had dreamed of those eyes while he lay in that little casa in Cuba. He stood transfixed by the lovely picture she made, standing in front of the elaborately ice-frosted window.

"Mr. Moore—"

Her formality galled him. "I wish you would call me Gannon."

She gave him no answer but a slight lift of her eyebrows. "What do you wish? Have you come to tell me what I must do to make legal our annulment?"

He clenched his jaw against her tart tone. "I've wanted a word alone with you. You should know I wouldn't do anything till we had spoken." Her frosty demeanor didn't seem to hold the possibility of warm feelings toward him. The course open to a gentleman was clear, even if he never recovered from the blow. He should set Varina free—if that was what she wanted. "Why have you avoided me the past two days?"

She lifted her brows again. "I am merely busy. I do not know why we must talk if you only wish to annul our marriage. That was already decided in April."

His mind rebelled at her cool tone and colder words. "Aren't we friends, Varina?"

His question stopped her. She lowered her eyes. "I do not know. Our time together was so short. What we shared—" She broke off. "Do you want to be . . . friends?"

As she said the words, they plowed deeply and agonizingly inside him. How could he begin to tell her? Should he blurt out, "I love you"?

"You have no answer for me?" she murmured. Her dark thick lashes fanned against her ivory cheeks.

The sight fascinated him. "Varina, we started out backwards." He ransacked his brain for the right words. "We met at such a time in both our lives—me off to war, you to marry a stranger. How can we be just acquaintances? We shared such life-altering events together. We must at least acknowledge . . . we're more than friends, aren't we?"

"Do you not wish our marriage annulled?" She took a step closer to him, her gaze searching his.

Her fragrance, sweet lavender, stirred his memory. The same scent had clung to the letters she'd sent him. Her nearness made it hard to concentrate. He tried to explain, "Your letters meant . . . so much to me." Everything! Only to you could I speak what I was really thinking about how the Cuban peasants were being treated, or should I say, mistreated? Only to you could I be honest about my feelings about the war. I looked forward to each reply you sent. "When I was wounded, I felt you—as though you were very near to me."

"I prayed for you." She stepped closer, only a breath away. "I worried. When my letters came back, what was I to think?"

Sorrow clogged his throat. So much had happened to both of them. How did one go back and begin again? He folded her soft hand in his, wanting to connect with her, tell her what she'd meant to him. Until he touched her, he hadn't noticed she'd taken off her gloves to play the violin. Now, he marveled at the new softness of her hand. In April, her palms had been callused and brown. Now they were soft and white, lady's hands.

He didn't value her more now that she had lady's hands, but because only to her had he revealed some of his disillusionment in Cuba. Yet it was the sensation of her warm bare hand in his that rocked him. The temptation to press his lips to her palm . . .

He forced himself to speak. "I'm sorry I didn't communicate to you right away, but I was ill and you knew . . . my family . . . we agreed that our marriage would be secret . . ."

His words seemed to turn Varina into ice. Her aura of intimacy, of yielding, vanished. She nodded stiffly, and then slipped her hand from his. "Of course, your family would never—you married me to provide for me. For that I am very grateful. You have come back from war. You wish to get on with your life."

He heard the hurt in her tone. *No, that's not what I meant!*

She went on. "Do not delay. I will sign the annulment paper. You bring it to me." She edged away from him. "I must return to my hostess."

As she drew apart, his heart cried, *Come back!* She'd spoken the truth. His family wouldn't approve. Normally he wouldn't have hesitated to follow his heart. But only a year had passed since his parents had lost Annie. He'd just put them through his going off to battle, then a prolonged recuperation. How could he foist an unknown bride on them? It would probably break his mother's heart.

Another thought brought him up short: He was a shadow of the man he had been. Did he have the right to love Varina? He'd noticed the shocked and pitying looks he'd received in the past two days. Certainly, Varina, Chicago's new rage, could find someone who had more to offer than he.

Chapter Eight

At the Bagley's annual November ball the next evening, Gannon bided his time dance by dance. The rumor he'd overheard when he walked in tonight had made his blood pound at his temples. As soon as he'd heard it, he'd taken action to find out the truth tonight. He'd caught Varina as she strolled past him in her dazzling evening gown and secured the waltz on her dance card.

Since last night's encounter with Varina, he'd told himself to give her the freedom she appeared to want, get the annulment, and then go back to Wisconsin and try to forget her. But he'd found himself unable to do it. He couldn't free her. He'd gone over and over yesterday evening at the musicale, replaying Varina's words. He'd felt so close to her until—what? He couldn't reason out what had broken their communication.

The schottische ended and Gannon wrenched himself back to the present. He appeared at Varina's elbow. "I believe this is my waltz."

Varina thanked her partner and stepped into Gannon's embrace.

Holding her once again shocked him. No other woman warmed him body and heart as this slender dark-haired woman.

She smiled politely. "You look very handsome tonight, Mr. Moore—"

"Don't talk to me as if we were strangers." He pressed his hand tighter at the base of her spine, tucking her closer. "Why won't you call me Gannon?" This wasn't at all what he'd planned on saying, but every time she called him Mr. Moore, anger sparked through him.

Varina stared up at him with something inscrutable in her eyes.

To the lilting—maddening—waltz, Gannon twirled her in his arms, trying to think of how to ask about the rumor he'd heard. It couldn't be true, could it? It was unthinkable. She's married to me!

Waiting for inspiration, he realized that what he had to ask couldn't be said on the dance floor. He couldn't confront her here. It was time to risk it all! He waltzed Varina over to one of the French doors, opened it with a quick twist of his wrist, and swept her out onto the snowy balcony. It was past time for truth telling.

Still in his arms, she looked up at him, startled.

"Is it true?" His words poured out. "Are you going to accept an engagement ring from that upstart, Jason Canty?"

Frowning, she stared at him, then pulled away, stiff-shouldered. "Perhaps. How can I know if a man wishes to marry me until he asks?" She folded her arms and turned away from him.

Her white shoulders glowed in the light from the ball-room windows. He took them in his hands. In spite of the cool still night, they felt warm, full of life, like Varina, the woman he couldn't let slip from his grasp. He couldn't wait any longer. He rushed the fence. "Varina, I can't annul our marriage. Let's declare that we are man and wife and begin our life together."

Slipping from his grip, she swirled and challenged him with a proud lift of her chin. "Jealousy is speaking, not your heart."

"No!" *How to persuade her?* "Varina, we were meant to be, meant to meet on that train, meant to come to Chicago together," he blurted out. "God brought us together!"

She stared at him, her bare arms crossed against the chill. "That may be. But I ask you, Mr. Moore, to imagine telling your mother that you have married a girl—" she ticked each point off on her kid-gloved fingers—"born in the Austro-Hungarian Empire, who speaks with an accent, whose father is a poor farm laborer. Can you tell her? Can you?"

He did imagine it. They would be shocked. His mother would be devastated. It might even mean a break between his parents and him. But Varina belonged to him. This realization finally made his course of action clear. "I don't care about all of that! I love you. I will make our union public despite my parents' disapproval."

"Do you love me? But I am a shame to you. How can that be?" Varina's eyes flashed her indignation. "I am not ashamed of who I am! God made me! I am the person he wants me to be! Before, I did not know that God cared so much about each one of us, but I have read the Bible and now

I know! Until you are ready to marry me because of who I am, not in spite of it, we have no future!"

She swept to the French doors and with a swish of her gown, disappeared inside.

White-hot anger sizzled through Gannon. He'd declared his love and she'd refused him! Would she accept Canty's proposal while she was his legal wife? Gannon stalked inside. Without a word to anyone, he retrieved his topcoat and hat and left the ball behind.

Striding on the light coating of snow, he walked past the line of carriages waiting to take the merrymakers home later. *How had all this come to be?* He tried to blot out the image of Canty's smug face. How could Varina, his very own wife, flirt with another man? His conscience pricked him with the memory of the look on Varina's face that first night at the Aldriches': such hope and fear intermingled. *Why didn't I claim her then? If not as my wife, at least as my friend?*

Snow began to fall. The large, wet flakes flew into his face, melting on his cheeks. Passion spurred him on, but each soggy step he took lessened his outrage. In its place, remorse—a feeling that he'd been put to the test and failed—slowly crept over him. He recalled the April train trip—Varina in her simple shirtwaist and skirt on her way to Chicago to bravely marry a stranger. He couldn't connect that Varina with the one who laughed at Canty's lame jokes. How could someone change so in six short months?

"*Did she change, or is it just your perception of her?*" his unsympathetic conscience asked.

Gannon halted at an empty street corner. In the distance, bells jingled on a harness.

"Did she change, or is it just your perception of her?"

His inner voice spoke true. If Varina hadn't already had this talent for music and design inside her in the spring, she could never have learned or manufactured it in such a short time—or ever! Hadn't he sensed this bright promise inside her, this eager, artistic soul that only needed an opportunity to shine in its natural glory?

Though shy and unassuming, Varina had caught his notice that day and over the past months had only proved her worth as a person and her devotion. He'd been surprised by her shedding her cocoon. But what a magnificent butterfly she'd become!

Her words echoed in his mind: *"I am not ashamed of who I am! God made me! I am the person he wants me to be!"* She'd declared, *"I did not know that God cared so much about each one of us, but I have read the Bible and now I know!"* Everything he'd ever been taught agreed with her words. So why had he never once applied these truths to his everyday life?

Old memory verses from Sunday school played through his mind: *"I will praise thee; for I am fearfully and wonderfully made."* *"The Lord seeth not as man seeth; for man looketh on the outward appearance, but the Lord looketh on the heart."*

The truth of those words tightened Gannon's chest, making him gasp. This year he'd ventured beyond the usual bounds. Just like Varina, he'd been a stranger in a strange land—dependent on the mercy of people who didn't speak his language. He'd found them kind. If the Cuban woman hadn't carefully tended his wounds, he would have lost his leg. He could have died without her help. How could he forget that?

Images of Cuba flashed inside his memory—the gran-
deur of the green mountains, the magnificent rainbow
plumage of the wild parrots, the shabby clothing of the downtrodden peasants, their hungry eyes. *Surely, Lord, you have
clothed the earth in beauty, but we poor humans have degraded
each other.*

"*You made a promise. Will you keep it?*"

Gannon felt as if God himself might be speaking
through his conscience. His face burned with embarrassment,
guilt. *I admit it, Lord. I tried to shove it behind me.*

He recalled the day at the little casa when the captain
had come to take him and two other soldiers back to the U.S.
Army. As they had carried Gannon through the door, he'd
reached for the hands that the Cuban woman held up to him
in farewell. He'd said, "*Gracias, mucho gracias, Senora.*"
He'd wished he could say more, but he knew so little Spanish.
So he promised them in English, "I won't forget what you've
done for me. I will repay my debt. I won't forget!"

The woman and her family had waved and called after
him, "*Vaya con Dios!*"

*Lord, I wanted to forget the pain, the terror, I felt when I
thought that I might die so far from home, that my body would
be buried away from my family!*

"*Christ endured the lash, thorns, and cross—then died far
from home and was buried away from his Father!*"

The words Gannon's conscience fired at him drew his
heart blood. Tears coursed down his face. *I failed you, Lord,
when I told Varina that I would love her in spite of who she is.
Varina has become a new woman. I will become a new man—
one after your own heart! I can't forget your providing help*

when I needed it and the people you sent to save my life. I made a promise to them—really to you—and I'll keep it.

"How?"

I don't know, but as soon as the peace treaty is signed, I'll return to Cuba and assess what is needed. I have some money saved, and I can use it to help the Cuban family. My father is wealthy and generous, and I know he wouldn't turn a deaf ear to anyone who needed help, whatever their race or language. There are many others like him, too. I'll raise more funds, if needed, to start the work. I'll go, Lord. I promise.

"Alone?"

All his doubts and fears about declaring his love for Varina deserted him. If God could give him the chance to learn to peel away his prejudices, couldn't God give his mother the same opportunity? Who could resist Varina? She'd proven herself kind, strong, and honest. *And she has a heart for God. Why have I waited to tell the truth?*

He wiped the tears from his face. *God, you brought us together. You sent me to Cuba and brought me home. I'll never be the same forgetful person again. I see now a little of your plan—bringing Varina and me together. Her transformation shows what learning of your love and real opportunity can do for a person. I will try to do the same, starting with one poor family in Cuba.*

Looking up, he read the street sign at the corner. He'd come to a street only blocks from Mrs. Amberly's. He set out for her house with a light heart and a clearer conscience. His only fear was that Varina might doubt his change of heart. Even though Jason Canty's rumored proposal lurked at the back of his mind, he knew Varina wouldn't accept another man's proposal while married—even if the marriage was in name only. She wasn't that kind of woman.

Shivering in the cold but determined to talk to Varina again, Gannon watched from the shadows around Mrs. Amberly's porch. Before long, a carriage stopped at the curb. Varina stepped out onto the shoveled path, newly carpeted with the light snow of the night. "Good night, Mrs. Ryerson! Thank you!"

She didn't come home in Canty's gig! The import of this made Gannon weak at the knees. His faith in her had been proved! Mounting the steps, she pulled a large key from her muff and fitted it into the door lock.

"Varina!" he called in a low voice.

Startled, she spun around and pursed her mouth.

Gannon stepped out of the shadows and hurried to her side, fighting the urge to sweep her into his arms. "Please, may we talk?"

"That depends on what you wish to talk about, Mr. Moore." She frowned at him.

He smiled, finally realizing that Varina couldn't have told him of her feelings when he'd refused to be honest about his love for her. Then another thought slammed into his chest. Could he have misjudged her feelings toward him? *Varina, do you love me, too?* He touched the soft fur of her wrap. "Varina, I've been a fool. I love you and want my family, and everyone in Chicago, in America, to know that you are my wife, my wonderful wife!"

She stared at him, looking stunned.

He drew strength from his well of love for her. He took her hand and kissed her glove. "Varina, I love you. Can you forgive me for being—"

"You love me?" She sounded unsure.

He cursed his own muddled thinking and hesitance. "More than words can say. You're my beloved, Varina. I would face any challenge to gain your love. I should have told you that first night—"

Varina threw her arms around his neck and stopped his words with a kiss.

He wrapped his arms around her and returned her kiss with an ardor that he'd never felt before. Words of love flowed through his mind—*Varina, my own, my precious, my gift* . . .

"Varina," he whispered and kissed her again. It was as though he drew life and strength from her touch. He lost himself in her fragrance of lavender, her soft willing lips, and the plush velvet and fur of her pelisse. His words found his voice. "Varina, dearest love, my own heart."

A sob broke from her parted lips.

"Don't cry, my darling!" He pressed her closer, fiercely protective.

She leaned her head against his shoulder. "I love you, Gannon. I think I have loved you ever since the day I married you. At first, I did not recognize or believe it. But when my letters came back and I thought I had lost you, I knew my heart would break and never be the same."

He leaned down, temple to temple with her. He felt the rapid beat of her heart. He kissed away the glistening tears, which beaded and slipped down her cold-pinkened cheeks.

"Even when I was so near death that I had no conscious thoughts, I dreamed only of you." He pressed a kiss to her white throat. "Remembering your face was my prayer to survive." He couldn't speak more. Tears threatened.

She brushed away her tears with her gloved fingertips. "Your family—"

"My family will come to love you as I do. But there is something I must tell you." He held her still and braced himself. Would she understand his mission? "I plan to return to Cuba. I believe I have been called to repay a debt to the family who saved my life."

She glanced up. The moonlight radiated like stars from her tear-drenched eyes. "You plan to move there?"

"I don't know." His grip tightened around her. "I just know that I am to go and make good on my promise not to forget my debt to them."

"You will leave me again?" She ran her forefinger down his cheek.

He trembled at her touch. "I will never leave you again. I want you to see Cuba. Will you go with me?"

"I will go anywhere with you."

Her quick acceptance, another gift of her generous spirit, filled him to overflowing. He kissed her hand and pulled her close for another embrace. "I hate to leave you tonight."

She looked up into his eyes and smiled that teasing way he'd come to know. "Why do you need to leave me? We are husband and wife."

Her reply left him breathless. He crushed her to him for one more kiss; then he swept her into his arms, her velvet ball gown overflowing his arms. Pushing the door open, he carried her over the threshold. His heart pounded. Joyful phrases, words whirled in his mind, but only these bobbed to the surface: *Thank you, Lord, for this woman I will love above all others!*

Chapter Nine

Late the next morning, Gannon bounded up the steps to Mrs. Evens's boardinghouse. He unlocked the oak door and pushed it open.

"Here he is now." Mrs. Evens's voice from the parlor caught him by surprise.

He looked into the room and froze. His mother and father sat on a carved settee beside the fireplace.

Mrs. Evens smiled and walked toward him. "I told your parents that you must have stayed with friends last night after the ball. It went very late, didn't it?"

Gannon nodded and strode into the room, surprised but calmer than he thought possible facing his parents. He kissed his mother's cheek and shook his father's work-roughened hand. Mrs. Evens excused herself and closed the pocket door behind her, leaving him alone with his parents.

"I didn't expect to see you, so this is a welcome surprise."

"We were concerned about you . . . you've been so

ill. . . ." His mother looked at him as though searching his eyes.

"I was going to put through a call to you today. In fact, I came back this morning to change clothing and get that started. I have so much news for you."

His parents exchanged puzzled glances.

"Well, Son?" His father gestured for him to speak.

Gannon leaned forward, holding his clasped hands out in front of him. "What I am going to say may shock you, but I would like to say as a preface that this has been a very unusual year for me." He stopped, not knowing how to go on.

His father nodded at him encouragingly. His mother pursed her lips.

Gannon continued, his heart bobbing in a crazy rhythm. He didn't think he should mention telling his father about his friendship with Varina right now. He cleared his throat. "On the train to Chicago last April, I met a young woman. Her name is Varina." Saying these words brought the events of that day back to him vividly. "She . . . I . . . we—"

His father glanced at his wife. "Should we make it easy on him?"

His mother sighed. "Yes, it has been a difficult year for him—for all of us. Go on, Tom."

Gannon tried to figure out what they were getting at.

His father exhaled deeply. "Son, we know all about Varina. That she is your wife."

Gannon gaped at them, a charge of shock racing over his scalp. "How? I—"

Dad grinned. "In early May, I received a page from the *Tribune* from Mrs. Ryerson here in Chicago. It was the page that listed all the legal notices— births, deaths, bankruptcies, marriages. She'd circled the notice of your marriage to a Varina Schiffler. In all that fine print, Mrs. Ryerson had somehow noticed your full name, Gannon Watkins Moore. Didn't you remember, Son, that all births, deaths, and marriages are listed daily in the Chicago papers?"

His own stupidity flooded Gannon. He hit his forehead with his open palm. "I didn't think—"

"No, you didn't." There was a wealth of meaning in the way his father said that sentence, but then his father gave him a gruff nod. "In any event, I didn't tell Mother right away, didn't want to upset her. I couldn't understand why you'd married a woman you'd never mentioned and right before you left for war."

Gannon felt his face flush with embarrassment.

"Instead, I hired a Chicago private investigator to find out all about your bride. The investigator located Varina at Mrs. Amberly's, her parents in Plover Station, found out about how her fiancé had died, and kept me abreast of Varina's progress at Hull House. Mrs. Ryerson took it upon herself to go to Hull House and meet Varina. She was quite impressed with her."

"Varina, Varina—you kept calling her name in your delirium. I didn't know what to think. Who was Varina?" His mother wrung her lacy white handkerchief. "Your father didn't tell me she was your wife until you left for Chicago. But one night, you held my hand, thinking I was Varina. You said, 'I'm coming home to you. I need you.' I realized then that your love for this woman I'd never met was giving you the strength to survive even though the doctors gave us no hope." She sent a prim glance at Gannon's father. "Why Tom hesitated to tell me I still don't understand. Evidently, you two think I'm too frail to hear the truth!"

Gannon found it hard to meet her eyes. "I'm sorry I've caused you pain, so much worry. I didn't mean to—quite the opposite."

"Well, please don't do it again. I'm not a frail woman. Your father should know I'd rather be told the truth."

"I apologized, Flora." His father held up both hands. "I will never try to shield you again."

Gannon nodded in agreement. He was amazed by his parents' reactions. He looked from one to the other. "You both seem . . . so . . . calm . . . about Varina. I know she isn't the bride you'd have chosen for me."

His mother rose from the settee and rested her hand on his arm. "Son, I lost Annie. I very nearly lost you. A surprise bride—even one you thought I might disapprove of—pales in comparison. I only want you to be well . . . happy . . . and right with the Lord."

Standing, Father touched her shoulder. "I kept hoping you might mention your marriage to Varina to me." His father smiled suddenly. "Let's not talk of the past. Everyone seems to think your Varina's charming. Mrs. Ryerson says she's taken Chicago by storm!"

Gannon sat, bemused. His mother wasn't as fragile as he'd thought. *I should have told them the truth in May.* But perhaps his coming so close to dying had put everything into perspective for all of them. Both he and Varina had become sure of their love while separated—while he thought he might not live and Varina feared he'd died. "Varina and I didn't realize that we would fall in love, but through our letters and seeing each other again, we've become sure of our hearts."

Thank you, Lord. Thank you, Mother and Dad, both of you. "I apologize again for not telling you sooner."

His mother dabbed at her eyes. "I had always looked forward to your wedding and Annie's. I just wish we'd been there to see you marry."

Father patted her hand. "Now, Flora, you know why he married her. He was doing just what you would have wanted him to do. A young woman needed his help and he gave it to her."

She nodded and brought a smile to her face. "When do we meet your bride? We'll have to start planning a celebration to welcome her to Wausau."

Gannon felt the last of his tension release. "I can't imagine my future without her, and I want you to meet her today." Gannon realized he'd never spoken truer, more honest words. After months of deception and doubt, he finally tasted the freedom of living the truth again. His spirit soared.

Epilogue

In the receiving line in the foyer of Gannon's home, Varina stood in a stylish dress of white satin. At her side, Gannon kept one arm around her waist and shook hands with the other. Today was his parents' reception to celebrate the wedding of the new couple.

A chattering stream of well-wishers had started arriving in the late morning and would continue until most of Wausau and Plover Station had met the bride and groom and extended their congratulations to them. Even Mrs. Amberly, Opal, and Mrs. Ryerson had traveled from Chicago to attend. All three proudly wore dresses designed by the bride.

Varina's and Gannon's parents stood side by side in the receiving line—smiling, greeting, and bowing to the guests. Varina thought about the lonely April wedding she had expected to go through in Chicago with Mr. Ramos. Now she

349

had married the man she loved, come back to Wisconsin, and had been reunited with her slightly astounded family. Her prayer on that train last spring had been answered beyond anything she could have imagined. The verses she'd memorized flowed through her, deepening into a river of joy. *"I know that my redeemer liveth." "We know that all things work together for good to them that love God." Thank you, dear Father, for loving me and for bringing Gannon and me together. Let me always be a good wife to him. I love him so.*

Gannon turned and kissed her cheek. "I love you," he whispered only for her to hear.

Her heart rejoiced. Handel's "Hallelujah Chorus" played in her mind's ear. She wished she could bring out her violin and add a stringed voice to her delight.

●　●　●

Finally, all the well-wishers had greeted the newlywed couple. Gannon held Varina's hand and would not let her stray from his side as they circulated among the guests. Varina looked like a princess in a play.

"It's time for the toast!" Gannon's father called out. The servants quickly distributed sparkling red punch. Holding crystal cups, the people crowded together in the large front parlor, dining room, and foyer.

Gannon's father raised his glass. "To the bride and groom!"

All the people lifted their punch cups. "Best wishes to Gannon and Varina!"

Varina beamed.

Gannon kissed her and everyone applauded.

"Have you told your parents about Cuba yet?" she whispered into his ear.

"No, we'll save our plans to go to Cuba until after New Year's."

Beaming, Varina's father, wearing a new suit, raised his cup. "To my daughter and her husband, *nzdravya!* To your health!"

Gannon gazed at a photograph of Annie on the mantel. Her smile blessed him and Varina as she would have if she were present. He no longer felt a pang when he thought of her. *I'll make you proud, Annie.* He tucked Varina even closer to his side. *Thank you, Lord, for my bride, for my life, for our future together!*

A NOTE FROM THE AUTHOR

Dear Reader,

My heroine, Varina, is very dear to my heart since she is based on my husband's grandmother, Therese "Rose" Sifer. *Staramama* (which means "old mama" in Slovenian) was eighty-seven years old when I met her. She'd immigrated to America in 1913, married in 1915, and raised a family on the south side of Waukegan, Illinois, just down the street from the Slovenian Hall, where she often sang. She had a deep faith in God and had been known for her beautiful singing in the church in her home village in the mountains of Slovenia.

In Varina, I tried to capture Staramama's artist's soul, joyful spirit, and zest for life. When Staramama died a week after her ninety-ninth birthday, I told my children, "Staramama is dancing and singing with the angels today!"

Please let me know if Varina and Gannon's story touched your heart. Contact me by mail in care of Tyndale House Author Relations, P.O. Box 80, Wheaton, IL 60189-0080, or by e-mail at L.Cote@juno.com.

ABOUT THE AUTHOR

LYN COTE was born in Texas and raised in Illinois on the shore of Lake Michigan. She now lives in Iowa with her husband, son, and daughter. Lyn has spent her adult life as a teacher, a full-time mom, and now a writer. By the way, Lyn's last name is pronounced "Coty."

Lyn's previous books include *Hope's Garden*, *New Man in Town*, *Never Alone*, *Echoes of Mercy*, *Lost in His Love*, and *Whispers of Love*.

Lyn invites you to visit her Web site at www.BooksbyLynCote.com. She also welcomes letters written to her in care of Tyndale House Author Relations, P.O. Box 80, Wheaton, IL 60189-0080, or by e-mail at L.Cote@juno.com.

Visit www.HeartQuest.com for lots of info on
HeartQuest books and authors and more!

www.HeartQuest.com

HEART
QUEST.

CURRENT HEARTQUEST RELEASES

- *Magnolia,* Ginny Aiken
- *Lark,* Ginny Aiken
- *Camellia,* Ginny Aiken

- *Letters of the Heart,* Lisa Tawn Bergren, Maureen Pratt, and Lyn Cote

- *Sweet Delights,* Terri Blackstock, Elizabeth White, and Ranee McCollum

- *Awakening Mercy,* Angela Benson
- *Abiding Hope,* Angela Benson

- *Faith,* Lori Copeland
- *Hope,* Lori Copeland
- *June,* Lori Copeland
- *Glory,* Lori Copeland

- *Freedom's Promise,* Dianna Crawford
- *Freedom's Hope,* Dianna Crawford
- *Freedom's Belle,* Dianna Crawford

- *Prairie Rose,* Catherine Palmer
- *Prairie Fire,* Catherine Palmer
- *Prairie Storm,* Catherine Palmer
- *Prairie Christmas,* Catherine Palmer, Elizabeth White, and Peggy Stoks

- *Finders Keepers,* Catherine Palmer
- *Hide and Seek,* Catherine Palmer
- *A Kiss of Adventure,* Catherine Palmer (original title: *The Treasure of Timbuktu*)
- *A Whisper of Danger,* Catherine Palmer (original title: *The Treasure of Zanzibar*)
- *A Touch of Betrayal,* Catherine Palmer
- *A Victorian Christmas Keepsake,* Catherine Palmer, Kristin Billerbeck, and Ginny Aiken
- *A Victorian Christmas Cottage,* Catherine Palmer, Debra White Smith, Jeri Odell, and Peggy Stoks
- *A Victorian Christmas Quilt,* Catherine Palmer, Peggy Stoks, Debra White Smith, and Ginny Aiken
- *A Victorian Christmas Tea,* Catherine Palmer, Dianna Crawford, Peggy Stoks, and Katherine Chute

- *Olivia's Touch,* Peggy Stoks
- *Romy's Walk,* Peggy Stoks

HEART QUEST

COMING SOON (SPRING 2002)

- *Winter's Secret*, Lyn Cote
- *English Ivy*, Catherine Palmer
- *Elena's Song*, Peggy Stoks

HEARTWARMING ANTHOLOGIES FROM HEARTQUEST

A Victorian Christmas Keepsake—Return to a time when life was uncomplicated, faith was sincere . . . and love was a gift to be cherished forever. These three Christmas novellas will touch your heart and stir you to treasure your own keepsakes of life, love, and romance. Curl up next to the fire with this heartwarming, faith-filled collection of original love stories by beloved romance authors Catherine Palmer, Kristin Billerbeck, and Ginny Aiken.

Sweet Delights—Who would have thought chocolate could be so good for your heart? A cup of tea and a few quiet moments are all you need to enjoy these tasty, calorie-free morsels from beloved romance authors Terri Blackstock, Elizabeth White, and Ranee McCollum. Each story is followed by a letter from the author and her favorite chocolate recipe!

Prairie Christmas—In "The Christmas Bride," by Catherine Palmer, Rolf Rustemeyer can hardly wait for the arrival of his Christmas bride, all the way from Germany. You'll love this heartwarming Christmas visit with friends old and new from A Town Called Hope. Anthology also includes "Reforming Seneca Jones" by Elizabeth White and "Wishful Thinking" by Peggy Stoks.

A Victorian Christmas Cottage—Four novellas centering around hearth and home at Christmastime. Stories by Catherine Palmer, Debra White Smith, Jeri Odell, and Peggy Stoks.

A Victorian Christmas Tea—Four novellas about life and love at Christmastime. Stories by Catherine Palmer, Dianna Crawford, Peggy Stoks, and Katherine Chute.

A Victorian Christmas Quilt—A patchwork of four novellas about love and joy at Christmastime. Stories by Catherine Palmer, Peggy Stoks, Debra White Smith, and Ginny Aiken.